FREE FALL

FREE FALL

Fern Michaels

This first world edition published in Great Britain 2007 by
SEVERN HOUSE PUBLISHERS LTD of
9–15 High Street, Sutton, Surrey SM1 1DF.
This first world edition published in the USA 2007 by
SEVERN HOUSE PUBLISHERS INC of
595 Madison Avenue, New York, N.Y. 10022.

British Library Cataloguing in Publication Data

Michaels, Fern
   Free fall. - (Revenge of the Sisterhood ; 7)
   1.   Sisterhood (Fictitious characters) - Fiction
   2.   Revenge - Fiction
   3.   Suspense fiction
   I.   Title
   813.5'4 [F]

ISBN-13: 978-0-7278-6429-1

All Severn House titles are printed on acid-free paper.

Typeset by Palimpsest Book Production Ltd.,
Polmont, Stirlingshire, Scotland.
Printed and bound in Great Britain by
MPG Books Ltd., Bodmin, Cornwall.

Prologue

Yoko Akia walked through the small apartment behind her florist shop. It was dark outside, the rain drumming on the roof and windows, louder than she would have thought possible. Crossing her arms over her chest, she quickened her pacing. February was always so cold. She was nervous, full of anxiety as the day rushed to a close. Time to relax and meditate, time to pray.

Everything was in place – her mat, her incense sticks, the pictures lined up on a red and gold shelf. All she had to do was take her place on the mat, shift her mind into the neutral zone, and do what she'd been doing daily for years. Today, though, there was no sense of peace in the ritual. Maybe she should wait till later. A hot cup of green tea might calm her down. She reversed her steps and headed for the tiny kitchen where a pot of tea was always ready.

Yoko carried the fragile cup over to the table and sat down, her thoughts going in all directions as she tried to concentrate on tomorrow's trip to the Rutledge estate in McLean, Virginia. Finally, it was her turn. Her turn to get the revenge she'd hungered for all her life. The revenge that should have taken place a year ago but due to circumstances beyond the Sisterhood's control, had been put on hold.

What specifically was bothering her? Was it that her mission was the last one? Was it that the Sisterhood would be disbanded once her mission was complete? What would happen to Kathryn, Isabelle, Nikki, Alexis, Myra and of course Charles? And now they had a new sister, Anna de Silva. What would happen to Anna?

Would life just go on as though their past missions had

1

never happened? How in the world was that possible?

Yoko sipped at the hot tea. Her eyes watered at the heat on her tongue. Outside, the hard rain splattered on the window. Normally she liked the sound of rain, found it somehow comforting, but today the rain sounded ominous. Was it an omen of some kind? The tea was supposed to calm her. Why wasn't it happening? She slid off her chair and started to pace again as she struggled to find her inner core of calmness. It continued to elude her.

A roll of thunder outside the small building startled her. She poured more tea and sat down at the table, then jumped back up almost immediately. It was Charles! Charles, Myra Rutledge's partner, was bothering her. It had been Charles's decision to put her mission on hold this past year because he had business abroad. He hadn't seen fit to apprise the Sisterhood of that business. That's what was bothering her. Charles and their new sister, Anna. There, she'd given a name to her uneasiness.

The tea was cool now but she drank it anyway. Tomorrow all her questions would be answered when she made the trip to McLean. She smiled at the thought. She'd missed the sisters; they were part of her life now. All of them risked their lives and their reputations to help each other. She adored them all, especially the brash outspoken Kathryn whom she loved to spar with, Isabelle who mothered her, Alexis and Nikki who teased her constantly about her boyfriend, Harry Wong. Myra and Charles were like a doting aunt and uncle. She wasn't sure exactly what Anna de Silva's role would be. Perhaps another doting aunt. Tears formed in the corners of her eyes when she thought of Julia, their fallen comrade. Tonight she would pray for Julia.

Yoko washed and dried her cup before she replaced it in the cabinet over the sink. She was on her way to her prayer rug when her doorbell rang. She knew it wasn't Harry because he was out of town. She *never* had visitors. She padded over to the door and opened it. 'Alexis!'

'Yep, it's me! Can I stay here with you tonight? I even brought dinner,' she said holding up a bag. 'Sushi for you. The weather channel said the roads are going to flood tonight

2

so I thought I'd come here and tomorrow we can go to McLean together. We can have a hen party.'

Yoko frowned as she looked over Alexis's shoulders into the dark night. 'You brought chickens?'

Alexis burst out laughing as she hugged her friend. 'Hens as in female. We're females. Chicks.' At Yoko's puzzled look she said, 'You know, girls. You're a girl. I'm a girl. Ergo, hen party. Never mind.'

'Come, come,' Yoko said as she closed and locked the door. 'I am grateful for the company. I was sitting here thinking about tomorrow. You knew that, didn't you?'

Alexis nodded. 'When it was my turn, I was so wired up I thought I was going to explode. It's been a long year, hasn't it?'

'Yes, it has. I was thinking about that, too. Charles didn't really say much about that business he had to take care of. None of the others seem to know what that business was or is. I guess he took care of it. It is strange that his business came up just as we accepted a new member to the Sisterhood,' Yoko said as she started to set the table and lay out napkins.

'I think Charles's business had something to do with Anna de Silva. Indirectly, I think it has something to do with us, too. It's just a feeling I have. Have you given any thought to what's going to happen when your mission is over?'

Yoko looked at the pretty woman sitting across from her. Alexis's dark skin and even darker eyes made her look mysterious. 'Actually, I was thinking about that earlier. I have no idea what's going to happen. Myra invested so much money in the technology Charles uses to keep us operational. Then there's Anna de Silva's billions. Maybe they will tell us what's going on when we meet tomorrow. I do like Anna. Do you?'

Alexis bit down on her lower lip. 'I do like her. She isn't Julia, though. I'm not sure how I'm going to feel when she takes her place at the table in Julia's chair.' Exuberance rang in her voice when she said 'I missed you, girl!'

Yoko giggled. 'I missed you, too. That stuff,' she said pointing to the bag of cheeseburgers, 'will kill you!'

'And that seaweed and raw fish isn't going to kill you? So,

3

how are things going with Harry?'

Yoko giggled again. 'Very well. No, better than well. He loves me and wants to marry me. I said no. Are you seeing anyone?'

Alexis ignored the question. 'You said no! Why?'

Yoko burst out laughing. 'Because he is afraid of me. I like the feeling that gives me. No one has ever been afraid of me. It is a . . . delicious feeling. Kathryn says I have to be in control. I am in control. That may change one of these days. In my culture it is not a good thing when a woman can best a man. Especially in martial arts.'

Alexis leaned across the table. 'Listen to me, little buckaroo. Here in America the name of the game is you allow the man to win. Key word here is allow. After you snag him, then you let him know who's boss. Do ya get it?'

Yoko grimaced. 'That's cheating.'

'Uh huh.'

Both women went off into peals of laughter.

'I met this guy when I was filling my gas tank,' Alexis said. 'He was at the pump next to me and we struck up a conversation. He said his sister has a Mini Cooper, too. I gave him my phone number. He was a hunk. He said he plays football for the Redskins. Did I say he was a hunk? He's a tight end.' At Yoko's amused expression, she said, 'Don't even go there.' Both women went off into peals of laughter again.

Dinner over, the kitchen tidied up, they retired to Yoko's small sitting room with cups of tea. 'Do you want to talk about it, Yoko?' Alexis asked softly.

'No. Tomorrow will be soon enough. It hurts my heart to talk about it. I am very worried about my vengeance. The man involved is very powerful, a public figure. I fear Charles may say it is not possible. If that happens, what will I do?'

Alexis scoffed. 'And you think taking on one of the biggest HMOs in the country wasn't heavy duty? Don't forget the Vice Presidential candidate and that guy who was the National Security Advisor. Then there was that little trip to China and the diplomat's nephew . . . Or was it his son? Whatever, that was pretty high profile and yet we pulled it off. I can't imagine who your public figure is but whoever he is, he's no match for the Sisterhood. You can take that to the bank, kiddo.'

Yoko blinked back tears. 'Would you like to see a picture of my mother?'

'Yes, I would, Yoko.'

Yoko got up and ran to her prayer room to return with a small picture in an oval frame. She held it close to her heart for a moment before she handed it to Alexis.

'She's very beautiful. You look a bit like her. How old was she in this photograph?'

'She was very young, only fifteen when she was brought to this country. I was born when she was seventeen. The man who fathered me threw me out with the trash. My mother died a painful death a month later. My aunts saved me and spirited me away to more aunts. Not blood relatives, you understand. Just young women who were in the same position my mother was in.'

Alexis thought she understood. She slipped off her pile of cushions to gather Yoko into her arms. 'Don't you worry, Yoko, we'll take care of that powerful man who threw you away. We'll make him regret what he did. We'll make sure the bastard rues the day he was born. And you can take that one to the bank, too.'

Yoko cried as she'd never cried before. All Alexis could do was stroke her silky black hair and pat her shoulder. From time to time she mouthed soothing words until Yoko fell asleep in her arms. Alexis carried her to the mat she slept on in the small bedroom, stunned at how feather light the little woman was. She gently lowered her to the mat and covered her with a light blanket. The last thing she did before she left her room was to place the picture of Yoko's mother next to her.

One

Myra Rutledge fussed with her gray hair with one hand while her other hand fiddled with the pearls she was never without, a sign that she was worried about something. She looked across the kitchen to where Charles was basting a turkey. 'Do you think it's an omen of some kind, dear?'

Charles Martin looked up from the golden brown bird and smiled at the love of his life. 'Why would you say something like that, Myra?'

Myra continued to finger the pearls at her neck. She walked over to the kitchen door to stare outside. She flipped the light switch to light up the courtyard. Rain was coming down in torrents. Maybe it was sleet, she couldn't be sure. 'I can give you a hundred and ten reasons why, my dear.'

Charles closed the oven door. 'One will suffice.'

'The weather. The conditions are identical to those . . . the first time the girls came out here. Remember how Kathryn drove her eighteen wheeler through the gates. The power went out and we had to use candles. The girls slid down the bannister that night. I caught Kathryn when she whooped her way to the bottom. I think this is an omen of some kind. I really do, Charles.'

Charles peeked into a pot bubbling on the stove. 'That's it, the weather?'

Myra continued to peer outside. Her response was almost a whisper. 'The weather and the fact that this is our last mission. We have so many decisions to make tonight. Are we going to simply walk off into the night? Are we going to continue with the Sisterhood? It's come to an end so quickly. What will we do with ourselves if the girls want to . . . to, you know, stop?'

6

'I don't think that's going to happen, Myra. The Sisterhood has become a way of life for all of us. There are thousands of people out there who can use our help. Just because Yoko's mission is our last doesn't mean we're going to close up shop. It just means our members have been vindicated, and that includes you, Myra. Now, is there something else bothering you?'

Myra turned away from the window and walked over to the man she loved with all her heart, and the man who made the Sisterhood hum like a well-oiled machine. She stepped into his arms and laid her head on his shoulder. 'You can't fool me for a minute, Charles. I know you too well. You spent almost all of last year going back and forth to Annie's fortress in the mountains of Spain. We've spent fifty million dollars, maybe more, to . . . to . . . outfit the old monastery Annie inherited from her husband. You had Nikki research the laws of sanctuary. You didn't do all this . . . just in case. Just in case we have to flee to a foreign land is why you've been doing it. You've called in old friends from your old days in MI6. For all I know your best friend in England helped you out. We aren't supposed to have secrets from one another. I feel you are keeping things from me. You justify it to yourself by saying it is for my own good so I won't worry. I am a born worrier and I worry more when I don't know all the details. This is a very good time to tell me what prompted you to do all this.'

Charles chuckled as he led Myra over to one of the kitchen chairs. He sat down opposite her. 'If you remember, we discussed all this in great detail a year ago, Myra. We included Annie and Judge Easter in those discussions as well. The day may well come when we have to retreat to . . . a more friendly climate. It's simply wise to be prepared should that happen. The girls understand. We've been extremely lucky so far, my dear, but luck lasts only so long.

'*My people* whom we never see have been advising me that the . . . ah . . . legal climate has been changing this past year. It's something I've had to pay attention to. It's all under control and I saw no need to worry you or the girls. Are you telling me, old girl, that you no longer trust me? Or are you trying to tell me you want to close up shop?'

7

Myra clasped Charles's hand in her own. 'Absolutely not. I want to continue but as Kathryn says, it's been getting dicey of late.'

Charles chuckled again. 'Kathryn is correct. I just found out yesterday that Ted Robinson and Maggie Spritzer are back in town. They were seen having lunch with some agents from the FBI. My man told me that Robinson and Spritzer had a meeting at the DOJ.'

Myra reared forward. 'The Department of Justice! Oh, dear lord! I thought when you sent them to New York they were out of our hair. They have no proof of anything. Do they, Charles?'

'I'd stake my life on the fact that they don't, but Robinson and Spritzer have excellent memories. They also met with a man from the CIA. I am not going to pretend it isn't worrisome.'

Myra bit down on her lip. 'Charles . . . I think . . . I suspect . . . that Nikki has confided in District Attorney Emery. I can't prove this but I think he's on our side, strange as that may seem. It's just a suspicion. I couldn't confront Nikki because I didn't want to put her in a position where she had to lie to me. Our girl loves Jack Emery. Love is more powerful than loyalty in my opinion. Having said that, if I'm right, Jack is telling Nikki everything that is going on.'

'I more or less suspected the same thing but didn't want to say anything in case I was reading it all wrong. In addition to that, those two reporters are incredibly smart. I wouldn't be a bit surprised to find out they're setting Jack up. Emery's no fool, he's been around the block, and if our suspicions are right that he is on our side, someone has to warn him.'

'What about your men with the gold shields? Can't they do something?'

Charles clucked his tongue. 'They're on it, Myra. We may have to have a talk with Nikki sooner rather than later.'

Myra worked at her pearls, twisting and untwisting them. 'That makes me feel a little better but I'm not sure about the talk with Nikki.'

'The good thing is we don't have to make a decision on that right this minute. What we have to do right this minute is set the table and get things ready for the girls. They should be arriving any time now, weather permitting.'

Myra frowned as she got up to get the dishes out of the cabinet. 'I'm still going to worry, Charles.'

Charles laughed as he reached down to remove the turkey from the oven. 'I know, old girl!'

Twenty minutes later, Myra and Charles heard the air horn on Kathryn's rig as she whipped through the electronic gates. The others followed close behind. The monster gates closed with a loud banging sound.

Myra's eyes lit up like stars. 'They're here, Charles! Even Annie. Our girls are here! Everyone is safe and sound! I hear Grady and Murphy barking. Here they come!'

Jack Emery jerked at the collar of his overcoat as he walked against the wind. He was on his way to the last place on earth he wanted to go. As he rounded the corner on his way to the Squire's Pub he heard his name called.

'Hey, Emery, slow down,' Mark Lane shouted to be heard over the wind. 'I oughta kick your ass for calling me out on a night like this. I hope you know the roads are icing up. What the hell is so damn important that you arranged this little meeting? Why couldn't we just have a conference call?'

'Stop whining, Mark. So what if the road ices up. The roads are supposed to ice up in February. This is February. Why do you care anyway, you walked here.'

'I'm not whining. I'm pissed that you called me out on a night like this. I know I'm not going to like whatever the hell is going on. Days like this I wish I didn't know you. You're like a fucking magnet to disaster and don't deny it. How's Nikki?'

'As far as I know, she's fine. Why wouldn't she be?' Jack asked as he burrowed his neck deeper into the collar of his overcoat. 'But to answer your question, no, you are not going to like what's going on. Robinson and Spritzer are back in town. They've been meeting with the DOJ and the FBI.'

'Oh, shit!'

'Yeah, oh, shit!' Jack struggled to get his breath against the driving sleet. 'I wouldn't be a bit surprised to find out someone has a few questions about that last computer program you wrote for your ex-bosses at the FBI. You know the one you can hack into whenever you feel like it.'

'Oh, shit!'

Instead of commenting, Jack slammed against the door of the Squire's Pub and blasted into the steamy watering hole filled with lawyers and young women in short skirts sporting deep cleavage. As he craned his neck to see over the crowds, Mark wiped at his steaming glasses.

'They're in the back,' Jack said shouldering his way through the laughing men and women who were looking to hook up for the cold night. 'Just listen, Mark, and let me do the talking. Whatever you do, don't get pissed off. Just look bored. Tell me you understand everything I just said.'

'Yeah, yeah, yeah. Who's paying tonight?'

'Robinson, since he called this meeting. Eat hearty because he probably has an expense account.'

Jack could tell with one look that the ex-*Post* reporter was in an ugly mood. His partner, Maggie Spritzer, looked like she was in the same ugly mood. The ugly moods didn't seem to be affecting either reporter's appetites as they chowed down on ribs, baked potatoes, and coleslaw with a slab of hot bread that was a foot long and oozed butter.

Both men slid into the booth the moment they removed their soggy coats. Mark immediately held up his hand to signal a waitress and ordered quickly. Jack shook his head and ordered a beer. 'You have barbecue sauce on your nose, Ted.'

Ted Robinson shot Jack a hateful look and ignored the comment as he clamped down on a dripping rib.

Jack settled into the booth and decided to wait out the reporter. Ted and Maggie were the ones who called the meeting. His gut told him coming here was a mistake.

The Squire's Pub was the kind of place where secrets were told, rarely kept and assignations were the order of the day. The decibel level was at an all-time high, so secrets remained secrets. Waitresses in skimpy shorts and spandex tops hustled and flirted to ensure a good tip. Nikki had told him once that on a good night a waitress at the Squire's Pub could earn three hundred bucks. She'd gone on to say every night was a good night at the pub. Nikki had explained she knew this because she'd represented several of the waitresses in a discrimination suit against the owners. A suit she'd won.

It took a full ten minutes for Ted to finish his ribs, wipe his face, clean his hands with a moist Towelette before he leaned back in the booth and eye-balled Jack. 'The fibbies are requesting your presence at the Hoover building tomorrow at ten.'

Jack narrowed his eyes. Like he didn't know this was going to happen. 'Really.'

If Ted had hoped for a better reaction, he was disappointed. He tried again. 'The DOJ wants you in their offices at two tomorrow afternoon.'

'I'm busy tomorrow. I'm busy the day after and the day after that. Look at me, Robinson, you don't want to go where you're going with this.'

Ted settled his lanky frame more comfortably in the booth. One of his long legs brushed against Jack's ankle. Jack kicked him hard. Ted winced but ignored the kick. 'Don't shoot the messenger, buddy.'

Maggie was busy sucking on a bone, as was Mark. They appeared to be oblivious to the conversation but Jack knew their ears were tuned to every word.

'Hey, Mister Reporter, what are you doing back in the D.C. area? I heard you were banished to the big bad apple. As in New *Yaak* City,' Jack said, his eyes glinting dangerously. He watched as Maggie tossed her bare bone into a bucket on the table. She licked at her sticky fingers before she reached for a Towelette.

'How about I missed your ugly face, you son of a bitch. You and that herd of criminals out there in McLean were the reason Maggie and I went to New York. It wasn't like we had a choice as you well know. It took us a whole year to realize we hate New York. We love Washington, D.C. so we decided to come back. In order to do that we had to get ourselves some protection. As in FBI protection.'

Mark stopped eating long enough to guffaw at the statement. It was his one contribution to the evening's festivities.

Maggie was digging at her fingernails with the moist towel,

11

her head lowered. Jack thought he saw a tremor in her hands. He noticed a momentary spark of fear in Ted's eyes. It was gone almost immediately but he relished what he'd seen.

Jack tilted his beer bottle and swigged. 'Are they any match for the shields? Those guys never go away. There's a whole new crew these days and they are bad ass mean. You maybe want to think about that a little.'

Ted's facial muscles tightened. 'I told them *everything*!'

Jack's stomach tied itself in a knot. 'Did they give you the magic decoder ring for your efforts or did they just promise 24/7 protection for you and the little woman?'

'Go ahead, be a wise ass. When they throw you in the slammer you'll be begging me to write your side of the story and I'll tell you to go fuck yourself.'

Jack finished his beer and plunked the bottle down on the wooden table. Then he leaned across the table and grabbed Ted's shirt with one hand and a hank of Maggie's hair in the other, yanking them toward him. His face was mean and ugly when he hissed, 'Cause me one moment of grief and I'll kill you myself. I know how to do it, too. That 24/7 protection of yours will be worth shit. I'm leaving now. Give my regrets to your buddies. Watch your back, Robinson. That goes for you, too, Maggie.'

Mark already had his coat on and was threading his way through the swarm of bodies that was six deep around the bar.

It was still sleeting outside. Jack drew a deep breath. He looked up at Mark. 'Well?'

'I think they got your nuts in a vice, Jack. If he spilled his guts, and there's no reason to believe he isn't telling the truth, they're going to go after you. Look, I've been out of the Bureau for a while now. I'm just a programming geek. No one is going to listen to me. If I could help you, I would. Ah, shit, you want me to hack into their files, is that it?'

Jack hiked up his wet collar around his ears. 'You told me yourself you wrote the programs, installed the firewalls and created a back door that no one would ever find because you're so goddamn smart. Now's your chance to prove it. Robinson has no hard proof. None. Call me tomorrow and let me know what you find out.' He watched Mark walk off into the dark night. Now, he could shiver and cringe. The FBI he could handle. The DOJ was something else entirely. Maybe it was time to have a little heart to heart with the shields that were still dogging him night and day. Sometimes he almost forgot about them. Other times they were front and center, a reminder that he was breaking the law right along with the Ladies of Pinewood.

Jack moved away from the entrance and looked into the steamy pub. The crowd around the bar had shifted to be closer to the three-piece combo that was belting out something he'd never heard before. He had a clear view of Ted and Maggie arguing. He watched as the redhead belted her boyfriend on the arm, her mouth going a mile a minute. Ted appeared to be sucking up her abuse, his face miserable. Satisfied that things were going to get ugly in reporter land, Jack hiked back to the office to get his car.

Fifty minutes later, slipping and sliding all over the road, Jack parked and walked the three blocks to Nikki's house in Georgetown. He spotted the dark sedan two doors up from the house. He stopped, rapped on the window and said, 'No, no, don't get out, it's nasty out here. Tell your buddy Charles or whoever the hell pays your salary that Ted Robinson is back in town. Funny how you guys missed that. Anyway, Robinson issued me an invitation to meet with the boys in the Hoover building and the DOJ offices tomorrow. Now, I know you guys don't want me spilling my guts to every Tom, Dick and Harry who issues invitations, so squelch it. If you don't, things could get a little rough if you get my drift. By the way, what's with this 24/7 protection our government is offering those two reporters? I have a good mind to write or call my congressman and complain. You need to take care of that, too, otherwise I'm going to have to shoot the son of a bitch myself. Have a nice night. See you in the morning, you big lug.'

'Listen, Emery, who the hell . . .' But Jack was already sprinting up the steps to Nikki's house and was out of earshot.

Two

They were a happy group as they hugged and kissed Myra and Charles. The dogs barked joyfully, delighted to be in the kitchen with all the tantalizing aromas and belly scratching afforded them. Within seconds, the young women were mashing potatoes, setting out the salad, making the gravy, while Charles carved the delectable bird and Myra poured wine. Within minutes the feast was on the table. Charles offered up the blessing before the dishes made their way around the table at the speed of light. They all talked at once, manic about how good it was to see everyone after a year's absence. Myra positively glowed. Annie soaked in everything like a sponge, a smile on her face. Even Charles had a twinkle in his eye.

There was no doubt about it, the Ladies of Pinewood were a united family.

And then it was time for dessert, a creation called Bananas Charles that he'd doused in brandy and set on fire with a mini torch, then spooned into crystal dishes.

Yoko stood up and clapped her hands for attention. 'Alexis is going to have a new suitor very soon. He plays football! That's my news.'

It was all the women needed to hear as they pummeled the lady with the Red Bag of magic tricks. Alexis blushed furiously as she shook her fist in Yoko's direction. Finally she gave up and said, 'Girls, this guy is so *hot*, my toes curled up! He said he'd call. I met him at a filling station when I was getting gas.'

Myra winked at Annie who was so mesmerized, her mouth dropped open.

Isabelle focused on Yoko and said, 'And how is the romance with Harry Wong going, little miss?'

Yoko groaned. 'He is in Japan for trials. He will return with much money and many trophies. The romance is . . . is . . .'

'What? Give it a name, girl! We want the full year's worth of details,' Kathryn said.

'He is very . . . athletic.'

'What exactly does that mean?' Isabelle demanded in her most motherly voice.

When Kathryn asked if athletic meant doing *it* while swinging from a chandelier, Charles, his face a rosy pink, excused himself.

Nikki giggled. 'Be precise, Yoko.'

Annie looked around the table, knowing the others expected her to say something. She'd been welcomed into the little group but she knew she was on probation. She wanted desperately to fit in, to make Myra and the others proud of her. 'Sex is wonderful. I remember one time . . .'

When the tale was finished, the others gasped. 'Way to go, Annie! You are my kind of gal!' Kathryn said, getting up and walking around the table to slap her on the back. Annie glowed like a beacon, remembering what Myra had told her earlier – that if Kathryn welcomes you with open arms, you are *in*. At that moment she felt like she could take on City Hall and come out the victor.

In thirty minutes the kitchen was tidied, the dogs fed, the dishwasher purring. Arm in arm, the women made their way to the living room and the magic bookshelf that opened to reveal a set of stairs that would take them to what they called the Underground War Room.

Today Julia Webster's chair no longer sat in the corner. Today it rested next to Myra's chair. Annie waited for the others to sit. Myra held her chair and said, 'Welcome to the Sisterhood, Annie.'

Annie nodded and said, 'I want to thank all of you for welcoming me to the Sisterhood and allowing me to participate in whatever way I can.'

The women reached across the table to take Annie's hand, their show of acceptance.

'Ladies, ladies, it's time to get down to business. Is there any old business we need to discuss?' Myra asked, calling the meeting to order.

Nikki twirled a pencil in her fingers. 'I hate to sound like a broken record but is there any news on the Barringtons? They were, after all, my mission that we had to abort.'

Myra looked at the young lawyer, her adopted daughter, and said, 'Actually, dear, there is news and it's tragic. Three weeks ago Charles received a communiqué from Germany. It seems Miss Barrington and her companion were killed in a car crash on the Autobahn. She was driving at a speed of 130 miles an hour. It was a fiery crash and both parties could only be identified by their dental records.'

Myra wasn't surprised when no one looked pained or in grief over the two deaths. 'There is other news. Judge Easter has moved into the farm right on schedule. At this moment in time, we are the only ones who know this. Nellie,' she said using the judge's nickname, 'is keeping her apartment in town and does stay there occasionally. And Isabelle is going to be written up in *Architectural Digest*. Of course the day they photograph the farm, Nellie will be in town. I just thought you'd all like to know about Isabelle's achievement.' The women all clapped their hands the way they did each time one of their own was singled out for praise. Five minutes of congratulations worked wonders for Isabelle who preened like a peacock.

Myra took center stage again. 'Before we get down to Yoko's mission, Charles has a few things to tell us. I know you've all been wondering why we had to postpone Yoko's mission for a whole year. There was a very good reason but I'll let Charles explain it all to you.'

Charles stepped down from his perch high above them where he reined as king behind a solid bank of computers. He carried a bright yellow folder in his hands.

Nikki felt a sense of fear as she stared hard at the man she considered a father. She knew he was going to say something that she and the others weren't going to like. She risked a glance at the others and decided they felt the same way. She turned her eyes away and looked up at one of the sixty-inch monitors where Lady Justice overlooked them all.

Charles cleared his throat. 'It's been an incredibly busy year, ladies. But so much was accomplished in that time frame that I think you will all forgive the delay. But before I get to my overseas ventures I need to apprise you all of a few things. The two reporters from the *Post*, Maggie Spritzer and Ted Robinson, are back in the District. Much to my chagrin, I might add. That particular situation is more or less under control for the moment. Mr Robinson obviously had a lot of spare time on his hands while in New York and diligently worked his computer. On his return, he paid a visit, along with Miss Spritzer, to the NSA. I'm sure you all remember *him*. Unfortunately, I have no way of knowing what went on during that visit. However, a few days later, Mr Jack Emery was called into the Hoover building and the DOJ offices. Mr Emery flat out denied any and all allegations that the two reporters put forth. It turned out to be a case of he said versus they said. The National Security Advisor, as I understand it, is backing up the two reporters. Mr Emery was left to swing in the wind on his own.'

Charles walked over to stand behind Nikki's chair. He put the yellow folder on the table and then placed his hands on her shoulders. 'We are not, I repeat, we are not going to allow Mr Emery to swing in the wind. If you like, we can all pretend we don't know Jack has been Nikki's informant but I say we bring it into the open and work from there. I also want to say at this moment that love, trust and loyalty are a wonderful thing.' A second later the thin chain around Nikki's neck and buried under her sweater was in his hands. A small diamond winked in the overhead light. 'No more pretending. Put the ring on your finger where it belongs, Nikki.'

Nikki burst into tears as she removed the ring and slid it onto her finger. 'The others know, Charles. I told them. We would have gotten caught twice if Jack hadn't helped us. Oh, God, he's lying to the Department of Justice and the FBI. We have to do something.'

'I know, my dear. I should say, Myra and I suspected. As to helping Jack, the matter is being taken care of as we speak. Jack will not be attending any scheduled meetings tomorrow.'

Nikki's sigh of relief was so loud the others laughed. The

mood in the war room turned upbeat. The women turned to Charles who was still standing behind Nikki's chair. They waited.

'The reason this meeting today was delayed a whole year, and I apologize to you, Yoko, was because I had pressing matters to attend to in Spain. As you may or may not know, Annie has turned over her mountain monastery to us; the Sisterhood. It's a difficult place to reach and all supplies have to be helicoptered in. That accounted for many delays and if you add bad weather spells, time will get away from you. I am happy to report that this room,' he said waving his arm around, 'has been duplicated on that very mountain top. Actually, it's larger, more high tech. I want you all to tuck this information in the back of your mind. The day may come when we make a mistake, when we have to move on. That mountaintop is where we will head. Later, I will be giving you each a small folder that you will need to familiarize yourself with in case things get . . . what is it Kathryn says? Ah, yes, dicey. It may never come to pass but it is best to be prepared for any and all eventualities.'

'The two reporters seem to be at the root of our problems. Can't we do something about them?' Kathryn asked.

'The wheels are in motion,' Charles said briskly. 'I think we should now get to Yoko's mission. She's waited long enough. Myra will hand you your folder. Peruse it while Yoko tells us her story. Then we'll decide how to proceed. Yoko, the floor is yours, my dear.'

Yoko licked at her lips as she sat up straighter. 'I cannot believe my time is finally here. I want to show you a picture of my mother. I never knew her but she was very beautiful and I am told a very gentle, loving person. She was fifteen years of age when this photo was taken and she was brought to this country.

'My mother came from a very poor family. So poor my grandfather, who I never knew either, was forced to sell his daughters. I understand he was given a princely sum of money for my mother by a very rich American who promised he would love, honor and respect my mother and her family. I am not sure of the amount but understood it to be five hundred

American dollars. What my grandfather did not know was this rich American was involved in a prostitution ring. He brought many, many young women from Asian countries to satisfy his and his friends' sick fantasies. When he tired of them, which didn't take long, he sold them to other sick people like himself. These women were passed around and around until they became sick and diseased and then left to fend for themselves with no homes, no money and no place to go. Unfortunately for my mother, she became pregnant. She told no one except the women she was forced to live with in very squalid conditions. When the man who is my father found out, he sent her to others. He was done with her. Before you can ask, there was no means of escape. Only two women ever escaped this man and they are the women who raised me. I always called them Aunt out of respect but they are not blood relatives. My mother gave birth to me and the others whisked me away immediately. My mother was immediately sent back on the . . . circuit . . . I do not know the word. She bled to death. She was seventeen. The others told my aunts she was tossed in a ditch and covered up. I think my mother would have loved me even under the circumstances. I know I would have loved her.

'My aunts died of the same disease as my mother. Others took me, were kind to me, fed me, housed me. They educated me the best they could. I am grateful to all of them.' Yoko's voice broke when she said, 'There was no one to love me. Not even from the man my aunts arranged for me to marry. More than anything in the world I wanted to know what that feeling of love was like. I found out when I met all of you. I am so very grateful to all of you.'

Because they were women with hearts, they were all off their chairs in a heartbeat, clustered around Yoko, patting her back, her arm, stroking her head, mouthing soothing words of comfort until the little woman was ready to go on.

'I want to expose the man who killed my mother. I want the world to know what a sick pervert he and his friends are. There is this club he has where men pay astronomical sums of money for people like my mother. I want him to suffer physically and I want to see him publicly scorned and to end up in prison in a tiny cell. I want to be his warden until the day he dies.'

Myra struggled to get her tongue to work. 'Did your aunts give you this man's name? Do you have anything to help us track him down, dear?'

Yoko leaped to her feet. 'Oh, I know who he is. I know where he lives. I know his name and everything that has ever been printed about him.'

Even Charles was stunned at the announcement. 'You actually know who it is! Who is it, child?'

'His name is Michael Lyons. They call him Mick.'

The women bellowed as one. They looked at Yoko in disbelief. The disbelief turned to belief when they saw the tears rolling down her cheeks.

'The movie star!'

'America's heartthrob!'

'The President's Ambassador of Good Will!'

'At fifty, the sexiest man alive!'

'Oh, my goodness,' Myra said.

Charles was speechless, but only for a moment. 'The man they call Mister Perfect! The man who has won three Oscars! The benevolent philanthropic Michael Lyons! It's unbelievable. Yoko, are you absolutely certain?'

'I am certain, Charles. I have very little in the way of proof but what I have is enough. It is all in my car. Michael Lyons is my father. He is the man responsible for my mother's death. And now it is time for him to pay for what he has done.'

'It's not that I doubt you, Yoko, it's just so hard to believe a man as famous as Michael Lyons could be involved in something like this. There was something in the *Post* yesterday about him. He was nominated for another Academy Award in March. I think the article said his people are campaigning for him. Something like that,' Charles said.

'I read the same article,' Alexis said. 'I saw the movie, too. It was excellent. They were touting him for an Oscar before it hit the screen. I didn't think I'd like a movie called *A Pocket Full Of Stars* but like I said it was excellent. Lyons is a terrific actor. No offense, Yoko. Now, though, after what you said, I hate his guts.'

20

'I used to know a lot of people in Hollywood,' Annie said. 'I even bankrolled several musicals. I imagine I could get in touch with some of those people if need be. Of course that was a while ago but I assume they are still around.'

'One of my clients has a brother who is a big honcho at Paramount,' Nikki volunteered.

Isabelle chirped up. 'When I had those temporary offices in the District, one of the men who signed on was from California. He told me he designed several houses for big name movie stars. I can get in touch with him if need be.'

Ever practical and ever verbal, Kathryn looked around at the others. 'How does someone of that stature get away with something like this? The man has to have a flaw in his armor somewhere. Think about it. Yoko is 33. Her mother died giving birth at the age of 16 or 17. That's a lot of years. How is it he's never gotten caught? Don't people like that get disgruntled and rat each other out? He must have one hell of a network in place is all I can say.'

'The Internet is an amazing tool,' Charles said. 'The man's an actor. Obviously we have to mount a campaign of sorts. We'll meet up tomorrow morning and run through possible scenarios. I'll start now while you ladies retire upstairs to discuss this among yourselves at greater length.'

In the kitchen, Nikki made coffee while Isabelle sliced a fresh pound cake that was sitting on the counter. Alexis set out plates and silverware. Myra and Annie huddled with Yoko, assuring her that justice would be done. At Yoko's skeptical look, Myra hastened to assure her things would work out. 'Look at it this way, my dear. If you had to place a wager on us versus the man who is your father, who would you place that wager on?'

Yoko smiled for the first time that evening. 'With all of you, of course.'

The others clapped her on the back before they gave her a resounding hug. 'Good choice, sweet cheeks,' Kathryn said.

'Excellent choice,' Nikki said, and grinned. 'God, I can't wait to get my hands on that bastard!'

'Spoken like a true sister!' Alexis said.

'Let's all sit here in Myra's lovely kitchen and drink coffee while we come up with suitable punishments. Whoever comes up with the best punishment gets a prize,' Annie said, excitement ringing in her voice.

'What is the prize?' Yoko queried.

'You'll see. Now, let's get to work!'

Three

Yoko tossed and turned, looked at the beside clock for the hundredth time, and finally got out of bed. She tried to be quiet so as not to wake Kathryn and Murphy who appeared to be sleeping soundly. Wrapping a blanket around herself, she crept to the window seat, curled up and stared out into the dark night. She had never felt so alone in the whole of her life. Within minutes she felt Murphy's cold nose prodding the blanket. She moved slightly so the big dog could join her on the window seat. She wrapped her arm around his neck for comfort as she gave way to the tears she'd been holding in check.

Once, way back in the beginning, actually the first day she'd met Kathryn and Murphy, she'd been terrified of the dog. Kathryn had shown her no mercy either, telling her to get over it. For all of an hour she'd hated Kathryn and the ferocious dog. A whole hour. Now, she couldn't imagine her life without Kathryn, Murphy and all the other sisters. She cried harder into the blanket she was wrapped in. She felt Murphy leave her but didn't see him pad over to Kathryn's bed and tug at her blanket and then paw at her shoulder. Kathryn stirred, disoriented, and then swung her legs over the side of the bed, thinking the dog had to go out. He nudged her leg to follow him to the window seat where Yoko sat curled up crying.

Kathryn was wide awake now. She gathered Yoko into her arms. 'What's wrong? Are you sick? Do you want me to make some tea? What is it?'

'I am so very sorry, Kathryn. I did not mean to wake you. It is everything. I am not ready for tomorrow. Today, really. There is something I need to do first. Something I have wanted to do for a very long time but I did not have the courage to do it.'

23

'I don't think it's a problem, Yoko. We'll just tell Charles you need more time. The girls will understand. Do you want to tell me what it is you want to do? Maybe I can help you.'

'I want to go to Japan! I *need* to go there!'

'Ah, I see. Because of Harry Wong. You miss him.'

'No, no, you don't understand. Not because of Harry. I need to find my mother's people. My grandfather, my grandmother, any brothers or sisters of my mother. It has been so many years. I do not even know if they are alive but I need to see where my mother was born and lived. I want to know my family. Before I can commit to anything further concerning my mother I must understand everything. I cannot marry Harry even though he has asked me many times until I . . . am I wrong, Kathryn?'

'Not at all.' Kathryn got up, put on her robe and tossed Yoko's to her. 'Let's go, little sister. I'll wake the others and together we'll get this puppy up on four legs. Come on, shake it!'

'It's three o'clock in the morning!' Yoko protested.

'So what? We're up! The others have had enough sleep. I'll get everyone up and put coffee on. I'll even make breakfast if you want.'

'All right.'

Kathryn jerked at the belt on her robe as she left the room. She shouted at the top of her lungs, 'Everyone up! Crisis mode! Come on, come on! The house is on fire! Let's go, people!' She swatted Murphy on his butt. The dog did his part and let out an ungodly howl. Doors opened, everyone babbling at once. 'Downstairs, downstairs, no questions. Hop to it, everyone! I'm making coffee.'

Grady, Alexis's dog, raced out of the room and down the hall to follow the fast-track shepherd. Kathryn grinned when she heard Annie say, 'I must say, Myra, you run an interesting household. Do you always do fire drills in the middle of the night?'

'Shut up, Annie. This is a first for us. Something's up!' Myra mumbled as she joined the wild push to get downstairs.

'How exciting! I don't see any smoke. I don't ever remember having coffee at three o'clock in the morning. I guess we won't be going back to bed. I do hope it's flavored coffee. I adore flavored coffee. Especially the hazelnut,' Annie babbled.

'If you don't shut up, Annie, I am going to shove my foot in your mouth,' Myra shot back.

Annie clamped her lips shut as she marched into the maelstrom in the kitchen where Kathryn was banging on the counter with a wooden spoon. 'Listen up, everyone! Our little buddy here,' she said pointing to the diminutive Yoko, 'says she can't proceed with her mission until she goes to Japan to find out about her mother's family. The coffee will be ready in a minute so let's kick this around and see what we can come up with.'

Kicking around Yoko's problem lasted exactly five minutes with everyone agreeing Yoko should go to Japan. Annie rounded off the decision by volunteering the use of her private jet that could be ready in ninety minutes. 'I'll even go with her.'

'Well that settles *that*!' Isabelle said heading for the stairs.

'Yoko, dear, are you all right with this?' Myra asked as she poured coffee.

'Oh, yes. You're all too kind. I thought you would . . . I don't know what I thought. I can be ready to leave in one hour. I always carry my passport with me.'

Annie looked around trying to decide if she'd been too impetuous or stepped on anyone's toes or was out of line in some way. Myra smiled at her and gave her a discreet thumb's up.

'Then let me call my pilot so he can file a flight plan. I, too, have my passport. I'll call my chauffeur to pick us up in,' she looked down at her watch, 'ninety minutes. We can be wheels up ten minutes upon arrival. Does that work for you, my dear?'

'Yes . . . but how will we find my grandparents? I know only that they were very poor and lived outside a small village on a little farm. Will it not be like looking for a noodle in a haystack?'

'Needle, dear, not noodle. I'm sure by now Charles has some information that will be helpful. He's been working through the night. If he doesn't have sufficient information by

25

now, he'll certainly have it upon your arrival in Japan. It's an extremely long flight to Japan so that will work in both yours and Charles's favor.'

Annie, her arm around Yoko's shoulders, led her up the back staircase so they could get dressed while the others prepared breakfast.

'What's going to happen if they can't locate the grandparents or worse yet, they're dead? It's going to be such a crushing blow to Yoko,' Nikki said, agitation ringing in her voice.

Kathryn stood at the window peering into the darkness. 'Isn't it better to know than spend the rest of your life wondering and regretting not going to check things out? There's bound to be a few cousins somewhere. If Yoko can just find one relative, she'll be happy. I know exactly how she feels and my heart breaks for her.'

'You're right,' Isabelle said, having changed her mind about going back to bed. 'I also think Annie is the right person to go with her. Have you all noticed how motherly she is? Yoko just eats it up and that's the way it should be.'

Alexis tied an apron around her middle. 'I'm going to make breakfast. I'm making one thing not six different things so decide what you want.'

Nikki threw a wadded-up paper napkin at Alexis. 'Bacon and eggs, toast and more coffee.' The others agreed.

The only sound heard in the kitchen was the hiss of the frying bacon and Alexis cracking eggs into a big yellow bowl.

The Ladies of Pinewood settled into a holding pattern.

Anna de Silva's luxurious Gulfstream landed smooth as silk at Tokyo's international airport. Thirty minutes later the two women were whisked through customs and out the door where they climbed into a waiting chauffeur-driven car. The moment the women settled themselves, the driver handed Annie a manila folder. In stilted English he said, 'I am to drive you to your destination, ladies. There is fresh coffee and tea in the thermos containers as well as fresh baguettes. There are also two copies each of the *Tokyo Sun*, the *Washington Post* and the *New York Times* for your reading pleasure. It will take us seven hours to reach our destination.'

26

Annie reached for the thermos that said COFFEE on the top in big red letters. Yoko reached for the one that said TEA. 'I guess we have Charles to thank for all this. It is so like him. He is a master at taking care of details. Not that these are details – more like absolute necessities. I'm babbling again. I don't know why I do that. Myra is forever telling me to be quiet. I guess I'm just nervous. Do you want to read whatever is in this folder since it concerns you or do you want me to read it?'

Yoko sipped at the hot tea. 'I would prefer for you to read it. I have some . . . some limited difficulty reading English.'

Annie shuffled the thick sheaf of papers in her lap and put on a pair of wire-rimmed reading glasses. She skimmed through the papers before she started to read. 'How does the man do all this?' she said more to herself than anything else.

'Charles can do anything. He really can. He calls the Queen of England Lizzie and they speak on the phone.'

'Imagine that!' Annie said adjusting her glasses. 'All right now, here we go. As you know, your mother's name was Suki which means beautiful and beloved. She had or has three sisters who are named Yayoi which means born in spring, Yoshe which means beauty, Ran which means water lily and a symbol of purity. There were four brothers named according to this as first born, second born, third born and fourth born. Their names are Taro, Jiro, Saburo and Shiro.

'Your grandfather's name is Kiyoshi which means quiet. Your grandmother's name is Umeko which means she is a plum-blossom child. So, you have three aunts and four uncles if they are still alive. You also probably have many cousins. Do you know what your mother's last name was?'

'No, the aunts did not tell me. I don't know if they knew. They just used the one name.'

'Well, the name on this paper says your mother's last name was Naoki which by the way means straight tree. However does that man do this?' Anna puzzled. Your mother's name was Suki Naoki. A very pretty name. Do you feel better now, Yoko, that you know your relatives' names?'

Yoko rolled the name off her lips several times. 'Yes, oh, yes. Now I don't feel like an orphan. Even if it turns out that

27

we can't find any of them I will be content knowing this. I brought my mother's picture with me to show . . . my . . . my family. Annie, do you think they are alive? Do you think they will like me?'

Annie's throat constricted. 'I don't know, child. What I do know is if they are alive, they will love you with all their hearts.'

'It's kind of you to say that. I want to believe it. Perhaps now that we are just hours away I will be able to sleep. Do you mind if I do not keep you company?'

'Not at all. I'll watch the countryside and read all these papers and the newspapers to make the time go faster.'

The moment Yoko slipped into a sound sleep, Annie relaxed and leaned into the corner of the comfortable car. She, too, was asleep within minutes.

It was a small rag-tag village with lopsided stores, vegetable stands, rusty pickup trucks, chickens and ducks waddling across the road scratching for food. Old people and little children walked slowly as they moved about. Yoko could only gasp. Annie wasn't as shocked as Yoko. She'd seen villages like this when she and her family had first retired to Spain. Her husband had worked tirelessly to improve conditions for the people and for the most part had been successful. To this day she funded those same villages, leaving the disbursement of funds to the padres.

The car ground to a halt. The driver got out of the car and walked up to one of the old ramshackle buildings. 'I wonder if he speaks Japanese,' Annie said. Yoko opened the car door and sprinted to the same building. She couldn't wait for the driver's halting use of the language. She was like a runaway train, her words tumbling over one another as she asked for directions to the house of her grandparents, Kiyoshi and Umeko Naoki.

Annie watched as the young woman and the aged one conversed. There were a lot of hand movements and nods. Finally, Yoko wiped at her eyes and bowed low in respect to the aged one. Both the driver and Yoko returned to the car. This time, Yoko sat in the front seat so she could offer directions in English. She turned around, her eyes wet and glistening. 'My grandparents are alive but unwell. They live on the same small farm. The man told me there are no aunts. He said they are all gone and he does not know where they went but it was many years ago. One uncle lives in Tokyo and comes one time each month and brings much food and medicine. One uncle is in Saigon and only comes one time a year. Another uncle stays with my grandparents and the last uncle is a no good bum. He does not know where he is. I didn't ask about cousins. I have a family. I really have a family. Oh, Annie, thank you so much for making this trip possible. I will never be able to thank you.'

Annie smiled. 'I just provided the transportation. Charles found your relatives. I am happy for you, child. Oh, your grandparents are going to be so surprised when they see you.'

Yoko started to cry. 'I brought no gifts. We should have brought food and presents. What will my grandparents think of me?'

'We can do all that later, little one. You did bring a present, the picture of your mother. I think for now the picture will be gift enough.'

'Annie, you know about such things, what would I have to do to take my grandparents to America where I can take care of them?'

'Slow down, little one, not so fast. It won't be an easy task but I'm sure Charles can arrange things if your grandparents are willing to make the trip. If they are not well, they might not want to leave their home.'

'I'm sure I can convince them to visit. I will wait on them hand and foot, shower them with love and good food I cook myself. I will give my grandmother flowers every day. I do not know what you do for a grandfather but I will find out.'

'Perhaps a big hug every day,' Annie said.

'That would work, too. Oh, we're slowing down. This must be the farm.'

Annie looked out the window. The farm was exactly what she expected, no more no less. Very poor people lived here trying to eke out a living and to stay alive. Well, she could change all that with one phone call. She watched as Yoko leaped out of the car before it came to a complete stop, and raced across the dry patch of ground that led to the door of the house.

Annie climbed out of the car along with the driver, who looked as tired as she felt. They both leaned against the side of the car. Neither spoke.

What was going on indoors? Was the reunion a happy one? Childishly, Annie crossed her fingers. Her eyes on the door, she continued to wait. She jerked to attention when Yoko appeared and shouted, 'Come, come, I want you to meet my grandparents!'

The driver, a burly man who looked like a sumu wrestler, grinned as he took Annie's elbow to escort her into the little farmhouse.

Four

The driver elected to stay outside, mumbling something that sounded like, 'I have no wish to intrude on a family reunion.' Annie shrugged and walked into the tidy, spartan room where two old, wrinkled, wizened people sat in little chairs. She was immediately struck by how tiny the aged ones were, just like Yoko. Their eyes in their wrinkled faces were bright and alert, the grandmother's full of tears. The old couple inclined their heads and Annie bowed in respect.

Annie looked around for a chair but there were none, just mats and cushions. Yoko indicated she should sit wherever she wanted as she dropped to her knees and reached out to take one hand of her grandmother and one hand of her grandfather. 'They are happy to see me. They say I look exactly like my mother. They want to know everything there is to tell about my mother. I must tell them many lies to make them happy. I will tell them she died from problems in her chest and that she owned a lovely flower shop that she gave to me. I will tell them the handsome American who . . . who purchased her also died in a car crash. They have not seen my other aunts once they were sold. My grandmother's heart is heavy. She said all her daughters were beautiful. My grandfather says his sons are selfish and uncaring. The one who is a no good bum takes drugs and is in jail a lot of time. The other sons want no part of him although one son does bring food and medicine, when he thinks about it. His heart is also heavy.'

Annie couldn't think of a thing to say so she simply nodded. She crossed her legs and tried to get comfortable on the cushion she was sitting on. How was this all going to end, she wondered?

31

An hour passed and then another. Annie tried to unobtrusively stretch her neck. Her legs were getting cramped. She wanted to stand up and go outside but she didn't want to cause a diversion. Finally, Yoko stopped talking and turned to Annie. 'My grandparents have no wish to even temporarily go to the big city. They say their son, the one who comes once a month, lives in the evil city. They do not wish to go to America. They want to stay here where they will die. They have only one wish and that is to go to a Shinto shrine but they cannot do even that because they are too sick and frail. They asked me to go and light the joss sticks. I said I would do that. My grandmother wanted to know what my mother's favorite flower was and I said a lily. I have no idea if that is true or not. She smiled. She, too, loves lilies. Once she said she had a flower garden. Now all she has is a small vegetable garden. A little boy in the village comes to tend it.'

Annie looked around. 'What do they do all day, Yoko? There is no television, no radio, no newspapers. How do they pass the day?'

Yoko offered up a wan smile. 'They sit. They smoke their opium pipes. They eat their rice and vegetables and they . . . dream. Of what I'm not sure.'

Annie felt tears gather in her eyes. She wanted to ask if they had regrets about selling their daughters but she bit her tongue. Yoko, as if reading her thoughts, said, 'They speak to each other every single day about their daughters as they try to imagine the wonderful lives they have. They pretend they have twenty grandchildren from their daughters in the far-off land of America where the streets are gold and money hangs from trees.'

'Don't they wonder why their daughters never came back to take care of them?'

Yoko sighed. 'No, they simply accept their absence. As you can see, they are simple people with no desires. It is breaking my heart but I must accept it. We must leave now. They do not wish me to stay. I . . . I thought they would want me to stay with them for a few days but they say no, I must return to my life and to remember them in my prayers.'

'Then I'll wait outside for you so you can say your final

good-byes,' Annie said as she untangled herself from her cushion. 'I must be getting old,' she mumbled to herself as she groaned at the stiffness in her legs. Unsteady on her numb feet, she bowed low and said, 'Sayonara.' The old ones nodded.

When the door closed behind Annie, Yoko moved closer to her grandparents, still on her haunches. She talked quickly, tears streaming down her cheeks. She wanted to ask them if they loved her, if they loved her mother and her aunts, but the words stuck in her throat. She took a liberty and moved even closer to lay her head in her grandmother's lap. She waited, hardly daring to breathe. Would she pat her shoulder? Would she stroke her hair with her old, gnarled fingers? When she finally felt the light touch she almost fainted. And then there was another touch to her shoulder. She grew light headed with relief. They loved her. If only she could hug them. Squeeze them close until they returned the feeling. She accepted that it was not their way. Using her hands, she pushed herself upright and bowed low.

Should she leave the picture of her mother? It was the only thing in her life that she treasured. She bit down on her lip as she withdrew the little oval picture from her pocket and held it out. She was surprised when her grandfather instead of her grandmother reached for it. 'Suki.'

'Yes, Suki, grandfather. My mother.'

The old man nodded. With a long bony finger, the old man touched his wife's arm. She got up and tottered over to a low wooden chest. She bent down and opened it. When she returned to her little chair, she held out her hand. Yoko looked down to sec a seashell comb. Clearly she was meant to take it.

'It was Suki's,' the old lady said. 'The picture for the comb.' Yoko wanted to scream, no, no, I want the picture, but she didn't. Instead she fixed the comb in her hair and smiled. The aged ones nodded and then motioned to the door. She was to leave.

It was all Yoko could do not to cry. 'I will not say good-bye for I will come back soon. I will. I promise.' She waited a heartbeat to see if there was a response but there wasn't. She closed the door softly behind her.

Outside in the cool afternoon sunshine, Yoko swiped at her

eyes. She straightened her shoulders and marched over to the car. She heard a dog bark, saw a bird swoop down to scratch in the gravel. She noticed but she paid it no mind. She took a few moments to stare at the little farmhouse, wishing she had a camera. It didn't matter; she committed everything to memory. She turned to Annie, her eyes glistening.

'What is it, little one?'

'When it's all over, when I have avenged my mother, I will come back here for a period of time. I will plant a garden with flowers and vegetables. I'll clean the house, especially the windows so my grandparents can see the garden. I may even plant some cherry blossom trees. Big ones in full leaf. I'll cook good nourishing food for them, make them tea and try to wean them off the opium pipes. I want to be a good granddaughter. I will shower them with love and kindness for all they have been forced to endure. That man will pay for all of this. Will you help me, Annie? Will you see that he pays for my grandparents' last days?'

'As Kathryn would say, absolutely and you can take that to the bank.'

Yoko smiled through her tears. She turned for one last look. She waved even though she knew the old ones couldn't see her.

She would return.

Jack Emery propped his feet on his desk, leaned back in his chair and closed his eyes. He knew he should go home but he was mentally whipped, tired beyond tired. He needed to get his second wind before starting for home. Now, if Nikki was at the house he would have crawled all the way to Georgetown no matter how tired he felt.

He was up to date, though, where the Ladies of Pinewood were concerned. He now knew that Myra and Charles were aware of his silent membership in their little society. The fact that they were okay with it boggled his mind. Who knew?

Jack's cell phone rang. He debated not answering it but the thought that it might be Nikki forced him to reach for the cell on his desk. He snorted when he saw the number that was displayed on the little window.

'Yeah, Harry. How did things go in the trials? Did you wipe up the floor with all that fancy footwork and kicking?' Like he really cared. 'Harry, Harry, get a grip. How the hell would I know where your lady love is? Maybe she took a vacation if the shop is closed. I'm sure she'll return your calls. You called thirteen times! What did I tell you about being over eager?'

Sometimes he really hated all the lying he had to do since he got involved with the ladies out in Pinewood. Sometimes.

'Listen, Harry, I'm half out the door. It's been a long day and not one minute of it was good. Will you stop that. Her dead body is not going to show up in our morgue. Goodnight, Harry.'

Jack took the elevator to the first floor, crossed the lobby, waved or called goodnight to several people and walked outside to see that it was snowing heavily. By the time he got to his car in the lot, his Brooks Brothers loafers, his favorite pair of shoes, were sodden and he was sliding all over the place. He cursed and grumbled under his breath as he cleared the snow off his windshield. His hands were cold and numb by the time he got to the back window. Now, he was really in a foul mood. All the way home he thought about a hot shower and a cozy fire with a couple of beers and some left-over Chinese food.

As he crept along the snow-filled road, Jack tried to shift his thoughts into the neutral zone. It wasn't the snow that had him in a foul mood. It was something else he really didn't want to think about but knew he had to. He knew Charles Martin had a long arm and entry into some very high places but until today he had no idea how powerful the quiet unassuming man really was. At the eleventh hour the fibbies had called and cancelled his ten o'clock meeting and actually apologized for any inconvenience. Then at 12:30 some chick with a sexy voice from the DOJ called and did the same thing. His boss had looked at him suspiciously but hadn't said a word.

It was snowing harder, drifting in places. Normally, he liked snow, especially a good snowstorm, but tonight Jack was relieved when he rounded the corner and found a parking space one door up from Nikki's house. He looked at his gas gauge. Shit, he was on E for empty. Oh, well, he'd worry about that in the morning. He was out of the car and in the house within seconds. He started to strip down the minute he locked the door behind him and set the alarm. He was down to his underwear when he reached the living room where he threw some logs in the fireplace and struck a match. He turned the heat to eighty and galloped up the stairs. He heard the phone ring but he ignored it.

Thirty minutes later, Jack was heating the leftover Chinese food, wearing flannel pajamas with tiny red hearts all over them, a gift from Nikki. He was glad there was no one to see him.

He was half way through his food, slouched into the corner of the couch, when he remembered hearing the phone ringing when he first got home. He reached behind him for the portable phone and looked at the caller I.D. Mark Lane. Contortionist that he was, he managed to stretch behind him to replace the phone and not spill the food on his plate. The phone rang in his hand before he could replace it. Startled, he dropped the plate and watched his shrimp chow mein splatter on the floor. Shit!

'Yeah,' he barked irritably.

'It's me, Jack,' Mark Lane said. 'Just calling to make sure you got home okay. How'd it go today with the fibbies and the DOJ?'

'They both called and cancelled. Even apologized. I can't figure it out. You want to make some calls, Mark, to some of your old buddies in the Hoover building, maybe get a bead on all of this? I can't make any sense of it. Robinson made it all sound like a slam dunk when I talked to him yesterday. He was so damn cocky I had the feeling they were going to lock me up and throw away the key. Hell, you were there, you heard him. Now this.'

'They apologized? Jack, the FBI does *not* apologize. Never as in never. I think the Department of Justice operates under the same policy. Somebody pretty powerful must have intervened on your behalf. I can't think of any other explanation. You said yourself Robinson had no hard proof. It was just his and Maggie's side of it. I'll make some calls but don't get your hopes up. The guys I know aren't players, just field agents who try to keep their noses clean and not get involved in bureau politics. What do you think happened?'

'Don't know, Mark. It was a relief, I can tell you that. I wasn't looking forward to a debate with the fibbies. With the exception of you, they're all hard asses. Those guys at the DOJ are just as bad. Think about it, Mark. If Ted Robinson has the National Security Advisor on his side, they should have dragged me kicking and screaming to the Hoover building. Maybe Ted was just blowing smoke but I had the feeling he had some kind of backup, and it's got to be the ex-National Security Advisor.'

'Well, shit, Jack, I heard, just like you and half of Washington the rumors floating around when the NSA had his . . . accident. It was fodder for weeks. The administration cut him loose when those tales of spousal abuse hit the rumor mill. That's the reason those Pinewood ladies took him on, right? I heard he was beating up his wife pretty bad and the Pinewood ladies stepped in and did a tit for tat kind of thing. More tit than tat or so the rumor goes. I can just see Robinson teaming up with him. The NSA wants vengeance. If spilling his guts to a fast track reporter is the only way he can strike out at the administration, then that's what the bastard will do. The fibs have to pay attention and investigate any and all complaints, you know that. Plus, they don't want the press, especially the *Post*, riding their asses. The DOJ is no different.'

Jack eyed the chow mein on the carpet. Nikki was going to kill him. 'That's kind of my take, too, but I need more info. Nose around, you might come up with something.'

'Just don't get your hopes up. Who do you think is your guardian angel? That guy Martin? Nikki doesn't carry any weight so that lets her out. Maybe Myra Rutledge or the new lady from Manassas. That's a lot of heavy fire power. I'm thinking you shouldn't be looking a gift horse in the mouth. Maybe the wise course of action is to leave it all alone and count your blessings.'

The chow mein on the floor was bothering Jack. He had to get off the phone and clean it up. 'Do what you can, Mark.

I'll call you in the morning. I have a feeling the city is going to shut down if this snow continues. You might be able to get hold of a lot of people at home if the roads aren't open.'

Jack poked at the chow mein with his big toe to see if it had stained the beige carpet. Yep. 'See ya,' he said ending the call.

Thirty minutes later, the carpet looked reasonably clean. He'd probably have to call in a professional at some point but for now the stain was barely noticeable. While he was returning the cleaning supplies to the kitchen, he looked out the window at the falling snow. He could see a huge drift in the tiny back yard. Too much snow could mean Nikki wouldn't make it into the city from the farm. He wondered why she hadn't called him. Things were probably hopping out at Pinewood. He shivered as he contemplated what the devious women would do for Harry's girlfriend.

A fluffer nutter sandwich in one hand, a beer in the other, Jack made his way back to the living room. Before he started to eat, he tossed another log onto the fire. Sparks shot upward as the new log caught fire. He wished Nikki was here so they could curl up in front of the fire. He looked down at the sandwich, Nikki's favorite. She said Myra used to make fluffer nutters for her and Barbara when they were little. Bread, butter, peanut butter, marshmallow fluff and thinly sliced banana on top crowned by a second slice of bread. A very filling sandwich but he really needed the beer to wash it down.

Jack flopped down on the sofa to devour his sandwich. Right now, a big dog keeping him company would be nice. Even a cat. Damn, why didn't Nikki call? He eyed the portable phone on the cushion. He could call her. Now that everyone at Pinewood knew he was an active member, and Nikki's inside informant, he didn't have to sneak around. He shrugged. She would call him when she had something to say. God forbid he should disrupt one of Martin's heavy-duty meetings. He grimaced as he wondered if he would ever be invited to attend one of those top secret meetings. He finally decided his job was outside the circle.

What a shitty place to be.

Five

Charles Martin stepped down into the empty war room and sat down at the round table that normally accommodated the seven ladies of Pinewood. Today he was alone and he was glad. Nothing in his long illustrious life and career prepared him for what he'd found out about Michael Lyons, Yoko's American father. Things he wasn't yet ready to present to the members of the Sisterhood. He had to be dispassionate when he presented his findings so that they could come to a satisfactory resolution where the movie star was concerned. Now simply wasn't the time.

Charles felt heartsick. How depraved could one human being be and yet have people, fans, dignitaries, worship at his feet? His gaze swivelled around the compact room to light on one of the oversize monitors and then to the green folder he'd placed in the center of the table. For the first time in his life he questioned Lady Justice. And like the women of the Sisterhood, he questioned the entire judicial system that allowed scum like Lyons to live among decent human beings. He moved his hands off the table, not wanting to touch the thick green folder. He'd give anything never to touch it again. Such a foolish thought.

Charles dropped his head into his hands as he roll-called his distinguished life and how he'd gotten to this place in time. He'd gone into service at MI6 as a young man and had worked tirelessly as a covert spy. He'd done Black Ops, Black Bag jobs, anything he was called on to do. The Queen had knighted him. Then his cover had been blown and the powers that be had sent him across the ocean where he signed on as head of security of Myra Rutledge's huge Fortune 500 candy company. There he renewed his relationship with Myra that had started in their teens when her parents brought her to England.

They weren't married but it wasn't for his lack of proposing. Perhaps this year. Myra said she didn't need to be made an honest woman. Only God in heaven knew how much he loved Myra and how much Myra loved him. How else could he have agreed to help her with his expertise to set up the Sisterhood to win justice for those who fell through the cracks or when Lady Justice looked the other way?

He loved being back in the game, loved that he could call on other operatives to help him. Loved that he could help the sisters with his expertise and Myra's unlimited funds. With more than one close call, they'd all managed to stay ahead of the authorities, thanks in part to Jack Emery, Nikki's fiancé, who had started out as an adversary but now was one of them.

Doubt cloaked him now like a shroud. Could he bring this all together for the sisters? If it were up to him, he'd simply seek out the bloody son of a bitch and blow a hole in his head. Unfortunately, that wasn't an option. He thought about Yoko and wondered how she would handle the sordid details. Alexis said Yoko was a tough little cookie but tough or not, she might not be able to handle the information in the thick green folder.

Clearly he was going to have to call in extra help. It shouldn't prove to be a problem since he'd called in so many favors he'd lost count just to get the material in the green folder. The Internet had proved to be an invaluable tool. Without it, he wouldn't have the information he had and Michael Lyons wouldn't be in the business he was in. He instantly realized the latter part was a lie. Men like Lyons would simply find other ways to do their trafficking. The Internet, aside from anonymity, simply made things a hundred times easier.

Charles swiveled around in the chair and glared at Lady Justice. 'You truly are blind, my dear, especially in this case.' The statement didn't make him feel one bit better. Now he had to pick up the green folder and take it back to his work station and continue until he couldn't stand it a moment longer.

Three thousand miles away, the object of Charles Martin's investigation stepped out of the shower. He didn't bother to dry off but wrapped a thick, thirsty black towel around his middle. He marched through the oversize bathroom into the dressing room where he popped in his summer blue contact lenses before he ripped off his towel to view his entire body in the full-length mirror. He was totally tanned like George Hamilton, thanks to his tanning bed.

Hollywood's Super Stud fingered the hairline scars all over his body. Liposuction was a wonderful thing, provided that one had a doctor who knew what he was doing. The hair implants had been done in Switzerland, along with his various surgeries in his fight to ward off age. He smiled at himself. His teeth, mostly caps and expensive veneer, glowed in the early morning light. He had many smiles – winsome, a wicked grin, his honest smile, his devious smile and then the smile his adoring public never saw. He called it his lust smile.

Michael Lyons was between pictures which meant he had a full month to do nothing but indulge himself and his *squirrely* appetites. He smiled at himself again before he got dressed. As always, his dress was impeccable even if he planned on staying indoors the whole day. Today he wore khaki slacks and a blue cashmere sweater that matched his eyes. Mr Casual himself. Someone might stop by.

Mick, as he liked to be called, meandered through his ten thousand square foot house to his office where life sized posters of himself graced the walls. His Oscars stood sentinel on the mantel. Above the Oscars was a full body portrait of himself sitting by the beach in a colorful striped beach chair. It was his favorite picture of himself and each morning, sometimes in the evening, too, he saluted it.

Five different state-of-the-art computers sat in the middle of the room. When they were installed he had only one demand: 'I want them to be impregnable.' And that's what he got, to the tune of millions of dollars. The White House would find it difficult to duplicate what stood before him.

His *hobby*, which is how he thought of his perversion, called for such secretive measures. His work, or his day job, was relegated to a different computer in a small alcove. When you were one of Hollywood's golden people, others took care of publicity, guest appearances and schedules. His business manager kept those funds separate from his other income that stopped just short of billionaire status. Sins of the flesh paid well.

Sometimes, like now, he stopped to think about what he was doing and how long he'd been doing it without anyone suspecting that Hollywood's idol was something other than what they saw on the screen. His adoring public saw him donating vast sums of money to Animal Rights, the Red Cross, the homeless, children's rights and any worthy cause that came his way. All funded from his nefarious activities. He'd been invited to the White House more times than he could remember. He played golf with the governor. He'd even had an audience with the Pope, even though he was a Baptist. Before he left Rome he'd left behind a ten million dollar check at the Vatican for the poor souls who needed help. The Pope had blessed him and called him 'my child.' The truth was, Mick Lyons was an atheist even though he claimed Baptist status and never saw the inside of a church.

The private phone line, complete with scrambler, rang, a pleasant tinkling sound. Mick Lyons hated loud noises. What he hated even more than loud noises was the sound of whimpering crying women when they found out what he was all about.

Lyons's voice was husky, sensual, his public voice when he said 'Hello.'

'Mick, it's Lyle. I thought you were going to call me back yesterday. I need you to say yes or no to the script I sent you. The studio wants an answer by noon. It's a great script, I read it twice. It's you through and through. You could do it with your eyes closed,' the agent said.

'I got sidetracked yesterday, Lyle. The answer is yes, and you're right, it's a good script. I want a double of my choice for the fight scenes. And, I'm going out of town for the whole month so don't call me unless the head of the studio dies or the check bounces.'

Mick broke the connection and booted up his computer. This was the part of the day he liked best; when he opened his secret email to see what was forthcoming from the four corners of the world. Today he was expecting to hear when his next Asian delivery would take place.

In seven short minutes, the handsome movie star's mood turned ugly. His adoring public would have run for cover if they'd seen him in this mood. He used up five full minutes tapping out equally ugly messages, the gist of which was that clients were waiting and if delivery wasn't on time, there were others standing in line for the opportunity to go on his cash payroll. Now, his whole day was ruined. He would spend hours on the phone trying to appease his sick perverted friends and clients.

Charles Martin tightened the collar of his jacket. Of all the months of the year, February was the month he hated most. Myra had wanted him to cancel the meeting when the snow reached the three-foot mark but the man he was to meet had been explicit. A no show would cancel any further contact. He also hated secret meetings that took place in Lafayette Park across from the White House. He'd debated long and hard before he had consented to this particular meeting, prefer-ring scrambled telephones or secure email. It wasn't that he didn't trust the man he was meeting; he did. No matter how careful, how diligent you were, something or someone could foul things up royally just by going on with their daily lives. Snow, an act of nature, could prove to be disastrous.

According to Steve Landry, one of Charles's operatives, Alan Nolan was the best computer hacker in the world. The operative had stressed the word *world* and in constant demand which translated meant he picked and chose those cases that challenged him. The description given to him was of a nerdy looking young man who lived in the gray shadows of the world, offering his services to anyone who could afford his astronomical fees. A man, the operative said, who knew how to deliver and who kept his mouth shut. As far as Landry was concerned, if you wanted his services, you showed up with a knapsack full of green. No checks, no credit cards and no promises.

Charles Martin did not look like Charles Martin today. Alexis and her Red Bag of tricks had altered his appearance just enough that even under intense grilling by the authori-ties, Landry wouldn't be able to make a positive identification where Charles was concerned. He wore an old watch cap to cover his gray hair, glasses that were plain glass, and gray contact lenses. The down jacket was padded and puffed him out, making him look heavier than he was. He wore leather gloves and his fingerprints were not on the knapsack or the bills inside. Five hundred thousand now and the rest when Landry delivered the passwords to Michael Lyons's computers and access to his stored files.

Charles stretched his arm out so he could roll back the cuff to see what time it was. Two minutes to go. With thirty seconds to spare, Charles looked through a tree bare of leaves to see a man plodding toward him in the deep snow. At first glance the man looked like the nerd his operative had described. On second glance, Charles knew the man was not a nerd. His eyes were sharp and shrewd behind glasses like the ones he was wearing. Meaning, of course, the man was in disguise just as he was.

Charles took the initiative. 'You were told what I want. Can you do it?'

The response was succinct. 'Yes.'

'Delivery time?' Charles asked coolly.

'Three days. Payment is half now, the other half on delivery.'

'Guaranteed?'

The nerd angled his head toward the White House to stare at the gawking tourists. 'Absolutely. Where do you want to take delivery?'

'The Lincoln Memorial.'

The nerd pondered the delivery site. 'Okay. This is the only time we'll meet. Someone else will make delivery. Use a gray knapsack. Dusk, around five-thirty. Does that meet with your approval?'

Charles sucked in his breath. 'Satisfactory.' He released the knapsack from his shoulders, set it on the ground, and walked away. He wondered if he'd just squandered a half a million dollars of Myra's money. His gut told him he hadn't.

An hour later, after changing taxis twice, riding the Metro, and then hoofing around the mall, Charles felt confident that he wasn't wearing a tail when he climbed into his own SUV and started the engine. He sat for a few moments waiting for the heater to click on. Standing in the park in deep snow for close to an hour had left him numb with cold. The temperature gauge on the dashboard said it was seven degrees. And it was still snowing. His best bet would be to check into the Hay Adams instead of trying to make it back to Pinewood.

His decision made, Charles inched his way out into traffic. Another car, parked six cars to his right, pulled out behind him. Ted Robinson smacked his hands together and cackled happily. 'Gotcha, you fucking spook!' He hit the speed dial on his cell phone.

Maggie Spritzer bellowed into her own cell phone. 'I'm on him, Ted and he's *walking*. How come I have the shit detail while you are sitting nice and warm in the car? For your information, I can't feel my feet. I'm frozen stiff. In case you haven't noticed the snow is up to my belly-button.'

'Stop whining and don't lose that guy. We need to know who he is.'

Maggie suggested he do something that was an impossible feat. Ted cackled again as he followed Charles Martin.

'This time I gotcha, you bastard.' Ted patted the small camera he carried in his pocket. It was a nice one, smaller than a package of cigarettes, half as thin, with five pixels. 'Gotcha,' he said again. While he wasn't sure what he had, he knew he had *something*.

Six

The hour was late, well past midnight, when Charles sat down on the chest at the foot of the bed to remove his shoes. Myra thought she'd never seen him look so weary, so distraught. She sat down beside him on the chest and started to rub his shoulders. 'I'm a good listener, Charles,' she said softly.

Charles closed his eyes and allowed Myra's strong hands to work at the knots in his neck and shoulders. The fire crackled in the fireplace but did little to warm the drafty old room in the farmhouse. Outside, snow fell softly, covering everything with pristine whiteness. He'd been shocked to see that it was snowing again when he entered the main part of the house from the war room. Earlier in the day he'd looked outdoors to see that most of the snow from the previous storm was all but gone, and now this.

Charles struggled for just the right words for Myra's benefit. He decided he was simply too tired to sugar coat anything. 'I think this is the worst thing I've ever worked on in my entire life. I can't tell you how many times I wanted to call the girls to tell them I didn't want any part of Yoko's mission. I can't seem to feel clean these days. I know there is decadence, filth, perversion in the world but this man . . . this man is the Devil. He moves among society, receives accolades, adoration and is in such demand it makes me question society as a whole. He's been doing what he's doing for years and years and no one, no one, Myra, has a clue as to who this man really is.

'So many times I wanted to rush to Yoko, to gather her close and explain who her father really is and that she should forget about her mission. I'm not sure what she's going to do when we bring it all out into the open. That little lady is so honorable, how will she react when she realizes all the sisters will know?'

Myra continued to knead Charles's shoulders. 'I think Yoko can handle anything you present to her. The girls will handle it too. This is what we *do*, Charles. We right the wrongs where possible. Now, if you're telling me you don't think the Sisterhood is capable of taking on Michael Lyons, that's a different story. None of us lives under a bush, my dear. We know what goes on in the world.'

'Myra, the papers report a pornography ring, the authorities round up a group of perverted souls, and then the story disappears until the next one surfaces. Lyons isn't just involved in a few porno films. He's into everything. Slavery, pedophilia, sick sex clubs that defy description, the buying and selling of human beings to satisfy his and his cronies' sick sexual desires. The Internet is the perfect tool for someone like him. And the man has been nominated, again, for an Academy Award. Why hasn't someone stumbled onto his sick perversion? Every instinct I possess tells me that people have voiced dissatisfaction and he had them taken care of. I have no doubt the man is capable of murder. I want to kill him with my bare hands.'

'The Sisterhood stops short of murder, Charles. Weather permitting, we'll make a decision in the morning when the girls get here. Now, I want you to take a nice warm shower while I build up the fire. We're going to sit on the sofa and drink some really wonderful wine. The whole bottle, Charles. Then we're going to go to sleep.'

Charles stood up, his eyes grateful as he patted Myra's shoulders before he headed for the shower.

Myra made her way over to the fireplace where she threw in two huge birch logs. A shower of sparks shot upward before they cascaded downward. She was opening the bottle of wine when she felt a light touch to her shoulder. She whirled around, the color draining from her face.

'Hi, Mom. Don't work that screw so hard, do it gently and the cork will pop right out.'

'Darling girl, is it really you?' Myra sat down on the sofa. She loved it when her daughter *visited*. 'Is something wrong?

You never . . . *talk* to me this late at night. It's Charles, isn't it. You're worried about him. I am, too, dear.'

'*Mom, Michael Lyons is a man. Do I need to say more?*'

'I guess you mean a bunch of women can take him down. Did I say that right? I think that's the way Kathryn would phrase it.'

'*You got it, Mom. You guys are gonna take this guy down big time and make him rue the day he was born. Don't worry about Yoko. She knows most of it and suspects the rest. She can handle it. What she couldn't handle was not knowing she had a real family. Now that she knows a little more about her mother, she'll handle anything you throw at her.*'

Myra's mood lightened. 'Hearing you say that makes me feel better.'

'*Mom, you're going to have to toughen up. Charles needs you right now to be strong. The girls will know what to do and they'll all handle it. Here comes Charles. 'Night, Mom. Kiss Charles good night for me.*'

'I'll do that. Good night, darling girl.' Myra sighed and leaned back on the sofa. These were the moments she lived for, the moments when her *spirit* daughter visited her.

'Now, this is what I call a nice evening. It's actually cozy in here now. Ah, this is a fine bottle of wine. Did I hear you talking to someone or was it the telly?'

Myra laughed. 'I was talking to this confounded cork. Sometimes talking to myself makes me relax.'

'You can't fool me, Myra. You were *talking* to our daughter Barbara, weren't you?'

'Yes, Charles, I was. She said Lyons is a man and we're women. She also reiterated what I said earlier about Yoko. Our darling girl says Yoko can handle anything you toss at her. Now, let's drink this wonderful wine and if we don't fall asleep perhaps we can do some other things.'

'Myra, I do love your back-ended invitations,' Charles said clinking his glass against hers.

Myra giggled.

Kathryn Lucas pulled her eighteen wheeler into a truck stop. Murphy reared up and looked out the window. 'It's still snowing, boy. I think we're going to have some guests for the ride out to Pinewood. Don't bark now, I have to make some phone calls.

One by one, Kathryn called the sisters. Annie was the only one who didn't answer. Kathryn's message was the same to all of them. 'If you can make it, meet me at the Shell truck stop, and I'll get us to Pinewood.' She gave directions to where she was parked. The sisters promised to battle the elements. With that promise, Kathryn climbed out of the truck to get a late breakfast or an early lunch, whatever Zack Wilson was serving at the moment. 'Come on, Murphy, this is Zack's station and you know how he loves you. I bet he has Tillie with him.' Tillie was a female shepherd Zack used to patrol the truck stop. Murphy woofed and hopped out of the truck.

Zack Wilson held the door open for Kathryn and Murphy. 'Tillie knew you were here the minute you hit the lot, Sis. What the hell are you doing out there in this weather? Where you headed? They closed the Interstate but I guess you know that.'

'I'm riding empty, Zack, and I'm headed out to McLean. I think I can make it but I need to wait for some people who are going to the same place. I'm starved, you got anything good?'

The big burly man who looked like Grizzly Adams laughed. 'Everything my wife cooks is good, you know that. Today we have stuffed pork chops, beef stew and fried chicken. I made some bread at four this morning and nine cherry pies. It's gonna be a light day so eat hearty, Sis. Don't worry about Murphy. Tillie is showing him some new toys the other truckers bring in for her. She's got about a dozen new ones since you were here last. So, what'll it be?'

'Some of everything. And some pie to go. Maybe two pies to go. You need to feed Murphy for me.'

Zack walked behind the counter where he started to dish up Kathryn's food. 'Mandy will feed him. She lives to feed people and animals. She has fourteen cats out back that she says belong to us so she feeds them. You step on this property and we own you. Food wise that is.'

Kathryn ate until she was stuffed. 'You have the best food

on the east coast, Zack. I wish I could eat that pie but I can't. I will have some more of that fine coffee if you don't mind.'

Kathryn looked over at the television sitting on a far corner of the counter. 'Academy Awards time. Who do you think will win?'

'Not a clue, Sis. Mandy's the movie buff. Probably that guy Lyons she lusts over. She has all his DVDs. Personally, I can't stand to watch him prancing around. I sure as hell can't figure out what you women see in him.'

'He's got good PR people. Don't like him myself. Seems too good to be real.'

'I said the same thing to Mandy but she said he dropped a bundle to the Pope. To the Pope no less. Makes you kind of wonder what he was sucking up for. You know, that confession thing.'

Kathryn shrugged, her eyes glued to the screen. He was a good-looking man. Nice smile. She liked Tom Cruise's smile better with that little crooked tooth of his. Cruise was real. The guy on the screen was as phony as a three-dollar bill.

Zach poured coffee for a couple of truckers before he returned to where Kathryn was sitting. 'Mandy says the guy is a cross between Clark Gable and Errol Flynn. Course you'd probably liken him to Damon and Pitt. I think he's a *wuss*.'

Kathryn burst out laughing. Calling someone a *wuss* was the worst thing Zack would ever say about anyone.

Forty minutes later the door opened and Alexis and Yoko entered the diner. They immediately sat down at the counter and asked for coffee. Even Yoko who was a tea drinker asked for coffee.

'I picked up Alexis in the shop van. Will it be all right to leave it here?' Grady stood uncertainly at his mistress's side as he sniffed out his playmate. Murphy came on the run, barked, whirled around to turn back to Tillie, Grady on his heels.

'Sure, but you'll have to park it back by the dumpster. We'll pick it up tomorrow. Oh, look, here's Nikki.'

Kathryn looked over at Zack. She grinned. 'My bridge club members. Is it okay if they leave their cars in the back by the dumpster?'

'No problem, Sis. He poured coffee for Nikki who was rubbing her hands together.

'The government shut down. That's twice in less than ten days. Supposed to get ten inches of snow by tonight. Are you sure you can make it in the truck, Kathryn?'

'Oh yeah. Anyone hear from Isabelle?'

The door opened. Isabelle entered, stomping her feet. She looked like an Eskimo. She gratefully accepted the cup of coffee Zack held out to her.

Kathryn placed some bills on the counter while Zack packaged up the two cherry pies she'd ordered to go.

Nikki leaned closer to Kathryn and whispered, 'This guy has seen us all together. Is that going to be a problem?'

Kathryn turned on her stool and whispered in return, 'They could stick lighted match sticks under Zack's toenails and he wouldn't admit to anything except to discuss the weather. We're safe. Trust me.'

Kathryn whistled for Murphy who herded Grady toward them. Each of them had a paper sack in his teeth.

'Soup bones for the trip,' Zack said.

'Thanks, Zack. See ya,' Kathryn said as she shrugged into her hooded parka.

The drive to McLean under normal weather conditions took at most an hour. Today they'd been on the road three hours and they were still ten miles from the turnoff that would lead them to Pinewood.

It was late afternoon when both dogs in the crowded cab barked to indicate they knew they were at the farm. The women heaved a collective sigh of relief.

Kathryn's rig rolled up to the electronic gates where she pressed in the code that allowed the huge monster gates to open wide. She gave the airhorn a loud yank. The sound ricocheted around the farm. The women leaped down as they did their best to straighten out their cramped limbs. The dogs raced through the snow barking and howling at the glorious white stuff that was so much fun to romp in.

'Hurry, hurry,' Myra called from the doorway. 'I have hot chocolate with loads of marshmallows for all of you.'

'And I have the pies to go with it,' Kathryn said holding

up the bag pies.' She whistled for the dogs who ran past her into the warm kitchen where they shook the snow off their heavy coats. They immediately raced into the den to lie down by the fire.

'I'm so glad you all made it safe and sound.' Myra smiled at them, her relief apparent as she hugged them one at a time.

'Charles is where he usually is when we're ready to start a mission. He expects us in the war room in one hour, just enough time to drink our hot chocolate and eat this wonderful cherry pie. Dinner is roasting in the oven. It's one of those everything-in-one-pan dinners, the kind you all like because it cuts down on the dishwashing.'

While they drank their hot chocolate and ate the delectable cherry pie, the women talked about the snow, the government shutting down, and the possibility they could do some playing in the snow with the snowmobiles in the barn that Myra had once given them as Christmas presents.

'They're gassed up and ready to go. Charles did it early this morning. How well he knows us,' Myra said.

Nikki looked around. 'Oh, my gosh, I forgot about Annie. Where is she?'

'With Charles. She arrived before it got light out. When she saw how bad the weather was getting she decided to leave early. She arrived safe and sound. We're all here. This is good pie, Kathryn. As good as Charles's pies but don't tell him I said that.'

Kathryn laughed. 'One of these days I'm going to take you and Charles to Zack's diner. Everything is home made from scratch.'

Myra played with her pearls. 'Yes, yes, someday we'll have to do that. If you're finished, I think it's time to go below and get on with Yoko's mission. There have been enough delays.'

As one, the women knew Myra was worried about something. The mood turned solemn as they cleared the table and fell into line behind her as she led the way to the secret bookshelf.

The women were still solemn when they took their places at the round table where Annie was already sitting. They offered up greetings, discussed the snow storm for a few minutes until Myra called the meeting to order.

Myra looked up to see Lady Justice gracing them with her presence. She took a deep breath before she shuffled the papers in front of her. As she started to speak, she fingered the pearls at her neck.

Nikki, who knew Myra better than anyone except Charles, knew that her adoptive mother was worried. Big time.

Seven

Nikki's hands itched to open the folder in front of her. She tried not to stare at Yoko who looked, in her opinion, incredibly calm. Since returning from Japan and the meeting with her grandparents she seemed to have moved to a higher plane of serenity. She risked a glance at Charles and was stunned to see that his normally ruddy complexion was pasty white and strained. To her experienced eye, Myra was decidedly uncomfortable. What they were about to see and read must be really bad. Right that moment she wished she was with Jack in Georgetown.

Nikki was jarred from her thoughts when Kathryn spoke. 'When are we going to run this,' she said tapping the green folder, 'up the flagpole?'

'Right now, dear. I was just about to tell you all to open your folders and read the contents. I don't see . . . Charles and I don't feel we need to discuss the contents aloud unless you all vote to do so. When you're finished reading, we'll move to the punishment phase. Are there any questions?'

The only sound in the room was the whirring of the oscillating fan overhead and a few beeps and chirps from the bank of monitors under Charles's command as Lady Justice watched over them.

Above the main floor, Charles watched the women carefully for their reaction to the reading material in front of them. All, it seemed to him, with the exception of Yoko, were stunned. Kathryn, while he couldn't hear her words, was cursing up a storm. Annie was speechless, her eyes wide in horror. Alexis wiped at her eyes while Isabelle chewed on her lower lip. Nikki was stiff with anger, her hands trembling as she turned the pages and looked at the downloaded pictures. Myra looked like she did when she was in bed with the flu; sick. Just the way he felt sick.

Minutes ticked by so slowly Charles felt like he was going to jump out of his skin. He forced himself to look down at Yoko whose expression hadn't changed. At that precise moment, Kathryn closed her folder and pitched it across the room. Words he'd never heard before spewed from her mouth. She then slumped back in her seat as if someone had let all the air out of her body. Even from where he was standing he could see tears on her cheeks. Hard-boiled, tough as nails Kathryn crying!

All eyes turned to Yoko when she closed the green folder and stood up. Her eyes were bright, her shoulders stiff, her expression grim. She inclined her head slightly. 'I wish to apologize for what you were forced to read. I cannot imagine what you must think of me. I . . . No one should be forced to deal with a man like Michael Lyons. I cannot ask you, my friends, to deal with this hateful person. I withdraw my mission. I will leave now and offer up my thanks for . . . for your friendship.'

Isabelle, who was sitting next to Yoko, gave her a push. Yoko landed back in her chair. 'Like hell you're leaving!'

Kathryn bounded out of her chair, ran around the table, gave Yoko's chair a wide swing until she was facing her. 'Kiddo, nothing in this life will give me more pleasure than going after that man. Read my lips, Yoko, we are all for one and one for all or however the hell that saying goes.'

Tears rolled down Yoko's cheeks. 'But . . .'

The others joined Kathryn and squatted next to Yoko's chair as they said all the words she longed for and needed to hear.

'We can take care of this man, my dear,' Myra said. 'I want you to trust all of us. Can you do that?'

Yoko's head bobbed up and down. 'That man . . . that sick person is my father.'

'Yeah, well, sometimes shit like that happens. Don't give it another thought. He's just a sorry sack of crap we're going to take care of,' Kathryn snarled.

Alexis reached for Yoko's hands. She took both of them in her own. 'Look at me, Yoko, and listen to what I'm going to say. You know, you all know, how terrified I am of going back to prison. I will *gladly* go back to prison if I can help you put that man out of his misery.'

'And I'll go to the wall defending you. If I have to sleep with the judge and all of the jury, I'll do it,' Nikki said.

Annie cleared her throat. 'And when it's all said and done, you'll make me a happy woman if you allow me to adopt you. I miss having a daughter. You don't have to decide right now, honey, the offer will always be open.'

Kathryn whooped. 'She accepts!'

'Of course she accepts, and I'll do all the legal work for free,' Nikki said.

Charles, his color back to normal, approached the women. 'All you have to do is tell us what you want us to do, child.'

Yoko cried openly. Isabelle cradled her, whispering in her ear. A wan smile tugged at Yoko's lips as she nodded.

Myra handed her a wad of tissues. 'Are we ready to get back to business?' she asked.

Kathryn moved quickly to gather up the contents of her folder. 'I'm sorry I lost my cool before. It won't happen again. Before you can say it, Charles, I am focused.'

In spite of himself, Charles smiled. When he had the women's attention, he started to press buttons on his computer. Lady Justice faded away to be replaced with a series of photographs of Michael Lyons from the moment he set foot in Hollywood until the present day. The women stared at the pictures but refrained from making comments as, year after year, the life of Hollywood's Golden Boy filled the large screen.

'As you can see, Mr Lyons is a very handsome man. On the big screen he plays athletic, virile heroes. He's played just about every type of character there is, even a priest. He won an Academy Award for his performance in Sins of My Father where he played the part of a priest. His performance was so sterling, he was invited to Rome to visit the Pope.

'I've had to enlist the aid of some of my . . . my old friends to get the information we need. I was only partially successful until last week when I managed to secure the passwords to his very private email accounts. I'm still working on those and will have them ready to include in your folders in a day or so. They are not . . . enjoyable reading.

'I've been able to trace some of Mr Lyons's early activities when he emerged onto the Hollywood scene. The money and the fame came very quickly to him. He had it all by his mid 20s which is when he started to look . . . for other forms of . . . gratification. He started wearing disguises and frequenting sex clubs. The sex clubs appeared to be profitable so he branched out. He realized, I suppose, that if anyone found out, he would no longer be Hollywood's Golden Boy. He became a voice in the business that no one knew. At first he used his own money but as the money started to pour into his sex clubs – whose membership fee, by the way, was a hundred thousand dollars a year – he managed to separate the two. Any one club could have as many as two hundred sick perverted clients. From his 30s to his 40s he owned, or different holding companies and corporations owned, twenty such establishments. I'll leave it up to you to do the math.

'Lyons's customers all had different fantasies that he catered to. Depending on the perversion, the client was charged extra. Money poured in like a tsunami. The demands were so high that Lyons was forced to go overseas for his . . . victims. He bought human beings, mostly young women like Yoko's mother. He didn't stop with the young girls. He bought children for his pedophile clients. Pure and simple, Lyons operated a slave ring. There was no such thing as medical care, decent food or shelter. These poor souls were used, abused and discarded where they eventually died of one disease or another. Those that tried to get away were always caught and simply disappeared never to be heard from again. A very few out of the thousands the man brought to this country got their freedom. Yoko's mother was one of the very few who died on the outside when her *aunts* found her baby and did the best they could for her.

'Actor Lyons is his own best customer. He has an affinity for tiny Asian women. Some of the women he brings to his harems, for want of a better word, are his special property where he will single out one or another and actually take them into his home and pretend they are servants. He uses them for a while, then when he gets tired of them, he puts them on the sex circuit or sells them to some of his sick friends. I could go on and on about his perversion but I think you are all getting the message here. Actor Lyons, as of today, is still flourishing. Right now he is between pictures. This is when he heads to foreign countries where he buys his victims. He does this twice a year. Do any of you have any questions?'

Alexis leaned forward. 'Don't any of the families complain when they don't hear from their children?'

'Who would they complain to, Alexis? Selling one's offspring, even in foreign countries, is against the law. Lyons has a secure operation. He's an absolute wizard at covering his tracks.'

'Not true,' Isabelle said. 'You infiltrated his organization. Obviously, it's not impenetrable.'

'Only because I was able to tap into old friendships, enlist the aid of others' expertise. On my own, I could never have done it. Some of the information is suspect but taken as a whole everything I've told you holds up and fits into the man's profile.'

'Is Yoko's mother the only woman who got pregnant? How did that happen?' Annie asked.

'The usual way, my dear. I'm sure there were others, since Actor Lyons doesn't appear to be a man who practices birth control. From what I've been able to gather, should a pregnancy occur, the woman is sent out on the circuit until she simply dies. There are no files, no records of children being born that we've been able to come up with. Yoko is the exception. I'm not saying there aren't others, just that we couldn't trace any.'

'The man is a murderer,' Nikki said.

'Yes, he is, Nikki.'

'If he's going to start traveling to . . . to *buy* more victims, how are we going to get him?' Kathryn demanded.

'I'm working on it as we speak, Kathryn. That's my job. Your job now is to come up with a punishment that will satisfy Yoko. We'll meet up again tomorrow at the same time.'

Myra ended the meeting. The others followed her from the

room, more sober and thoughtful than they'd ever been in their lives.

The occupant of the wheelchair stared at the two reporters with hate-filled eyes. His gaze swiveled to his wife Paula who was watching his every move and listening to the conversation. He knew he would be wasting his time asking her to leave. Instead, he glared at Maggie Spritzer and Ted Robinson. 'I no longer work for the United States government as you can see. I have nothing to say to either one of you. My wife made a mistake inviting you into the house.'

Spritzer, ever mouthy and never shy, said, 'But you said you would talk to us. Why did you change your mind? Don't you want to see the people who put you in that chair brought to justice? We can tell you who they are but we can't prove it. Did something happen to change your mind?'

Paula Woodley, the ex-National Security Advisor's wife, gin and tonic in her hand, spoke. 'My dear husband has mood swings. One day he's gung ho and the next day he just wants to wallow in self pity. I don't think he knows anything that can help you. And, no, he doesn't want to know who put him in that chair. The reason he doesn't want to know is because the FBI and the DOJ were here a few days ago and while they were quite nice, they were equally firm about my husband accepting his tragic *accident* and getting on with his life. It will be dark soon so you should leave now. I'm asking you nicely not to come back and if you call, I'll hang up on you. We don't talk to the press. Ever.'

Ted ignored the woman and her little speech. 'But sir . . . even though we don't have hard proof, my associate and I have information that would allow you to seek justice. What and who are you afraid of? I can get you protection 24/7. The administration owes you that much.'

The man in the chair laughed, a bitter hateful sound. His wife joined in before she drained her gin and tonic.

Maggie Spritzer had a sense of deja vu. Either that or she had just slipped down the rabbit hole. Who were these people? They both looked deranged to her. Maybe it would be a good idea to leave. She tugged at Ted's sleeve.

Ted wasn't about to give up. He wasn't afraid of the dark and he didn't share Maggie's feelings about the rabbit hole. According to Jack Emery, he was also stupid.

'There's a first time for everything, Mrs Woodley,' Ted said ignoring the tug on his sleeve. 'How is it possible that you and your husband don't care to know who put him in that chair? Don't you want to see the guilty parties punished?'

Ted shivered at Mrs Woodley's eerie laughter. 'The answer to your question, Mr Robinson, is no.'

It took Ted a full minute to come to terms with the woman's response and the eerie laughter. Jesus Christ, did this weird woman pay those kooks at Pinewood to beat up her husband?

Maggie tugged at his sleeve again. Ted started walking toward the door. He turned back and handed Karl Woodley his business card. 'Call me anytime, day or night, if you change your mind.'

As Ted urged Maggie forward, she turned around in time to see Mrs Woodley snatch the card out of her husband's hand and tear it to shreds. 'Open the damn door, Ted, and get us out of here before . . . those strange people do something to us.'

Outside, Ted looked around, trying to come to terms with what had just transpired. 'Are those people crazy or what? What's with that guy anyway? Shit, I heard some of the rumors way back when they said he was a wife beater but I didn't believe it. She certainly appears to be in total control now. The guy hates her and is scared to death of her. Didn't you see it?'

'Yeah, I did see it. Hey, if he was beating her up, I'm on her side,' Maggie said. 'The guy's a real shithead.'

'Well, if it's true that he beat on her then maybe she's the one who hired those women at Pinewood. I bet that's exactly what happened.'

'If true, you aren't going to get anything out of her. By the way, don't wait for Woodley to call you. She snatched your card out of his hands and tore it up.'

'Oh, shit, don't tell me that.'

'I saw her do it, Ted. Now what?'

Ted took a deep breath. 'If bad comes to worse I might have to suck up to Jack Emery.'

'Bad move, Ted. Don't go there.'

'We'll see,' Ted said. 'No promises.'

Eight

Maggie Spritzer stood at the living room window of her new apartment watching the falling snow and the snarled traffic moving inch by inch up the road. From her position behind the window it looked like the drivers were fighting a losing battle. She liked snow, unlike Ted who hated it. She was angry and trying to conquer her feelings by watching the snow. It wasn't working.

'Look, Ted, I think I've had enough of those women out at Pinewood. Everything we've done, and we've done some scary things, just isn't cutting it. They're too damn powerful.'

Ted squirmed around so he could face his partner and lover. 'Even powerful people can be toppled. You can't get away with breaking the law forever. Sooner or later someone like me is going to bring it all into the open.'

'You're obsessed, Ted. You had me mesmerized. I thought we could get the goods on them but they thwart us at every turn. It's not going to happen. We have to move on. Look, we got our jobs back at the *Post*. Let's not jeopardize them. I want to grow old so I can wear outlandish getups and do outrageous things that I can blame on being old and crotchety. You need to think about the fact that we defied Charles Martin and left New York. Now, that bothers me.

'Another thing, I really like this apartment. It's big and we can afford it. You can't beat having two bathrooms, a decent kitchen and an office, and it's a doorman building. I feel safe here. Are you listening to me, Ted?'

'Yeah, yeah, I'm listening. How many times do I have to tell you this is Pulitzer prize stuff.' He looked around, eying the cartons that were stacked everywhere. The game plan had been to unpack the boxes three days ago but that hadn't happened. Ted wondered if he should suggest it just so Maggie would shut up.

'Why do you think the NSA blew us off? Last week he was all set to cooperate and then he switches up. Do you think it's the wife or the fact that those guys behind the initials paid him a visit. Boggles my mind that a man like him could be scared off. He's got to be one sick dude not to want to know who put him in that wheelchair. He's no longer on the government dole. As a private citizen he has rights.'

Maggie laughed bitterly. 'Yeah, like we had rights when Charles Martin forced us to relocate to New York. That man and the people behind him stomped and trampled our rights and no one did a damn thing about it. You were as scared as I was and don't deny it, Ted. So the NSA is scared. He's not going to open up since he's been warned and that wife of his watches him like a hawk. That lady is in control. You just backed the wrong horse, you should have gone after her, but it's too late now.'

Ted eyed one of the cartons that said Kitchen on it. Maybe he should unpack it so Maggie could cook a decent meal. He was sick of Chinese and fast food. He decided he was too tired to unpack anything. Arguing with Maggie was about all he could handle. 'Why are you always so negative?'

Maggie brushed at her wild hair, finger combing it before she pulled it back into a pony tail. She clenched her teeth. 'Because there is nothing to be positive about, that's why. You came up dry from that stake-out in Lafayette Park and then again at the Lincoln Memorial. Can we just move on, Ted?'

'No, Maggie, we can't simply move on. You're right, I am obsessed. I did not exactly come up dry when I staked out Charles Martin. Whatever he was doing, he needed a disguise to do it. The man he met was also disguised. They weren't even good disguises. That tells me dirty work is afoot. And I thought I heard the name Lyons or maybe it was Lynus and the Lincoln Memorial mentioned. I grant you I don't know what it means or who Lyons or Lynus is. It's a common name. On the other hand, it could be a place. I think a meeting of some kind was scheduled for the Memorial but I staked it out and Martin was a no show. I didn't see the other guy either.

After four days I had to give up. Hell, for all I know it could have been a late night meeting. Or, I just thought I heard what I think I heard. I admit I was psyched so anything is possible.'

'I guess that's another way of you saying you're not giving up,' Maggie snapped.

Ted stroked his two cats who were sitting in his lap. 'Yeah, that's what it means, Maggie. Look, that guy Martin scared the piss out of both of us. We went running with our tails between our legs. Well, I'm done running. That guy isn't going to tell me what to do. If he blows the whistle on us, I'll take the fall and do jail time but my mouth will be going a hundred miles an hour. I'll do my best to keep you out of it. I'm running a computer check on the name Lyons as well as Lynus. There's a *kazillion* of them in the data base.'

'Then why bother? It's got to be a dead end.'

'It's not like I have a lot to do, dear heart. I want to run something by you. Tell me what you think.'

Maggie looked around the living room at the stacked cartons. 'We should start to unpack these. I'm not going to like whatever it is you want my opinion on, right?'

'Negativism is not becoming even in someone as beautiful as you are. We have all weekend to unpack those boxes. Fetch us a beer and some munchies first, though, okay. I'd get it but Minnie and Mickey are asleep and I don't want to disturb them.'

Maggie snorted as she made her way to the kitchen. She wished she could shake the anger she was feeling. She wasn't even sure what she was angry about. Ted? Charles Martin? Circumstances in general? Maybe it was something as simple as missing her dog Daisy Mae that her mother was taking care of.

Maggie handed a beer to Ted along with a bag of onion flavored potato chips. 'Let's hear whatever it is I'm not going to like.'

Ted stuffed his mouth with chips and then washed it down with a slug of beer. 'Just hear me out, and don't say anything until I finish. What do you think about me going to see Aaron Frist and telling him our story? I know he's retired but he ran the *Post* for a hundred years. I revere the man. I'll lay it all out to him, all the things we did, why we did them, the whole ball of wax. That man cannot be intimidated. He doesn't have a problem thumbing his nose at the administration. He'll help us if he thinks we're on to something. We need someone in front of us, Maggie, someone with clout. That paper has been in his family for generations. Just because he stepped down doesn't mean he isn't keeping his hand in things.'

'If he tells you you're nuts will you back off and leave it alone?'

'Well, yeah. He is/was the head guru.'

'He's going to want to see our notes, our files. Martin confiscated everything. You don't have anything to show him.'

'That's true but I have a good memory and so do you. We'll spin it out like a story. If we're onto something, he'll smell it. I even know where he lives. I was there for his retirement party. It was before you came to the paper.'

'They say he was a holy terror.'

'Among other things. He was tough as rawhide but fair. He knew everyone's name at the paper right down to the janitor. He even knew the kids' names of his employees. Always asked about them. He's probably one of the smartest people in this country. A week didn't go by that he wasn't invited to the White House. And he knows *everyone*. When you first meet him you walk away thinking you just made a good friend. I think he'll listen, Maggie. He'll like being back in the game even if it's just to offer advice. If he doesn't like my story there's every possibility he'll kick my ass all the way to the Pennsylvania Turnpike. So, are you with me or not?'

Maggie pretended to think. 'I'm with you if you swear on my life, your mother's life, the life of these two cats, my dog, my mother's life, the pope's life and every single relative in your family that you will walk away if Frist tells you to take a hike.'

Ted stretched his long lanky frame. 'You drive a hard bargain, Maggie Spritzer. Yeah, okay. I sure could use another beer.'

'Yeah, I could, too. It's your turn.'

Ted was no fool. He shifted the cats to their own cushion before he got up. 'Let's go early tomorrow morning. He retired to his summer home he has up on the Chesapeake. He hardly ever comes into the District these days.'

'How old is this guy?' Maggie asked curiously.

'Eighty on his last birthday. Walks five miles a day, plays a little tennis if his knees permit, and he does the *Times* crossword puzzle every week. I made it my business to study up on that guy because I knew a day like this was going to come. I'll tell you all about him tomorrow on the drive. Let's fool around.'

'What do you have in mind, Robinson?'

He told her. She had giggled all the way to the bedroom when she realized her anger had disappeared.

The following morning when the two reporters woke, Ted rolled over so he could see out the window. Shit, it was still snowing.

Maggie squirmed, her leg stretching out to find his for warmth. 'Is it still snowing, Ted?'

'Yeah, but lightly. Listen, either I dreamed all night or my subconscious was at work. Hell, maybe it's one and the same, but I changed my mind about going to see Frist. Maybe it's my reporter's intuition or my gut. Whatever it is, it's saying don't do it. I had another thought, too. Jack Emery is the key to all this shit that is going on. I know it as sure as I know I have to go outside and go to work. That bastard is in this up to his neck. For all we know the son of a bitch is calling the shots. Yeah, yeah, we have to concentrate on good old Jack.'

'Hmmm, okay. C'mere, pussy cat and keep this little kitty warm.'

Ted didn't need to be asked twice.

Nine

Myra Rutledge's heirloom dining room table was awash in laptops, yellow legal pads, pencils, coffee cups and seven angry, disgruntled women.

Kathryn threw her pencil across the table, the expression on her face beyond furious. 'I cannot enter another chat room to listen to that crap! Why doesn't someone do something about those sick perverts? I refuse, do you hear me, I refuse to download one more page of that horrendous filth.'

Isabelle looked across the table at Myra who was doing her best not to show the disgust she felt. 'Why is Charles making us do this?'

Myra cleared her throat. 'To show you the enormity of what we're up against. At any given moment there are three million four hundred thousand active chat rooms that can be accessed by anyone who so desires, even children who know their way around computers or children whose parents are not computer savvy. We haven't even begun to access one percent of them.'

Alexis's pencil joined Kathryn's on the floor. 'We'll be here till eternity. I can't do this anymore. It makes me sick. I don't want to pretend I'm one of . . . of those . . . those people.'

'I agree,' Nikki said. Her pencil joined the other two on the floor.

Yoko stood up, her eyes moist. 'This is a mistake. I am so sorry. None of you should be subjected to this. I want to call it off right now. I agree with the others, I cannot keep doing this. We should be speaking with the police, somebody, anybody who will listen to us. We need to lodge complaints.'

Annie stood up. It was obvious she was as agitated as the others but her voice was a little more calm. 'Ladies, ladies, listen to me. I know I'm new to all this and I am as sickened

67

as the rest of you, but we can't walk away from this. People like those we've been meeting in the chat rooms don't deserve to breathe the same air we do. Now, let's all put our heads together and see if among the seven of us we can't do something to at least cripple some of these organizations. If word gets out that someone is invading their space they might make a mistake. This is a job and we can't let our personal likes and dislikes interfere with our brand of justice.'

'Annie's right,' Myra said.

Nikki was shredding a paper napkin with a vengeance. 'We all need to get real here. We only have a few weeks if our target date for Yoko's mission is the Academy Awards. How can we infiltrate these clubs and organizations in a few weeks? These people aren't stupid. They know how to play the game so they don't get caught. We don't know the name of the game much less the rules. They use key words and ask innocent questions we don't know the answers to. They aren't playing doctor nurse here. This is hard core. We haven't even come up with a word or phrase that would indicate there is some kind of slave ring out there.'

'All of us have been at this for over nine hours. Collectively, that is 72 hours and the only thing we know is there's a lot of pornography out there. Nikki's right, we haven't come across one thing that will lead us back to Michael Lyons. Not one single thing,' Kathryn said.

'Maybe that web site I set up last night on the fly will produce some results,' Isabelle said. The others hooted at that statement.

'Don't be so quick to negate my endeavors,' Isabelle said. 'We announced the site in every chat room we entered today. The site I set up is geared to people who like Asian women. Alexis gave Yoko seven different looks, we photographed her and then scanned her likeness onto the site. The caption under her pictures says that she and her sisters and cousins are looking for a new home. I also added, reasonable fees. I just hope that was the right lingo. I bet by now we have at least fifty hits.' At the others' skeptical expressions, she said, 'It's a gamble, okay. If it doesn't produce results, we'll try something else. We did learn something whether you realize it or not. Any posting is immediately picked up and spun around the world within minutes. Who wants to be the first to check out the counter?'

'I'm bringing it up right now,' Annie said. Her face suddenly contorted as she looked over at Isabelle. 'How many hits did you say you expected.'

Isabelle's voice was defensive. 'I said fifty. Maybe I was a little over confident. Okay, maybe 25. There's nothing spectacular, no gimmicks on the site. How far off was I?'

Annie turned her laptop around. As one, the sisters gasped. Myra's death grip on her pearls was fierce. Alexis was the one who gave voice to the number flashing on the screen; '977,000 hits.'

'*Un-be-lievable!* It hasn't been twenty-four hours,' Kathryn said. 'Did any of those perverts write messages?'

'The Guest Book is full. We'll have to print them out so more can come through,' Isabelle said. 'In a million years I would never have believed this.'

'Are you saying we have to respond to this smut?' Alexis demanded.

'That's what it means, dear,' Myra said. 'We need to discuss this with Charles. This is just a guess on my part but I think each reply has to be authentic in case any of those . . . those people know one another. As Nikki said, they're careful and they know how to play the game.' She looked down at her watch. 'We need to pack up our things and go to the war room now.'

Charles looked up when the jabbering women entered the underground room and then looked down at his watch. Time had gotten away from him. But it was worth it. The man Steve Landry had put him in touch with had delivered what he had promised. In his sweaty hands he had Michael Lyons' passwords to five different email accounts. He could hardly wait to tell the sisters.

Myra called the meeting to order, and Charles waited until the women turned silent. 'Before we go any further, Yoko has to tell us what she wants in the way of punishment for Actor Lyons, at which point the rest of you will give us your input. Only then will we discuss whatever it is that has you all so excited. I'm also bearing in mind that the award ceremonies are just weeks away. Now, let's get down to business and do what we do best.'

Yoko stood up, her small hands gripping the edge of the round table. 'I have given this moment years of thought. For some reason I could never get beyond my aunts' description of my mother's death. Now that I am faced with saying the words out loud, I do not . . . what I want is beyond what we swore never to do, commit murder. I must settle for something less. Prison, disgrace, poverty? I want the world to see how ugly the man is. I want him to know I am the one who brought about his downfall. I want to look in his eyes so he will know I am the one. I want his downfall to happen at the Academy Awards.' She lowered herself into the swivel chair and looked around at the compassionate faces staring at her. She dropped her head and waited, her tiny hands clasped in front of her.

'I see it as doable,' Isabelle said.

'A work in progress,' Nikki said, looking down at Michael Lyons's heavy file.

Alexis looked fretful. 'This is Virginia. Lyons lives in California. Are we going to hijack him or are we going out there?'

Kathryn looked as fretful as Alexis. 'We don't have much time if we want to pull this off at the Academy Awards and get safely away, assuming we all go to California. I suspect this little caper is going to take a lot of planning. We need a plan. A good one.'

'Does that actor surround himself with security?' Annie asked.

Charles stepped forward. 'No, strange as that may seem. The persona he presents to the public is that of the guy next door who just happens to make movies for a living. Oh, his estate has the usual security to keep fans out, but he doesn't have bodyguards, gate keepers or anything like that. He drives himself and most times uses a battered pickup truck. He likes to go among the masses in a baseball cap and sunglasses. He does appearances, goes to premieres, but he doesn't do the party scene. The people who work for him on his estate go home at night. No one lives in. He is so far under the radar it's mind boggling.'

'If all of that is true, then our work shouldn't be too hard,' Annie said. 'Earlier you said Lyons goes abroad between movies. If he's going to be away for the next few weeks, we could set things up and be ready for him when he returns.'

Charles held up a copy of *Variety* and waved it about. 'According to this latest issue, Mr Lyons left aboard a commercial flight for Japan two days ago. He's expected to return five days before the award ceremony. If he runs true to form, he gives his help a month off with pay. He notifies them before he returns so the house is ready. If you believe any of this,' Charles said, pointing to a stack of files, magazines and books, 'the guy is an open book, just your typical guy next door who is the next thing to a saint. He's rich, handsome and generous to the world at large.'

'A modern day trifecta,' Kathryn snorted.

Myra tugged at her pearls. 'How are we going to get the proof we need to . . . to . . . nail him, Charles?'

Charles smiled. The women relaxed, even Yoko. He was still smiling when he said, 'I have operatives in place as we speak who are the best in the business even though they're retired. Mr Lyons cannot make a move that isn't being recorded. I expect some reports momentarily. What I want you all to do right now is to come up with a plan. Give me something to work with and I'll make it happen for you. Get on with it, ladies, I have work to do.'

The ladies of Pinewood decided to get on with it. Ideas from the bizarre to the surreal popped out of their mouths, their voices going from normal to strident to angry in seconds as they threw out idea after idea.

On the dais above the women, Charles listened with half an ear as he tapped out messages to his operatives abroad. He stopped when he heard Kathryn say, 'Let's go with a home invasion. Charles can get us a helicopter and we can drop down onto the grounds and swoop in like those guys in that movie where they used those Black Hawk helicopters. Of course Charles would have to turn off the power to Lyons's house ahead of time and somehow scramble his cell phones.'

71

Of course, Charles thought. He wondered how hard it would be to get his hands on a helicopter. The women were clapping their hands. Obviously, they all liked the idea of jumping out of a helicopter. He shuddered at the thought of Myra and Annie dropping out and doing a double tuck and roll without breaking any bones. He tapped some more as he continued to listen.

'How about this?' Alexis said. 'We somehow manage to get in. For the sake of argument, by invitation. Myra and Annie go in. Annie says she wants him to chair some charity she's working on. Once they get inside, she pretends to collapse and die. Myra dials 911 and we all arrive in a hearse. Or an ambulance. Charles does his thing with the power and disables the cell phones.'

That would work, too, Charles thought. He stopped tapping to give the conversation a hundred percent of his attention.

'And then what?' Nikki asked.

'We're just getting started here, Nikki. Let's kick it around. We're in, we got him in our clutches. Let's go, people, what do we do next?' Kathryn demanded.

'Search his house, find his records, maybe he has secret rooms,' Isabelle said.

'Yeah, yeah, yeah, that's the easy part. Then what?' Kathryn shouted, her words echoing around the war room. All eyes turned to Yoko.

Yoko chose her words carefully. 'What we do to Mr Lyons, I think, should depend on what we find when we search his house. Whatever we decide, I get to go first. If there is anything left to him except his shoes, you can have them.'

Charles frowned. He didn't realize he was holding his breath until he saw the women nod in agreement. This was, after all, Yoko's mission.

'What if his house turns out to be just a house? What if he doesn't keep records or pictures there? Maybe he has another place, you know, his place of business where he does all that ugly stuff,' Nikki said.

Then what indeed, Charles thought.

Kathryn got up and slammed her clenched fist into the open palm of her hand. 'Then we beat it out of him. Ooops, Yoko beats it out of him. One way or another, he'll cooperate with us. I guarantee it. I'm not above voting to cut his dick off if need be. In case you've forgotten, we have experience along that line. I for one paid attention to Julia when she was doing the quick and dirty. The man hasn't been born who can deal with seven women holding sharp knives threatening to turn him into a soprano. Without anesthetic.'

Charles flinched at the enthusiastic response to Kathryn's solution. He went back to what he was doing as the women waxed on and on and on.

An hour later Myra signaled Charles that they were ready to make their decision. He joined them at the table, wondering what their plan was going to be. If he was a betting man he'd go with the Myra/Annie/hearse solution. He felt rather smug when the decision came down just the way he'd expected it to. The helicopter might have presented more of a challenge than he wanted to admit.

'Now what?' Kathryn demanded. 'Do we have to continue to invade those chat rooms because in my opinion it's an exercise in futility. If we use those five days after Lyons gets back we should be able to get everything we need from him personally.

'I just read earlier that there are over thirty-four million web sites on the Internet. There's no way we can get a handle on all of that. For whatever my opinion is worth, I say we shelve the chat rooms and the porno sites and take it on as a separate mission later on. Anonymity is the best defense to getting caught. Think about it, those people have no clue that the seven of us invaded their space. Let's vote on it, girls.'

'It's unanimous,' Kathryn said, scanning the circle of raised hands, grateful that she wasn't going to have to converse with another pervert even if she couldn't be physically seen and heard.

Nikki looked up at Charles. 'Do you have Lyons's passwords?'

'Yes, but I can't give them to you yet. I have to traverse the firewalls and make sure all the doors are closed so he doesn't know his operation has been compromised. Patience. Another day and we'll be good to go.'

Myra called the meeting back to order. 'All right, ladies, let's make our plans to get to California. Nikki will make notes so we don't overburden Charles. I rather think he has his hands full right now. For starters, we'll need a hearse. I guess the safest thing would be to buy one. Fully outfitted of course. We'll need temporary quarters in Los Angeles, several rental cars, maps, and of course airline tickets. We should fly separately on different airlines as opposed to going together or taking the company jet. To do so might raise a red flag. Did I forget anything?'

'A lot, Myra, but not to worry, we know what to do. While we're doing it, you and Annie get your story together and remember, this guy is an actor so you'll have to be convincing.'

'Oh, this is so exciting!' Annie said. 'Just *talking* about it is so exhilarating. I can't even begin to imagine what it will be like to be an active participant. I won't let you down.'

Tongue in cheek, Kathryn glared across the table at their newest sister. 'You better not, sister, or your ass is grass.'

Annie blinked and then grinned when she realized Kathryn was pulling her leg. 'Gotcha!'

Ten

Maggie Spritzer walked around the block for the third time, trying to get the lay of the land. Breaking and entering was not something she took lightly. The last time she and Ted did a little B&E, she'd just been along for the ride. This was a whole new ball game, one she was definitely wary of. The last time there had been deadly repercussions when Charles Martin and his goons banished both her and Ted to exile in New York, and it was a whole year before they got the guts to thumb their noses at him and return. Facing the music on their terms, Ted said, was better than letting some schmuck from England call the shots. And, here she was, freezing her tits off outside Alan Nolan's apartment building on O Street. Alan Nolan, the *dweeb* she'd been dogging for days now. The same dude she'd followed that day in Lafayette Park when he met up with Charles Martin.

Ted had run a check on Alan Nolan but the most he could come up with was that the man was a computer genius of some kind. Probably a big time hacker was her personal opinion. A good, as in very good, big time hacker, if Martin was meeting up with him.

One more circle around the block and she would be ready to make her move. With the cold weather, few pedestrians were out and about; even traffic was light for mid morning. As she trudged forward fighting the wind, Maggie reviewed what she knew about Alan Nolan. He lived alone. Definitely a nerd. He worked the early morning shift in a bakery. He got off work at noon, went back to his apartment for an hour and then went to his second job where he managed a cyber café from two till eight in the evening.

Three days in a row she'd gone into the bakery and bought

a bagel and coffee and three days in a row she'd used the cyber café. It wasn't until yesterday that Alan had actually noticed her. She'd openly flirted with him, hoping to draw him out, and she had, but the man was incredibly shy. He blushed. She'd suggested going for a bite to eat when he closed the café at eight o'clock. 'Just a burger,' she'd said. She followed that up with the fact that she was new in town and really didn't know many people. When it looked like he was going to turn her down, she decided to feed his ego by telling him he had to be the smartest computer person in the world. 'All those people who come into the café think you're the best.' He'd puffed out a little at that and finally agreed to a burger and a beer at Snuffy's Bar and Grill.

Two hours of non-stop talking later she knew nothing more than when she entered Snuffy's. Alan Nolan's contribution to the conversation was that he liked baking bread at three o'clock in the morning because he didn't sleep much. He liked managing the café because it paid well and he met people who were interesting. He did admit taking on private clients from time to time, for a fee, when the situation called for expert computer skills. Not that he was an expert, he'd hastened to add, but he did know his way around cyber space.

Maggie had cooed and purred in what she thought were all the right places. 'You mean like people who don't know a cable box from the DVD machine?' she asked. 'Something like that,' had been his response. She'd sucked in her breath then, her bosom jutting forward, a feat that did not go unnoticed by Nolan, and said, 'Look, here's my problem. I moved here from New York to get away from this guy who's hassling me. I don't know how he does it but he can get into my email and he's sending me threatening messages. I'm getting scared. I change servers and passwords and the guy still finds me. I'm thinking about going to the police but I'm not fond of cops if you know what I mean. So how much would you charge for something like that? Assuming of course you had the time to do it and I realize you just met me. Things always happen for a reason,' she babbled on hoping to spark interest in the man sitting across from her.

Nolan hedged, squirmed in his seat. 'Well, I am kind of busy, booked up, you know.'

'Oh, Alan, I would be soooo grateful if you could get this man off my back.' She leaned across the table and batted her eyelashes. 'I think he could be dangerous. And to think I *almost* slept with him. God, I get sick just thinking about it.' She continued to babble, a desperate tone creeping into her voice. 'You're kinda cute when you wrinkle your forehead like that. Okay, okay, I can see you don't want to help me. Don't worry about it,' Maggie said, squirming around to get her coat and backpack. She pulled a five dollar bill out of her pocket and laid it on the table. 'See ya tomorrow when I come in for my bagel.'

Maggie was already outside and walking down the block when she heard her name being called. At least it was the name she'd given the cyber geek: Julie Jett. Who would fall for a name like Julie Jett? Alan Nolan, that's who. He caught up to her and said he could probably help her out on the weekend since he didn't work in the bakery Saturday or Sunday. They exchanged cell phone numbers before they sauntered off to go their separate ways.

Now, here she was, just hours later, about to break into Nolan's apartment.

Maggie squared her shoulders, took a last look around before she marched up the four steps that led to the front door of Nolan's apartment building. She was grateful for the warmth of the lobby. She scanned the area before she headed to the bank of mailboxes. There he was, A Nolan. Apartment 202. She headed for the stairs and walked up the two flights. It was warm in the hallway. She hadn't seen a single person. She wondered if she should call Ted. No, that wasn't a good idea.

Lock pick in hand, Maggie walked on trembling legs down the hall to apartment 202. At the end of the hall she could hear music. Someone on the floor above was banging on a piano. A dog gave off a squeaky bark as she passed 206 and 208. A small dog by the sound of it. Then she was in front of 202. She pretended to knock as her right hand dug the pick into the keyhole. In the movies it always looked so easy. It

77

wasn't working. Maybe she was too nervous. Maybe she should call Ted. Maybe she should just calm down and work the pick. She talked to herself the whole time until she heard the tumbler roll over.

Maggie's heart was beating so fast she grew lightheaded. She had to lean down and put her head between her knees until the feeling passed. 'I'll never make a crook,' she muttered.

The apartment wasn't overly large nor was it small. The perfect size. Maggie wondered how much rent Nolan paid. What really surprised her was how tastefully the apartment was decorated, with deep comfortable furniture, large screen TV, colorful Chagall prints on the wall, lots of greenery, nice plush carpeting. Book shelves with the classics and rows and rows of computer manuals.

The kitchen was small and compact. A place to heat food, as opposed to cooking it, although everything needed to prepare a meal was in evidence. She suspected Nolan was a take-out kind of guy.

The bathroom was white tile with bright blue towels and area rugs. Nothing here. The bedroom was small, a twin bed with a colorful quilt. There was no greenery or pictures on the wall. Just a place to sleep. The closet was a surprise. It held a rack of good looking suits, custom shoes, and then a rack of scruffy clothes and underneath those, seven or eight pair of sneakers.

The last room had to be a spare bedroom. She opened the door and gasped. The entire room was lined with computers, printers and all manner of high tech appliances. It was cool in here, the vents in the Off position. This wasn't some computer nerd's lair. This was something else entirely and Maggie knew she was out of her depth. She fished around in her backpack and withdrew her new digital camera. She clicked steadily for a good ten minutes. Ted would have to figure all of this out. When she was finished, she shoved the camera back into her backpack.

This equipment didn't come from Staples. She took a wild guess, knowing what she'd paid on the retail market for her last computer and knew she was looking at a quarter to a half million dollars in high tech equipment. There appeared to be miles of cable and different wires. How did this guy do it? Didn't he blow the circuit breakers? 'Computer nerd my ass,' Maggie muttered to herself. Nolan was no small time cyber freak. Nolan was . . . what, she didn't know.

There was no way in hell she was going to touch *anything*. But, she could look around, peruse anything she found. She crossed the room to a stack of spiral notebooks and picked one up. Nothing but a jumble of numbers and letters. Codes? She shivered as she whipped out the digital camera a second time. She clicked steadily for several minutes.

Maggie looked down at her watch. Time to leave.

Maggie was shaking like a sapling in a high wind when she exited Alan Nolan's building. She hailed a taxi and gave the *Post*'s address. She didn't draw a calm breath until she was seated in her swivel chair in her cubby hole at the paper, Ted leaning over her shoulder.

Maggie dug in her backpack. She shoved the camera into his hands. 'What does all that,' she said jerking her head in the direction of the camera, 'mean?'

'I think it means Nolan isn't exactly who he says he is. I think I might take a ride up to Aaron Frist's house to run this by him or else I'll call him and send him these pictures. The notebook stuff might be codes or it might be just innocent stuff only computer experts can relate to. This is way over my head. You did good, Maggie. Now what?'

'Now I'm going to get some lunch and then I'm going to the cyber café and chat this guy up some more. He likes to have his ego stroked. Like most men,' Maggie said, a bit of a giggle in her voice.

Ted didn't miss the giggle. 'You need to find out who some of his clients are, particularly the one in Lafayette Park that day we staked out Martin.'

Maggie grimaced. 'We know who the client was. We want to know what the client wanted.'

'Yeah, yeah, that's what I meant. Find out.'

Disbelief rang in Maggie's voice. 'Just like that, find out!'

Ted's face turned sour. 'I haven't been able to come up with even one negative where that guy is concerned. He's just what

79

he appears, a computer nerd. This might or might not blow you away but he has a degree in Computer Science from M.I.T. Since you know so much about men, and according to you, men like to brag, get him to brag a little. Ask him if he could hack into government files just for the fun of it.'

Maggie looked around the busy newsroom. With all her extracurricular activities, she hadn't even started on her column that dealt with the beltway gossip. Thank God she was one day ahead. She'd be up all night as she tried to parcel out the slim gossip to stretch it into a couple of days' reading. 'It's snowing again. I think I'm catching a cold. I could get pneumonia out there, Ted. This guy is no fool. I just want you to know that.'

Ted looked at Maggie, a dumbfounded look on his face. 'And you think this place isn't riddled with germs! Everyone in this damn office has been coughing and sneezing all morning long. I'm not feeling so hot myself.'

Maggie said something totally inappropriate as she shrugged into her down coat, grabbed her backpack and headed for the cyber café where she would play with the computer until she found a niche of time to spend with Nolan.

'Are you going to be cooking dinner tonight?' Ted asked hopefully. Maggie shot him a single digit salute as she headed out of the newsroom.

Maggie's thoughts whirled and twirled as she hailed a cab to take her to the cyber café. She leaned back against the seat and closed her eyes. The driver had his radio on but she could still hear it. Her eyes snapped open when she heard the announcer's gleeful voice saying that an Alberta Clipper was on the way with an expected snowfall of twelve to twenty-four inches of snow. A groan escaped her lips. Just what she needed, more snow.

Maggie's thoughts continued to ricochet. Nolan lived in a fairly high rent district. He had quality furniture, expensive prints on the wall. Just how much money did he make in the bakery and the cyber café? Not enough to buy all that high end computer equipment, that was for sure. He'd be lucky if his rent was covered with what he earned working both jobs. It was possible he was independently wealthy but she doubted it. The suits in his closet were off the rack but still expensive, as were his shoes. Maybe people like Martin paid him large sums of money.

Who did she know in the banking industry that she could put the squeeze on? No names came to mind. It took her all of two minutes to decide she needed someone just like Alan Nolan to hack into his files. That might be doable if she could come up with someone who would admit to being able to do such nefarious things. She didn't know anyone in that line of work either.

'That'll be ten-eighty, lady,' the cab driver said as he pulled to the curb at the corner.'

'Why'd you park here? Now I have to walk a whole block. Nine bucks, mister, that's it. You see that snow falling out there? Did you hear me sniffling? And you're making me walk a whole block! Eight bucks and a dollar tip. I shouldn't even give you a tip.'

'Just pay me and get out of my cab,' the driver shot back. Drivers behind them leaned on their horns as Maggie rummaged in her backpack for the fare. She was in no hurry.

Outside in the blustery snow Maggie realized being let out on the corner wasn't such a bad thing. This way Nolan wouldn't see her getting out of the cab. Why she thought that might be important she didn't know. She trudged to the café, again walking against the gusting wind, fine snow stinging her cheeks.

A bell tinkled loudly when she entered the café. The place smelled of fresh coffee and cinnamon buns, two of her favorite things in the whole world. Nolan looked up and smiled a greeting. She waved and sat down at the counter. The cyber end of the café was hopping, all the terminals busy. Snow must bring out the cyber bunnies, she thought.

Nolan ambled over as Maggie sneezed twice. He danced backward immediately to avoid any germs. 'Just hot tea with lemon,' Maggie said trying to sound as cheerful as she could. 'Maybe a piece of cheesecake while I wait for a free terminal. How are you this morning, Alan?'

'Fine. I'd ask how you are but I can see for myself that you aren't looking so good. You should probably go home.

The weather is only going to get worse. By the way, do you work?'

Maggie did her best to look indignant. 'Doesn't everyone work? I work at the Mall. In cosmetics. I love perfume. Part time, though. I take classes at Georgetown. I have one eight o'clock class and another one at seven. I'm going for my Masters. How soon do you think I can get a terminal?'

'At least an hour.'

'That long, huh? Well, we can spend the time talking. Maybe you can help me a little. You know, where that guy is concerned. A man's perspective. That kind of thing.' Maggie felt pleased with herself when Nolan preened like a peacock.

'Sure, if I can.'

Eleven

The hour was beyond late when Myra made her way into the war room to see her beloved Charles sitting at the table with his head in his hands. She knew instantly that something was wrong. Her hands searched for the pearls that were always around her neck but they weren't there. She was in her nightgown and robe since it was after two in the morning. She sat down at the table and reached for Charles's hands. 'Talk to me, Charles.'

Charles looked up. 'Myra!' he said, surprise echoing in his voice. 'What brings you down here at this hour? Is something wrong?'

'Of course something's wrong, my dear. I've been waiting for hours for you to come upstairs. The storm is increasing but that's not what's bothering me. What is it, Charles, why aren't you talking to me about whatever it is that's troubling you?'

Charles leaned back and closed his eyes as he massaged his temples. The headache he'd had all day was still with him. 'It's so overwhelming. I knew . . . I think most people know that pornography is out there. You clean up one little section and four more sites, a dozen more groups replace those four. It's impossible to get a handle on it. In plain old American terms, my dear, this little caper is kicking my English ass.'

In spite of herself, Myra smiled. 'I thought we agreed that we weren't going to take on the smut industry but just concentrate on Mr Lyons and his trafficking in . . . in his slavery ring.'

'That's true, but to get to that, I have to wade through all the other filth. I thought I was, for want of a better word, tough, but this perversion is making me ill.' His voice turned fierce. 'I want to get my hands on those people and rip their hearts out through their noses. I haven't been able to compartmentalize the way I should. I don't think I am the man for this job. There, I said it out loud. I'm failing all of you.'

'My darling Charles, you *are* the man for this job. You aren't in this alone. All seven of us are with you. We must persevere and in doing so, we will prevail. I truly believe this. We need to think of this moment as a bump in the road. A rather large bump but we can climb over it. We will, Charles. I don't want to hear another negative word. You are the man for this job. Now, I am going upstairs to make you something to eat. Do you want coffee or hot chocolate?'

Charles smiled. 'Food soothes the savage beast, is that it?'

'Something like that. I'll make you a hot roast beef sandwich.'

Charles nodded. He was hungry. He was also incredibly sleepy. Food and hot chocolate would either keep him awake or put him sound asleep.

When the secret door leading to the main part of the house closed, Charles felt his shoulders slump. He really did need to shift into the neutral zone or he was going to foul things up.

'Tough day, eh, Charles?'

Charles reared up and looked around. His tongue was so thick in his mouth he could barely get it to work. 'Barbara!'

'It's me, Charles. What can I do to help you?'

'It's true then. I can't believe you're here talking to me. Myra . . . dear child, how good it is to talk to you. I miss you, terribly. We all miss you.'

'I know . . . Daddy.'

Charles reared up again. Had he just heard the word he'd dreamed of all his life? 'You knew?'

'Of course I knew. Only a father could love me the way you loved me. I knew you and Mom had your reasons for not wanting me to know so I simply went along with it. I called you daddy in my dreams. Even though I called you Charles, I thought of you as daddy. I regret you never got to hear me call you by that cherished name.'

'It would have been music to my ears. I know this sounds

silly but are you all right? I . . . I don't know anything about the spirit world.'

'*I'm fine. Tell me what's troubling you, Daddy.*'

Charles leaned forward and then looked around again. 'Where are you?'

'*Right behind you.*'

Charles wasn't sure but he thought he felt gentle hands on his shoulders. The feeling was so warm and comforting, he relaxed immediately. The flood gates opened. 'It's the evil, child. I've never had to deal with pure evil before. In my other life when I was in service to Her Majesty, there was nothing like this. It was war and there were rules. I feel like I'm at war with the Devil and I'm losing the battle. I know that if by some miracle we succeed, there will be others just like Lyons waiting to step in his shoes. Right or wrong, if I fail Yoko and the others, I'm going to take it personally. I talked about this at great length with your mother. I had these visions of you and Nikki being ripped away from us by that man or someone like him and forcing you to do things only the Devil would demand. For some reason I cannot get past that thought.'

'*You have to get past it. It didn't happen. You and Mom would never have allowed that to happen. In third world countries there are no rules. You can't police the world, Daddy. You can't be the world's 911.*'

'I know that,' Charles said wearily.

'*Concentrate on Michael Lyons. Let Mom and the others help you. Please, Daddy, don't try to do it all yourself. I want your promise.*'

Charles laughed. 'Like I could deny anything you ask. Very well, my dear, I will do as you ask.'

'*Do you remember how you used to sleigh ride with me and Nik? Do you remember how beautiful the snow was when we'd start out? You used to say the snow was as pure as me and Nik. Of course we didn't know what that meant at the time. All we knew was you smiled when you said it and that made it wonderful. Now this is what you have to do, Daddy. You shift into your neutral zone and you damn well kick ass and take names later. You got that?*'

Charles choked on his own laughter. 'I got it.'

'I gotta go. Mom's coming. Love you, Daddy.'

'Dear God, how I love you, child.'

The secret door opened and Myra stepped into the room. She knew immediately that something had changed in her absence. Her smile lit up the room. 'She came to you, didn't she?'

Charles smiled from ear to ear. 'Yes, and she called me daddy. She said she always knew.'

Myra clapped her hands. 'Isn't it wonderful, Charles? Our daughter comes to us when things are the darkest. I'm so happy for us both. She talks to Nikki, too, you know.'

'No, I didn't know that, but it's right. They were so close just the way sisters are supposed to be. We were a family, Myra.'

'Eat, Charles. I made that sandwich with love.'

'And a lot of lumps in the gravy.'

'Shush. I made it with love and for my daughter's father.'

The ladies of Pinewood were sitting at the kitchen table the following morning finishing up a sketchy breakfast when Charles entered the kitchen. He was freshly shaved, dressed in corduroy trousers and a heavy wool sweater on top of a white shirt whose collar showed at the neck. He looked like a British scholar with his glasses perched on the end of his nose. He greeted everyone with a smile, helped himself to a bagel, spread cream cheese on it, and then accepted a cup of coffee from Alexis.

'I think we're snowbound,' Isabelle said as she pulled the curtains aside on the kitchen window. 'I suppose things could be worse.'

'Oh, yeah, how?' Kathryn asked, her tone combative. She hated being cooped up. What she hated even more was the upcoming two-hour Spanish lesson Charles had insisted on. Having lived in Spain for so many years, Annie was teaching them Spanish, saying her orders from Charles were that they all had to become fluent. Kathryn was doing badly, refusing to wrap her tongue around the alien sounding words. The others tried to help her but she refused their help. Even Yoko was starting to speak the language well, a feat that boggled her mind.

'I have no interest in learning to speak Spanish,' Kathryn said. 'I failed the subject in school. This time Charles is way off base and over the line at the same time. I refuse to attend one more class and I mean no offense to you, Annie.'

'None taken, dear. Humor me today and let's see if we can't make some progress. You're fighting me, Kathryn, and you know it. Being stubborn isn't helping. You're a smart woman. You have an engineering degree and a Masters so that tells me you have the capacity to learn. And you will learn if you stop being so belligerent. Now, get off your ass, go into the dining room and open the goddamn book. I'll be in in a few minutes.'

'Whoa,' Nikki said sotto voce as she scurried behind Kathryn into the dining room. 'The lady is on a roll.'

Kathryn's face flamed, but she was in the dining room with the book open in front of her. She wasn't about to give up, though. 'I thought we were here to work on Yoko's mission, not learn Spanish. I thought it was all a big joke. It's not a joke. Are you all going to kick me out if I don't learn the damn language?'

The ladies of Pinewood started to vent, in general and then at one another. Finally, Alexis slammed her fist on the table. 'Will you just listen to us! What's happening here? We're like a bunch of snarling cats caught in a rainstorm. Is there something going on that we don't know about? Something Charles isn't sharing with us? I think so. If I'm right, it's not fair.'

Nikki looked around at the angry faces, knowing her own face was just as angry. Still, someone had to be the voice of reason. 'Listen to me. I'm on your side. I'm sure you all heard how I'm butchering up the language but Charles always has a reason for everything he's asked us to do. We agreed early on that there would be things we wouldn't like, things we didn't want to do, but if Charles asked, we would do them. For the betterment of the Sisterhood.'

'Charles thinks we're going to get caught at some point. He always looks ahead to the future. It's called planning. Spain will be our getaway if that ever happens is what I'm thinking.

It's the only thing that makes sense. What that means, Kathryn, is this, shut up, buckle down and do your best. We'll help you.'

Kathryn suddenly burst into tears, hard sobs rocking her slim shoulders. The others looked on in horror. Kathryn Lucas crying. It was so unbelievable the women could only respond with stunned silence. As they struggled to get their wits about them, Kathryn swiped at her eyes with the sleeve of her flannel shirt. A second later she was speaking fluent Spanish, whole paragraphs, entire sentences, tears streaming down her cheeks.

'There, are you all satisfied? Why did you make me do that? It was all I had left.' At the women's stunned expressions she said, 'My husband taught me Spanish. We learned it on the road. He used to whisper all those soft love words to me that no one else could understand. It was a private thing, something I didn't want to share with anyone, not even you as much as I love all of you. You all know everything there is to know about me and my husband because I told you. This was just . . . it was . . . *mine*. Everything else is gone. At night when I can't sleep, I lie there and remember, often saying the words out loud. Damn it, do you understand?' Kathryn looked at the shocked faces staring at her. 'Okay, do you want me to teach this fucking class? I will. Maybe Annie can find something better to do than hassle me. Now, let's get to those verbs.'

The ladies of Pinewood fell to it with a vengeance.

In the kitchen, Annie and Myra smiled at one another. 'How did you know, Annie?' Myra whispered.

'Because she worked too hard pretending to be stupid. Kathryn is far from stupid as you well know. I wasn't sure but I thought it was something like that. I became convinced when I would say endearing words and her eyes would flood with tears. Those women in the dining room are a remarkable group, Myra. Absolutely remarkable.'

Myra fiddled with her pearls. 'I know. Every night I pray that nothing goes awry. Oh, Annie, listen to this. Barbara spoke to Charles early this morning. It was so wonderful. She called him daddy. I thought my heart was going to burst wide open.'

The two women hugged and smiled through their tears.

'Down to business,' Annie said. 'Tell me what you think of this idea, Myra. I couldn't sleep last night so my mind was racing. I fund a charity, along with a lot of other people, that benefits children. The foundation does wonderful work for children with disfigurements, sick children, and homeless children. Not just here in America but world wide. I thought, since I'm the one who started up the foundation years ago, that I would call Mr Lyons' agent and ask him if he would ask Mr Lyons to chair a special event with me. I'll tell him all he has to do is lend his name to the effort, have some pictures taken several days before the Academy Awards Ceremony which will be our way to getting into his house on his immediate return. I checked our donor list early this morning and the man has contributed robust sums of money to the foundation over the years. What do you think?'

'I think it's a splendid idea. Do you know the name of the agent?'

'I do and I even have his home phone number. It's still early in California so we'll have to wait at least an hour before I call him.'

'What if he says he's too booked up or he has no time until after the awards?'

Annie quirked an eyebrow at Myra as much as to say, c'mon, get real. 'I think I can be persuasive. I can always throw in a prize like a Range Rover but Lyons won't take it. He wants his public to believe he's above accepting material things like that for helping a worthy cause.'

'Should we tell Charles?'

'We could, but I think we should just do it. We can tell him later if we manage to nail it all down today. It certainly won't interfere with anything he's planning. Actually, if you think about it, it can only help. I called several of the people at the foundation when I got up this morning to alert them to all this. They're very excited. I also wanted them to be aware that Lyons' agent might be calling to verify the situation.'

'Annie, you fit right in. You're okay with all this then?'

'My dear, I am more than okay with all this. The best thing that ever happened to me was the day you came to the mountain and smashed my television set. I haven't looked back, not even once.'

'Spoken like a true sister.'

Annie grinned before her clenched fist shot high in the air.

Twelve

Michael Lyons could barely control his excitement as his driver brought the car to a full stop. This was it, *the moment*. His adrenaline at an all time high, Lyons stepped out of the car and walked up to the garish looking building with equally garish lighting where a bevy of young women would be paraded before him within minutes of his arrival. Flesh for sale. He'd attended horse auctions that operated the same way.

Lyons still managed to look like the movie star he was, even though he was dressed down in khakis, deck shoes and baseball cap. Not that anyone knew his profession; he'd gone to extreme lengths to cover his tracks. His scouting trips – that's how he thought of his trips to Asia – were for sinful pleasure even though the words were never spoken aloud. His nerves were twanging all through his body. It was always like this, the wild anticipation, the adrenaline rush as the young women were paraded in front of him. All he had to do was point a finger, nod, and the girl would step to the side. As always, he chose three girls for his personal use; the other six or seven of his choosing were for his clients. The next step was to negotiate with the father of the girl for hard cold cash. He was always amazed at how willingly the parent parted with his child. Goods for sale. It was that simple.

The small group of people seated in the back of the room were silent as they waited for the American to step forward to inspect his purchases at closer range. He always smiled and offered a token gift, usually a gold bracelet that eventually found its way back to him when the purchase was put out on the circuit. He had tons of gold bracelets. He touched the girls' glossy black hair, the porcelain skin of their cheeks. He liked the demure look of the young girls. He patted down the girls,

91

satisfied that their breasts were lemon size, just the way he liked them. He looked down at each of them from his six foot three height, knowing he was intimidating, and asked the one question that would finalize the sale. He spoke in fluent Japanese. 'Are you a virgin?' The shiny black heads always bobbed up and down at which point Lyons turned to the back of the room where the father stood to confirm that he was selling a virgin and Lyons was buying a virgin.

Lyons walked down the line handing out the gold bracelets. When he was satisfied, he stepped down off the crude stage and walked to the back of the room. He whipped out a wad of American dollars, paid for his purchases, left the building and didn't look back. His job here was done. Others in his organization would take over now and arrange for the women to be smuggled back to the United States.

He could hardly wait. His clients would be ecstatic with his choices. Now, though, he needed to get away from this foul smelling place and back to his hotel where he could take a shower and wait for the woman who would stay with him for the rest of the night. A professional who knew the ways to please a man.

Lyons's mind raced as the car barreled through the dark Tokyo night. This was one of his most productive trips to date. He'd trolled for young women since his arrival, going to a different place each night, like the one he'd just left. He'd bought twenty-seven women. Enough to keep his clients happy for the next few months. He'd paid a thousand dollars a head and would turn around and sell the women to his clients for a hundred times that amount.

Just like a horse auction. Prize flesh on the hoof.

Lyons closed his eyes and let his thoughts drift to his organization and the money he flipped around the world with the press of a button. What was he going to do with all the money he had squirreled away in off-shore accounts? He already owned everything worth owning. This was the part that always bothered him. What to do with his vast sums of money. He knew where these thoughts would eventually take him: to the child he'd fathered with Suki Naoki. He tried not to think of her and for the most part was successful, but when he came here to her mother's country she would invade his thoughts. Maybe he should think about making a will and trying to find the young woman. Maybe. Maybe she was dead. The thought didn't really bother him one way or the other.

The old hags, the worn-out women who had befriended Suki, had spirited the child away. What had she been told? Obviously nothing of importance or she would have made an appearance somewhere along the way. She must not be interested in his wealth or his celebrity. He wondered why that was. She had to be dead; nothing else made sense.

Screw it all. Now he was in a black mood. The evening's activities that he had looked forward to were now out of the question. He'd shower, have a late dinner and sleep. Tomorrow morning, with nothing on his agenda other than lounging in the hotel, his time would be free to do whatever he wanted to do. It would be a good time to make his way to the countryside to visit Suki's place of birth. Yes, yes, that's what he would do. Maybe then he could stop thinking about the child he'd fathered and knew nothing about.

Lyons dozed then and didn't wake until the car stopped at his hotel. He made several phone calls in his room, canceling his evening's entertainment, and retrieved his messages, none of which was important. The only call he returned was to his agent. He didn't give a second thought to saying yes to Countess de Silva's request. Of course he would lend his name to her project, of course he would donate handsomely to her project and of course he would pose for pictures. 'It's all about image, you know that,' he said before he ended the call.

Twenty minutes later, Michael Lyons was sound asleep on 1200 thread count sheets.

Lyons was dressed in the same attire as the day before – khakis, docksiders and baseball cap. Today his tee shirt said SAVE THE EARTH. As he stepped out of the car he couldn't help but wonder if the old couple would remember him. Hell, coming here was a spur of the moment thing. The people he was involved with said it wasn't a good idea, but he had told them to shut up. He called the shots, something they needed to remember. He supposed the parents could be dead but he doubted it. Japanese people for some reason lived long lives.

He felt nervous and wasn't sure why. Tingling with anticipation was not the same as being nervous. No, he was nervous, his hands clammy. His lips felt dry, his tongue thick. His hand was clenched to knock on the door when he thought better of the idea. He turned to walk away, only to stop and go back. He wasted no time and knocked. He heard a weak sounding voice telling him to enter. He did.

The room reeked of opium and a sour smell he couldn't quite define. Two wizened creatures sat on piles of cushions, their eyes bright and curious at his intrusion into their lives. When he'd seen the old man thirty-some years ago, he'd been whippet thin. Now he just looked emaciated. The woman could have passed for a Halloween witch. How could these two have given birth to such exquisite daughters?

Lyons spoke a greeting in Japanese and then sat down cross-legged in front of the old couple. He looked for some sign of recognition but there was none. He introduced himself. The old couple simply stared and then whispered among themselves. The crone said, 'My granddaughter said you were dead.'

Lyons thought his heart would explode right out of his chest. He had to say something they would believe. He then muttered something about modern American medicine that brought the dead back to life. They seemed satisfied.

'When was my daughter here?' Lyons asked

The old man picked up his pipe and puffed. He made no comment. The old woman held up three fingers. Days? Weeks? Months? What did it matter? He asked where she lived.

'The land of milk and honey where money grows on trees' was the response. He mouthed the word, California, and the old woman nodded before she picked up her pipe. Her rotted stumps of teeth clamped tight on the pipe while her hands rummaged under the cushions for something. Finally she had what she wanted in her hand and held it out. Lyons reached for it. Suki. Beautiful little Suki. He felt something stir in him.

'Where did you get this?'

'My granddaughter.'

94

'Is she coming back here? Do you know where I can find her?'

The old man made a sound in his throat, an ugly sound. Lyons inched backward when the old woman started to laugh. 'She is looking for you.' She cackled again.

A chill raced up Lyons's back. He wished now he had listened to the others and not come here.

'To kill you,' the old man said.

Stunned, Lyons could only gape at the old couple. 'You're a crazy old man, you don't know what you're talking about.'

The old couple laughed in unison. Lyons thought it was the deadliest sound he'd ever heard in his life.

'She talked to the other lady in English. We learned some English words when you took our daughters away in case they ever came back to us. The man at the store taught us the words. We wanted our daughters to be proud of us. Our granddaughter is more beautiful than her mother.' Quicker than a snake, the old woman snatched the photograph of her daughter from Lyons's hands. A second later it was back under the cushions.

Lyons was backing toward the door. 'She told the other lady you are a famous film star and she is going to kill you for what you did to her mother and to all the others. We wished her well.' The couple cackled again as they sucked on their pipes.

Outside, Michael Lyons ran to the car where he fought to quell the panic rising in his chest. What did those crazy old people know? They were so stoked up on opium they were lucky they knew night from day. Still, he had been the one who took that picture of Suki on her arrival in America. Obviously the old couple weren't as crazy as he would like to believe.

Lyons literally fell into the car. 'Drive and get me back to the hotel as quickly as possible. I have a plane to catch.' He had to get back home. Back to the States. Back to his life. He had to look upon this as a warning. Just hours ago he was trying to figure a way to leave his vast holdings to his daughter, provided that he could find her. Now, if what the old couple said was true, his daughter was searching for him with the intention of killing him.

The other lady. What other lady? In a million years he never would have believed the mummified couple would know even a smattering of English. What other woman? A cop? Someone in authority? Surely not one of Suki's friends. They'd be old now, in their late 60s. Who? The kid was a baby when Suki died. How did she know to come here?

Michael Lyons started to shake and couldn't stop. He was still shaking when he got to the hotel. Three double shots of scotch did nothing to calm his nerves. A fourth shot gave him a blinding headache.

A blizzard of phone calls later, Lyons had a first class seat booked on a flight that would leave in seven hours. He could be packed and ready to go in fifteen minutes. He made a second series of phone calls and when he hung up an intensive state wide manhunt was underway for his daughter.

By the time Michael Lyons boarded the jet that would take him back to Los Angeles he had consumed almost the entire bottle of scotch and his hands were still shaking.

Annie de Silva grinned from ear to ear. 'Mr Lyons has agreed to lend his name to the foundation and to make a sizeable donation. Are we in luck or what?'

Myra smiled. It was nice to see her old friend so alive these days. 'It's wonderful, Annie. I knew you could do it. I think we should reserve some rooms at the Beverly Hills Hotel in case Lyons wants to get in touch with us. We certainly don't want to compromise anything the girls do. I also think we should fly out ahead of them to make it look even more legitimate. Perhaps we can leak your arrival to whatever publication movie stars read on a daily basis.'

'That's a good point, Myra. I'll get right on it. Now, you can tell Charles. The lesson is almost finished so I'll join you when it's over. We're going to get him, Myra. We are going to make Yoko as whole as we can make her.'

'How did she live all these years knowing all that, Annie? I think I would have gone insane.'

Annie could only shake her head. 'How did Kathryn live with what happened to her? How did you live with Barbara's death? How did the others live with it? I think with the hope that someday, somehow, it would all be made right. Yoko

96

looks fragile, frail and so delicate and she is all those things, but she's also resilient, tough and she has nerves of steel. I would never want to meet up with her in a dark alley.'

'Charles calls her our little lotus flower.'

Annie patted Myra on the shoulder. 'It's going to be all right. It really is, Myra.'

'I hope so, Annie.'

Annie leaned over and looked into Myra's eyes. Her voice was soft, gentle, almost musical. 'How did we get to this place in time, my friend?'

Myra sighed. 'We walked a lot of miles, Annie. One day we were children and then we were all grown up. I so loved our childhood. There were no worries other than which hair ribbon to wear, should we wear our lockets, mind our manners. It was the grown-up part I didn't handle too well.'

'You fell in love, Myra. You don't have to make any excuses for that.'

'Yes, I did, and what a glorious love it was, and still is. My only regret is that we never told our daughter the truth. I can live with the shame my parents said I brought on them. I can live with the fact that I married a man I didn't love to give my baby a name. I was a good wife to my husband. When he died, I mourned him the way I was supposed to but my heart has always belonged to Charles, just the way your heart belongs to Armand.'

'We were too pampered. We weren't tough like *our girls*. What's that expression the young people use today? They have it going on. How I envy them. At their age, I wouldn't have had the guts to do what they're doing. We lived in the dark ages, Myra.'

'In some respects, I think you're right. But we're in the light now. We're doing something . . . illegal . . . but at the same time, we're righting old wrongs. I have no intention of quitting. As Kathryn would say, are you in this for the long haul, Annie?'

'Damn straight! I am living! I still cry at night. I think that's okay, don't you, Myra? I mean, I lost my whole family. That sense of loss is never going to go away.'

Myra reached for Annie's hand. 'Of course it's all right to

cry. I do, too. And, you're right, the sense of loss is never going to go away.

'Annie . . . have you ever thought . . . I don't know how to say this . . . but you, me, Nellie, we all lost our children. A parent is not supposed to bury a child. No one can explain this to me. All three of us, best friends for over fifty years and we all lost our children. Will we ever understand, will we ever be able to accept it?'

'No.'

The two friends clung together and cried. It was a long time before either of them stirred and dried their eyes.

'Would you look at all that snow. More and more I think we should all move to a warmer climate. It's on my list of things to do. How about you, Annie?'

'Your roots are here, Myra. You aren't going anywhere. It's nice to dream, though. Spring is just weeks away. But to answer your question, no, I have no desire to go to a warmer climate. Take heart, old friend.'

'On that thought, I think it's time for me to see Charles. I need to tell him again how much I love him.' Myra waved as she headed for the living room and the secret door that would take her to Charles and the war room.

Thirteen

Maggie Spritzer knew she'd dallied a few hours too long in the hope of getting some kind of information from Alan Nolan. She looked down at her Nike sneakers, knowing if she even tried to slog her way home, she'd freeze to death. The snow, according to the weather man on the small TV on the counter, had been falling at the rate of two inches an hour. 'And,' he said, ominously, 'it will continue to fall at that rate throughout the night and into tomorrow.' Then he gave a dissertation on the Alberta Clipper out of Canada that started the whole mess.

Maggie sat glumly at the counter. She was on her fourth latte and couldn't swallow another drop. She was stuck here with all the nameless people sitting at the terminals. Nolan was certainly no bundle of fun as he whipped up burgers and fries in the café section. The man was just too serious for his own good. Did he ever smile, did he ever laugh, did he ever tell a joke? She doubted it. She was tired from trying to draw him out. Better to think of ways to kill Ted when and if she ever got back to the apartment.

A plate with a grilled cheese sandwich on it slid across the counter. Maggie raised her eyes. 'Oh, thanks, Alan.' She reached for a pickle spear and crunched down on it. 'Looks like we're all here for the night. I hope the power doesn't go out.'

Nolan walked around the counter and sat down next to her. 'I have a generator out back. There's a little apartment with a full bath, too. We'll be okay. We were stranded a few years ago when a nor'-easter ripped through here. The place was full then, too, just like tonight.'

'What's your boss like, Alan? Doesn't he mind that you

99

give the customers free food and let them use the terminals for free?'

Nolan drummed his fingers on the counter top. 'I'm the boss. This is my café. I can do whatever I want.'

Surprise, surprise, Maggie thought. 'That's nice,' was all she could think of to say. She was just too damn tired of trying to keep the conversation going. She went back to plotting Ted's death in her mind.

'I own the bakery around the corner, too,' Nolan volunteered.

'Really. Guess you'll never starve then, huh?'

'Good investments. Listen, if you want to use the phone, go ahead. Don't you need to call someone to tell them you're okay?'

'I just moved here, remember? There's no one to call. Unless you want me to call that creep who's harassing me back in New York.' Maggie bit into the sandwich. It was surprisingly good, with strips of bacon and a slice of tomato in the center. She finished it, licked her fingers and went back to plotting against Ted for putting her in this position. She really felt lousy and knew by tomorrow she'd have a full-blown winter cold.

'I have some cold tablets in the medicine cabinet in the back if you want to take them,' Nolan volunteered when Maggie sneezed three times.

Maggie sneezed again. 'That might not be such a bad idea. Thanks, Alan.'

Nolan rushed off and returned with a bottle of cold tablets. He plunked it down and fetched a glass of water. 'Are you warm enough?'

Maggie swiveled around on her stool. He sounded like he really cared. 'Yes.' She swallowed the pills and pushed her plate away. 'It's going to be a long night. You usually close around eight, don't you?'

'Or nine. Rarely later. It really depends on how busy it is.'

'Then what do you do? Go home and watch the boob tube?'

Nolan grimaced. 'Hardly. I work. Sometimes all night till it's time to go to the bakery. For some reason I don't require much sleep.'

'Well I need lots of sleep. I can't function if I don't sleep. My body wears down and then I get a cold like now. Do you just, you know, fiddle around, or do you work at something? Like for money.'

'Definitely for money.'

'If I came to you and said, listen, I'm up to my eyeballs in debt, can you hack into the different credit card companies and erase my accounts, could you do that?'

'Sure. Piece of cake.'

'No kidding. Wow, I'm impressed. Bet you're in demand.'

'Actually, I am in demand but not for small stuff like that. I name my own price. I specialize in security, encryption, I can install barriers to prevent anyone wanting to crack into someone else's computer system. I can install backdoors, trapdoors, firewalls, worms, viruses, that kind of thing. I've done a lot of work here in Alphabet City that no one will admit to.'

'What's Alphabet City?'

'You know, the FBI, CIA, NSA, DOJ, Washington.'

Aha. Now we're getting somewhere.

'Let me get this straight. Are you saying you can hack into the United States government any old time you feel like it and read up on all the secret stuff going on?'

'That's what I'm saying. Since I'm one of the few people around who can do this, I installed wormholes. It's complicated. Of course I would never do anything like that but I could if I wanted to. I have ethics.'

Maggie was starting to get excited. 'Yeah, yeah, I'd never do anything like that either. These people who work in those places that use initials can make you disappear if they want to.' She thought about Ted's run-ins with the gold shields. She had to take this slow and easy now that Nolan was in a talkative mood.

'When you think of the government you think they have it under control. Let me tell you, they are vulnerable to people like me. If I wanted to, I could work for them and make a hundred grand a year. I make twice that much between the bakery and this café. Fifty times that much from my private clients. I don't advertise my talents and only take referrals. It's all pretty much secret so don't go blabbing this to anyone.'

Maggie managed to look indignant. 'Get real here. Who would I tell and who would be interested? This sure is a strange city. Everything is a secret. Do you know any *real* secrets?'

'More than you can imagine. In my line of business you're only as good as your reputation and I never talk about my government work. If I even hint at anything to you, I'd have to kill you.'

'Well, for God's sake, don't tell me then. I want to live to a ripe old age.' That sounded good, she thought. Careful now, she warned herself, he's loosening up. Careful, careful, careful.

Nolan smiled. Maggie was struck by how nice he looked when he smiled. Nerdy but nice. Rich, nerdy and nice.

'How'd you get so smart?' Maggie batted her eyelashes. 'Guess that was a stupid question. Either you're smart or you're not. I am not book smart but I have street smarts. I think street smarts are important.'

'You're right about that, Julie Jett. That's a nice name by the way. I like the way it sounds. But to answer your question, when I was little I was sickly, rheumatic fever. My mother was over protective. I read. I think I read every book in our library. When computers came on the market, my parents bought me one. I know this is a cliché but I took to that machine like a duck to water. As they say, the rest is history.'

'Fascinating. You parlayed that into what you do now. You must be rich.'

Nolan beamed. 'I could retire right now and live the life of luxury if I wanted to. If I did that, though, I wouldn't be able to help you this weekend, now would I?'

'No, I guess not.' He was suddenly in a talkative mood. Maggie wondered if it was the close quarters or if he just enjoyed her company. 'Do you have a girlfriend?' she asked bluntly.

Nolan turned pink. 'No. I dated a girl for a while but she kept trying to get me to play tennis, golf and she was into going to the gym. She didn't even know how to turn a computer on. She thought email was obscene. We didn't last very long. I date sometimes. I don't have time for a social life.'

'Yeah, I know what you mean. I'm sitting here thinking

about everything on my plate that I have yet to get to. I don't know how I would manage a relationship at this stage in my life. You know something, Alan, without sounding like a traitor to my gender, you're better off without that girl. You need someone who has the same interests you have.'

'Sometimes I get lonely,' Nolan blurted.

Maggie was about to respond when several customers meandered over and ordered sandwiches and coffee. More chatter followed as they made their way to the door to stare out at the storm. The decibel level of the chatter increased as they speculated about how far each of them had to go to get home. Cell phones were whipped out and the conversation escalated to an even higher pitch as other customers came over to the café side.

Maggie marched around to join Alan behind the counter. 'Let me help. It's the least I can do.' As people called out orders, Maggie worked industriously.

An hour later, the customers were back at the computer terminals and Maggie and Alan were left with the cleanup. They talked about the weather, Washington, New York and nothing important.

'What was the hardest or the most interesting job you ever did? Did you ever strike out?'

Nolan wiped down the counter. He appeared deep in thought. 'No, I've never failed. None of it is that hard. For me, that is. What I do is time consuming and frustrating for sure. Probably the most interesting was a job I just did recently. Now, that one kicked my butt. For a movie star you'd think he was into something sponsored by the government or the Chinese. That guy had so much deep encrypted crap on his computer I learned a whole new language. He was hiding something, that's for sure. I cracked it and turned over the information to the man who hired me, took his money, banked it and that's the end of that story.'

'You know movie stars! Who? I love the movies! I rent DVDs all the time. I'm a real movie buff. Do I know him or her?' Maggie gushed.

'Now you know I can't tell you his name. But, he's up for an Academy Award.'

Maggie managed to look disgusted. 'So is half of Hollywood. Jeeze, I thought you were going to make my day. He's probably cheating on his wife, right? Thinks his career will be ruined if anyone finds out. Does he even have a wife? Who hired you to get the goods on him? Another disgruntled actor? Smear your competition. That's how they do things in Hollywood. That figures.' She risked a glance at Nolan who looked like he was at war with himself.

'He's already won three Oscars. The news says he's a shoo in. He's not young. But he looks good for his age.'

'Is he up for best actor?'

Nolan nodded.

Maggie closed her eyes and ran the list through her mind. 'Michael Lyons?'

Alan Nolan smiled. Maggie laughed and then reached for his hand and patted it. 'So, do we want him to win or not? What do *you* think he's hiding?'

'I have no idea what he's hiding, if anything. I was paid to crack his computers which I did. Like I said, I have ethics. Whatever he's into is none of my business. What I will tell you is the government hired me, not an actor. At least I think it was the government. My contact has some pretty high clearance. He didn't balk at my fee either.'

Maggie was so excited she thought she would explode. The Mother Lode! Instinct told her to play it all down. She waved her hand about. 'Bet he fathered a child out of wedlock when he was 19 or something like that. Who cares? So, do you think you should get the guys in here to help shovel out front? The snow is drifting toward the door.'

'It's not necessary. All the shop owners chip in and a guy comes around in the morning to do the whole street. You're pretty, Julie Jett. I like red hair. When you have a free night would you like to go to a movie?'

Maggie felt the sudden urge to cry. She was no better than a lowdown skunk. She worked a smile into her voice. 'That would be nice.' Why would Charles Martin and the women at Pinewood want to know about a movie star; Michael Lyons in particular? She needed to find out more without tipping her hand.

'What's wrong? Are you feeling worse?' Nolan asked, genuine concern in his voice.

'I feel the same. I'm just upset about that movie star. I've seen all his movies. I hate it when people disappoint me. Now I am never going to feel the same about his movies. Heck, I probably won't even go to see them.' Maggie leaned across the table and whispered, 'Do you think he's a communist or something? Why would the government be interested in him? Why would they pay you all that money to get the goods on some Hollywood movie idol? I bet he's gay. Not that there's anything wrong with being gay. If you are, you are. Fans like me would accept that. It's bad when you deny it and then proof comes out the other way around. Oh, well, life will go on. How could you not have, you know, *peeked*, at what you were seeing?

Nolan looked at the young woman sitting across from him. He was coming up short in her eyes. He shrugged. 'I was just paid to crack the computers and get the passwords. Then I burn my records.'

'What?' The one word exploded from Maggie's mouth like a gunshot.

Nolan decided he needed to redeem himself. 'Well, they think I burn the records. I hide them. Trust me when I tell you the person hasn't been born who can crack *my* computers. But, you never know when something will come back to bite you. Does that make you feel better?'

Maggie wiped at her watering eyes. 'Well, yeah, but for you, not me. That was the first thing I thought about, those people coming after you. They probably don't have ethics like you do, Alan.'

'Exactly.'

Outside the wind howled and the snow fell. Maggie felt like she was enclosed in a tomb. And she felt lousy. Not just lousy but really lousy. She was about to say something when the lights flickered and then went out. They came on a second later and then went out again.

'Everyone! Stay where you are. I have a generator. We'll have power in a few minutes. Julie, there are some candles in the cabinet in the corner. Light them and put them around the café. I'm just going to power up the computer room to save on gas. We'll have minimal heat but we won't freeze.'

Five minutes later dim light could be seen coming from the computer side of the café. Alan appeared at Maggie's side. 'It is going to cool down here rather quickly. Since you're coming down with something, I suggest you go to the little room in the back and bundle up. There are plenty of blankets. Take a couple more of those cold tablets. I'll take care of things out here. I'll look in on you. If you need anything just send up a shout.'

Maggie wanted to cry all over again. Betrayal was such a terrible thing.

Fourteen

While the snow fell outside the farmhouse in Virginia, Charles called the meeting to order. Two stacks of folders sat in the middle of the table. The women looked at them curiously. In the past, when they were preparing for the crunch before a mission, they were given one single colored folder. Their curiosity caused them to squirm in their chairs as they tried to anticipate whatever it was Charles was going to tell them.

Charles reached for the folders and placed them directly in front of him. He spoke rapidly, his words clear and concise. 'When the storm passes and the roads are clear, Myra and Annie will leave for California to set up shop at the Beverly Hills Hotel. They will lay the groundwork for their meeting with Michael Lyons. With just weeks till the Academy Awards, everything must be in place. We've alerted the appropriate gossip columnists that both ladies are there to back several high budget films. One strong possibility is the new James Bond series if the studio can get Lyons to sign on for the role. The studios will be clamoring for their attention. The papers will carry articles and interviews every day until the rest of you arrive. By the time you get there, Myra and Annie will be household names in the industry.

'An old and dear friend, retired from the SIS in England, called me last evening when I put out word I needed his help. To you that means the British Secret Intelligence Service. My friend has been visiting his brother who lives in California. He is now actively on our limited payroll. He and a few operatives of his choosing will conduct surveillance on Mr Lyons who, by the way, has returned to the States weeks ahead of schedule. It would seem that Mr Lyons has been under the watchful eye of my countrymen for some time. No one as yet has been able to tell me exactly why. I do not know if this is true or not, but if it is, we have to work quick and fast if we want to get to him first.

'That's another way, ladies, of saying we have our work cut out for us on this particular mission. I want to show you the headline in yesterday's paper.' Charles pressed the remote in his hand and one of the oversize monitors overhead came to life with the front page of the *Los Angeles Times*. The women gasped as the black headline took over the large screen. THE LYON ROARS! was the headline. Underneath the bold black headline, above the fold, was a full frontal shot of Michael Lyons with his clenched fist in the air. 'He's thanking the Academy for the nomination of Best Actor in that photograph. His picture was nominated for eleven awards. The smart money says they'll take all eleven Oscars. They also say he's a hair away from signing on to be the next James Bond. Annie and Myra will be standing in line to offer their backing if he signs. I'm only guessing at this but I suspect this is how he came under the SIS's radar screen. We Brits are very cautious and outspoken when it comes to our English heroes and James Bond is right up there with Churchill. No giggling, please,' Charles said sternly.

'Mr Lyons is going to be getting a huge rush of publicity. That's where all of you come in. You're going to be feature writers for different media publications. We're going to inundate him with publicity. Alexis will alter your appearance just a little, as we don't want anyone knowing exactly who you are. I've had to make a few changes and I've decided that Yoko will be joining you.

'Now, something rather serious has happened. It's been all underground the past several days but my people have ferreted it out. Mr Lyons has initiated a nationwide manhunt to find Yoko. I'm not going to give you details on how, what, when and why this came to my attention. Just the word manhunt is enough to chill one to the bone. The man has the wherewithal to hire as many people as it takes to find her. That doesn't mean he will be successful.

'There are two other additional areas of concern you need

to be aware of. As I told you several days ago, we managed to hack our way into Actor Lyons's private computers and secure a wealth of information on his activities. However, that all changed as of yesterday when everything was shut down. Obviously, our hacker left some trace that he had invaded Lyons's files, and his people shut down his entire system.

'The second area of concern is that Actor Lyons, while in Japan, went to see Yoko's grandparents. We have no information on what triggered that visit since he has never done that before. Our operative visited with the grandparents shortly after Lyons left Japan, which was almost immediately. He was supposed to go on to Hong Kong but he canceled out and returned to the States.'

Charles fixed his gaze on Yoko and then Annie. 'The grandparents told Actor Lyons that their granddaughter, on her first ever visit to them, told another lady – that would be you, Annie – that she was going to find and kill Lyons for what he did to her mother. It seems that the old ones know a smattering of English taught to them by a man from one of the local stores in the village nearest them. In case their daughters ever returned, they wanted to be able to talk to them in English to make them proud.'

Yoko started to cry. 'Then they know what happened to my mother and my aunts! How stupid I was. That man didn't hurt them, did he?' she asked fiercely.

'No, he didn't, Yoko. You had no way of knowing, my dear. I don't want you to blame yourself. There is no way to know at this time if Lyons's visit was a spur of the moment thing or if he planned it. He went there to try and find out where you are. Perhaps he went as an errant father. Perhaps he went for devilish reasons. At this time we simply don't know. What we do know for certain is he now knows that someone, other than his network of perverts, knows about his activities. I suspect he returned home to work on damage control. That's all I have at the moment. I'm going to hand out these folders. Each one is different so when you finish one, trade off. What you will be looking at is the information we've taken off his computers. Attached to each folder is the biography and a picture of a man, wealthy, high-powered men, scions, captains of industry, doctors, lawyers, generals and admirals, people you would never believe could be a member of the Michael Lyons organization. I must get back to work now.'

The ladies of Pinewood looked at the pile of folders with narrowed eyes. Yoko was the first to reach for one. The others followed suit.

The man ranting and raving on his cell phone bore no resemblance to the smiling philanthropic actor dubbed the Golden Boy who almost daily graced Hollywood's media. If he had horns, this ugly person could have posed for the Devil. 'You told me that could never happen. You said you were the best of the best. You said even the CIA couldn't penetrate my system and now you're telling me I was compromised not once but twice. I paid you millions of dollars to make sure this very thing never happened. It happened, you asshole. Now what are you going to do?' Lyons screamed at the top of his lungs, sweat rolling down his bronzed cheeks. 'Well?'

The voice on the other end of the line was cold and professional. 'If you recall, Mr Lyons, what I said was that, to my knowledge, there is only one other person with the expertise to hack into your system. Since he works for the CIA and the FBI, I saw little chance of that happening. You agreed with me. I also told you since I, too, work on a consulting basis for both organizations, I was in a very good position to know when and if you were going to be compromised. That didn't happen. You agreed with me on that, too. It is entirely possible you have a disgruntled member who is disenchanted with you or your organization. The system I installed is so sophisticated I'm having trouble believing that Alan Nolan could penetrate it. If I were you, I'd purge all your files. I can build you a new system but it will take time and be costly. The decision is yours.'

'Purge the files! Purge the files!' Lyons screamed. 'I've already been compromised. My files have been copied already and God alone knows where they are. How do I find that guy?'

Dan Boatman knew exactly where Alan Nolan lived and worked but he wasn't about to give him up to the likes of

Michael Lyons. 'I have no idea, Mr Lyons. Check the phone book.'

'Don't get smart with me, Boatman, or you'll find yourself in a ditch somewhere,' Lyons roared.

'Don't ever make the mistake of threatening me, Mr Lyons. Since I know where the bodies are buried it would behoove you to alter your tone of voice when you talk to me. Now, do you want me to build you a new system or are you going to go with the one you have left that hasn't been compromised?'

Lyons bit down on his lip. 'I'll get back to you.' He threw the cell phone across the room. The back of the phone and the batteries rolled across the floor. He made no move to pick it up. Beyond livid, he stomped his way to his office where he picked up the phone to call Five Star Investigations. He asked for Paul Yarm and told him he wanted to locate Alan Nolan. He gave him what information he had and said he wanted the information yesterday. He ended the call and looked around helplessly. He knew what he needed to do but he couldn't bring himself to call his clients. Maybe this was nothing more than a little windstorm he could weather. If he played his cards right he would save himself and the others the humiliation of being found out.

What he should do now was enjoy being nominated for an Academy Award. He should start returning all the congratulatory calls. And he needed to call a few of the gossip columnists and give them a few sound bites. He'd always done it in the past so he had to do it this time, too. He couldn't do anything out of the ordinary to draw attention to himself. He'd never believed in secretaries and he sure as hell didn't believe in money managers or bodyguards or any of that claptrap other celebrities surrounded themselves with. When you led a double life like he did you had to be careful who was in your inner circle.

Who in hell was Alan Nolan? He wondered if that was the man's real name or just the name that Boatman knew him by. He decided it was the latter which did nothing for his mood. Did he really want to mess around with someone who worked for the CIA or the FBI? Hell, no, he didn't. But if it came down to his survival and reputation he would kill the son of a bitch if he had to.

111

His thoughts turned to his daughter that he'd never seen. Why she was consuming his thoughts he didn't know. Aside from the fact that she wanted to kill him, he knew nothing about her. It bothered him that she had the edge. She knew who he was, what he looked like and she could find out where he lived just by asking around. He knew nothing about her, except her age. He didn't know what name she went by. Suki might have given her a meaningless name just in case he ever tried to find her. The girl might be married by now with a whole new name. Finding her would be like finding a guppie in the ocean. All he could do was hope that Five Star Investigations lived up to its name.

Lyons walked around his house then just to have something to do. He stopped at each framed poster hanging on the wall. One for every movie he'd ever made. His own personal Rogue's Gallery. He loved each one of the posters.

And now the possibility he might sign to be the next James Bond was something he had to deal with. The studio wanted five pictures. One a year for the next five years. He could pack it in at the age of 55 and retire. Maybe he should think about retiring now. Hollywood would remember him as the man who walked away from the mega million dollar Bond deal. He could say he wanted to spend his time working for his various charities. He'd get out of Dodge and he'd fade off the radar. Yeah, yeah, that's what he should do. He'd make the announcement after the Academy Awards. Or, better yet, he'd make his announcement when he gave his acceptance speech, Oscar in hand. He wasn't going to carve it in stone just yet. The ceremony was weeks away and many, many things could happen between now and then.

One thing he did know now was his daughter's name. Yoko. Yoko what? A million names raced through his mind. Did Suki name her Yoko Naoki, her maiden name? Or did she pick an alias so he could never find her?

The phone on his desk rang. He looked down to see the Caller I.D. and winced. He picked up the phone and said, 'Hello.'

'Michael, it's Maxwell. I heard you were back in the States and didn't go on to Hong Kong as planned. Do you care to tell me why?'

'Actually, Maxwell, I returned for personal reasons. I plan to go back after the Academy Awards. You sound upset, why is that?'

'Because I was counting on some new merchandise. My people were expecting to sample the merchandise as promised. I don't like giving my word, accepting payment and then having to say things went awry. This would be a good time to tell me if there's something wrong.'

Lyons struggled to keep his voice light. 'Maxwell, have I ever let you down before? Leave the worrying to old ladies. I told you I came back for personal reasons. If you read the papers I'm sure you know the studio is trying to get me to sign on to do five James Bond movies. I have a business life in case you've forgotten. I have to pay attention to that business. Some of the merchandise will be arriving next week. As always, you get to view it first. I'll be in touch in a few days when the details are finalized.'

'See that you do,' the voice on the other end of the line snapped.

'Screw you, too!' Lyons snarled as he slammed the phone down.

Michael Lyons stretched out his foot to pull out the desk chair. He sat down and started to shake. Was his secret life about to come crashing down around him?

Would his daughter find him and try to kill him?

Would Five Star Investigations find Alan Nolan?

He wished he could see into the future.

Fifteen

Maggie Spritzer woke drenched in her own sweat. She struggled with the cocoon of blankets she was wrapped in before she looked down at her watch; 3:10. She'd slept for three hours. She lay quietly as her mind raced. She felt alert, less groggy than when she'd come back here around midnight. The cold tablets must have helped since she didn't feel as feverish. She wondered if it was still snowing. How was she going to get home in the morning?

The silence was so total, Maggie felt like she was sealed in a tomb. She could see dim light from the computer area which meant the generator was still on. Where was everyone? Probably curled up on the floor or on the chairs sleeping. She thought about Alan then and how nice he'd been to her. Then she thought about Ted who was waiting for her back in the apartment. She wondered if he was worried about her. She probably should have called him earlier but that would have blown her cover with Alan so she'd turned off her cell phone.

Maggie started to get excited then when she thought about what Alan Nolan had divulged to her just hours ago. Ted would go over the moon when she told him. *If* she told him. She needed to get up to use the bathroom. She heard the voice when she swung her legs over the side of the narrow bed. Someone talking. A voice that was agitated. She slid off the bed and made her way to the doorway. It was Alan Nolan talking to someone. Just one voice. Was he on the phone? People didn't talk to other people in the middle of the night unless it was serious. She shrugged thinking she was going to hear the computer expert talking about being snowbound. Her jaw dropped when she heard the Wizard, that's what Alan said his cyber name was, say, 'How reliable is this info, Scratch

Man?' Maggie wiggled her eyebrows. Scratch Man? Must be another cyber name. She continued to listen but she made a mental note of the name. 'You gotta be shitting me, Scratch Man! I can't cut and run. No way. I'll call the agency. Yeah, yeah, I sort of/kind of/*glanced* at the stuff. I knew you were the one who set it all up. That one look was all I needed to know I didn't want to be part of that mess. I can't believe you set that guy up knowing what he's into. Yeah, money is money but damn, that's over the top, man. You're getting out, too? You're really going to let the bastard swing in the wind? Damn! Okay, okay, soon as the roads are clear, I'll shut down both shops and head for the ranch. You're welcome to join me, Scratch Man. We'll both be safer there than the gold at Fort Knox. I don't know if it's a good idea or not but since you're close to the source, I'll take your word for it. Yeah, yeah, this is an encrypted phone, no one is listening in. What happened to those nerves of steel you're always talking about? What we should do is turn the son of a bitch over to the proper authorities.'

Maggie was so excited she thought she was going to pee her pants. Talk about being on the inside track. Pulitzer, here I come. She continued to listen to Nolan but he wasn't talking, just listening. She'd have given up her pinkie finger to know what the other party was saying. And then Nolan was speaking again. Maggie could hear the awe in his voice. 'Don't con me. We both know to crack Lyons's remaining system you need both passwords, the sender's and the recipient's. Don't bullshit me, cowboy. You cracked the recipient's code? Well, hot damn. I bow to you, Scratch Man.'

The testosterone was really flying, Maggie thought. She wished she knew what the two wizards were talking about. What remaining system? Who did it belong to? The movie star? Who was the recipient they were talking about? She pressed her ear against the door frame. 'I'll call you when I'm on the way. Thanks for the heads up.'

Maggie scurried back to the tiny bathroom and closed the door quietly. She waited a few moments and then flushed the toilet. She walked out to the bedroom, looked around and pretended to walk sleepily to the café side of the cyber café.

115

She pretended surprise at seeing Nolan sitting at the counter. She tried out her voice and was surprised to hear how normal it sounded. She didn't sound hoarse at all the way she had before she went to bed. 'Whatever those pills were, they worked wonders. Do you have any coffee? Guess everyone's asleep, huh?'

'Yeah, they pretty much all crashed around midnight. Did you just wake up? I made some coffee a few minutes ago. I'll get you some. Do you want anything to eat?'

'I woke up drenched in sweat. I must have had a fever and it broke because now I feel fine. Coffee will be real good. Is it still snowing?'

Alan walked around to go behind the counter. 'It stopped around one o'clock. The plow went past about twenty minutes ago. So, you're feeling better, huh?'

'Oh, tons better. I appreciate everything you've done for me. You're a really nice guy, Alan Nolan.' Maggie realized she meant everything she'd just said.

'You're pretty nice yourself, Julie Jett. Listen, I just remembered that I have to go out of town this weekend. I promise to work on your computer the minute I get back.'

Maggie winked at Alan. 'Big secret job, huh?'

'Yeah, something like that. Are you okay with waiting a little while?'

'Sure. I just won't turn my computer on. I'll give you my number and you can call me when you get back. Are you going far?'

'Far enough. I'll probably be gone, two, three weeks, maybe four. The movie will have to wait, too.'

'Hey, business first, I always say. Boy, this coffee is good. I saw you grinding the beans earlier. Guess that makes all the difference, huh?'

Nolan was back on the stool next to her. 'Yeah, it does make a difference. Grinding the beans I mean.'

Such drivel, Maggie thought. Maybe he wants to talk but doesn't know how to go about saying what he wants to say. Careful, Maggie, don't overplay your hand, she cautioned herself.

'So you just close up your businesses when you . . . ah, go

116

off on an assignment? I'm assuming you're going away on business.'

Alan tapped his spoon on the side of the cup. 'More or less. What other choice do I have? These two shops pretty much pay the bills. The special assignments put money in the bank and my retirement account. When the weather is bad like this there isn't all that much business.' Maggie thought he was trying to convince himself of what he was saying. He looked tense though, maybe even a little frightened. She couldn't decide which.

Maggie was off the stool and massaging Nolan's neck within minutes. 'You're way too tense, Alan. Relax. Things always work out. Look, I know we just met but you're a nice guy, and I'm a nice person so If you want me to keep the café open while you're away, I'll do it to help you out. I can't promise this but there may be someone in my apartment building who could help you out with the bakery. You get the dough ready made, right? Then you just punch it down and pop it in the oven. That can't be too hard to do.' Oh, God, she didn't just say what she said, did she?

'Damn, that feels good,' Nolan said as Maggie kneaded his shoulders. 'Are you kidding me? You'd really do the café? There's a possibility I'll be gone longer than a month. Are you sure you want to commit to this?'

'I can use the money, Alan. The move here left me with almost a zero bank balance. You can trust me if that's what's worrying you. I'll keep precise records.'

'Then it's a done deal,' Alan said turning on the stool to face her. 'Boy, you have strong hands. Can I make you some breakfast?'

Maggie felt sick to her stomach at what she'd just proposed. What kind of person was she to take advantage of a guy like Alan Nolan? 'No, the coffee is fine. But thanks for the offer. Maybe you should show me what I would have to do. Everyone is asleep and there's nothing else to do. Are you going to make a lot of money on your assignment? I'm sorry, that's none of my business and I never should have asked such a personal question. It's just that what you do is so . . . *so fascinating.*'

117

It was obvious to Maggie that Alan Nolan was not an accomplished liar. He looked everywhere but at her. 'No. It's phase two of my last project. I've already been paid. I always take my money up front.'

'Boy, that sure is smart of you. See, see, that's what I mean, it's all so fascinating. I bet you could write a book about what you do.'

'God forbid. I'd be behind bars the minute the proposal left my hands. Maybe when I'm old and gray with nothing to do, I'll consider it.' Nolan laughed then, a genuine sound of mirth. Maggie grinned. She was liking this weird guy more and more.

'So, how much will you pay me?'

'How much do you want?' Nolan asked.

'I don't know. I never managed a cyber café before. What's the going rate?'

'Well, guess what, Julie Jett, I don't have a clue because I've never hired anyone before to manage the café. How about half of whatever you take in for the day. You pay your own taxes. Make a deposit at the bank once a week. I have a safe in the back where I keep the week's money. If you don't want to mess with food, just serve coffee and Danish. If you want to do the food, I have an account with Schwan and they bill once a month. It's up to you.'

Maggie's conscience pricked her. 'I can't take half. I'm thinking an hourly wage would be better. What would half come to?' she asked craftily.

'Nolan laughed again. 'About eighteen hundred bucks a week, Julie.'

'Mercy! Okay, I'll take half.' How she was going to explain all this to the *Post*, she didn't know. 'Would it be the same deal if I can find someone to do the bakery? Does it generate as much revenue as the café?'

'More.' Nolan laughed again at Maggie's surprised look. 'And all the bread, pastries and muffins you can eat.'

Ted, you just got yourself a new job. Her next thought was they would both pork up big time. Her second thought was that would be okay because they'd both be fired from the *Post* but they wouldn't starve.

Nolan's face turned serious. 'What's wrong?'

'Nothing. This is just so generous of you. We hardly know one another and here I am, sick, you give me cold pills, let me sleep in your bed, you've fed all of us and now I'm going to run your business while you're away. It's a bit mind-boggling. I just want you to know you can trust me.'

Alan Nolan swiveled around on his stool so his back was against the counter. He wished he could tell the young woman sitting next to him that he wouldn't be coming back to the cyber café and the bakery but what was the point? In his line of work, he'd had to relocate so many times he'd lost count.

'It's going to be light out soon,' Nolan said. The words were no sooner out of his mouth when the power came back on. Maggie clapped her hands.

'It's a good thing. I only have about two more hours of gas for the generator. See, everything happens for a reason. Be right back. I want to shut off the generator. I think maybe we should wake up our customers and make them some break-fast. You start frying the bacon and I'll be right back to help you.'

Maggie wished she could call Ted. As soon as it was light enough she was going to attempt to make it back to the apart-ment. If bad came to worse maybe she could hitch a ride with one of the people in the café or even the snow plow if it was going her way. She tried not to think about what she was doing as she slapped bacon onto the mini grill behind the counter. If only she had heard the other half of Nolan's conversation. If only . . . words to live by, she thought.

The computer wizard returned and they worked side by side. One by one, the customers stirred. There was an imme-diate run on the small bathroom. Some of the young girls volunteered to help by setting the tiny tables and the counter with the stools. Two of the guys – hackers, she was sure – wanted to go back on the computers, coffee in hand.

Outside, the day was just beginning. Snow plows could be heard going up and down the streets. By noon, Maggie knew, Washington would be clear to travel.

'So, how am I supposed to get in touch with you while you're away, Alan? Are you sure you can't tell me where you're going?'

'I'll call you. I'm probably going to be moving around a bit. When I finally settle in for the last phase of this project, I'll let you know.'

That was all she was going to get and Maggie knew it. She started to mutter under her breath.

'What did you say?'

Maggie looked Nolan square in the eye, hating herself as she did so, and said, 'I said, it's just my stupid luck. Here I finally meet a really nice guy and off he goes into the wild blue yonder saying, yeah, he'll call me. Yeah, right. I've been around the block a few times. I know how *that* works.' She slid the cooked bacon onto a large plate and put more on the grill. 'I won't hold my breath waiting for your call. Just so you know that, Alan.'

The wizard frowned. A really nice guy. She thought he was a really nice guy. He almost told her then where he was going but he didn't. He, too, had been around the block and what he did was dangerous stuff. Early on he'd been taught by the experts to leave no trail of any kind behind. As much as he liked Julie Jett, he didn't really *know* her. She'd popped into his life just a little too conveniently. Scratch Man would tell him to zip his lips and that's exactly what he was going to do. 'I *will* call you, Julie,' he lied with a straight face.

Maggie decided it was time to become cheerful. 'Okay, but I still won't hold my breath while I wait. How many eggs should I scramble?'

'All of them. I think we have a hungry crowd here. I appreciate you pitching in. I'm going to close up here as soon as the roads open. Will you be able to open tomorrow?'

Maggie looked down at the yellow froth in the bowl in front of her. So quick? She'd thought maybe a week. She'd need at least that long to square things with the *Post*. 'Sure, no problem.' Liar, liar, pants on fire. 'Are you leaving today? Why did I think you . . . I don't know what I thought. Next week, I suppose.'

'When the client calls, especially a client who has already paid you, you have to hustle your butt and do what he says. In this business, you're only as good as your reputation. I'm sure the airport will be open by noon. I'll get the first flight

I can wrangle.' Nolan wasn't going to any airport. He was going to drive to his destination in his very own Pathfinder that he kept in a garage in town. A vehicle no one even knew he owned.

Maggie offered up a sickly smile as the scrambled eggs slid onto the grill. Where in hell was he going?

Sixteen

Charles Martin stood at the kitchen door looking out at the melting mountains of snow. Three days of sunshine guaranteed a flood in the yard. The roads were sopping wet but free of snow. He felt better sending off his girls, knowing they'd make it safely to the airport. He'd stood here in this same position at first light to send Myra and Annie off to California. He started to miss Myra the moment she walked through the door to the waiting town car that would take her and Annie to Reagan National Airport. With nothing on his immediate agenda other than his chaotic thoughts and seeing the rest of the Sisterhood off to their destinations, he opted to make a huge breakfast, everyone's favorites.

A chill washed over him when he saw the limousine arrive and park outside the gates. He took a deep breath, closed his eyes for a moment, and then opened them. Only time would tell if he was sending the women into danger. He'd worked tirelessly through the snowstorm and through the following three days to make their trips as foolproof as possible. He'd called in so many favors, paid and otherwise, that he'd lost count. It wasn't that he doubted any of their capabilities; he didn't. It was the unknown, the human element that could foul things up. Each of them was going to be alone this time around with absolutely no back-up other than their special cell phones.

He'd argued with himself, and with Myra, that what he was doing was best. Worrier that she was, she'd made him promise the girls would return unscathed and unharmed. He'd made the promise, albeit reluctantly. If he hadn't made the promise, Myra would have refused to accompany Annie to Los Angeles.

'Any last-minute instructions, Charles?' Isabelle asked as

she joined him at the door. 'Other than to wear sunglasses. I've never seen the snow look so blinding white.'

'No, I think we covered everything. Your meeting was confirmed at five o'clock yesterday afternoon. Retired General Josh Tappen has graciously given you ten minutes of his valuable time today at four o'clock. I think you will have his undivided attention by two minutes past four. Your return flight is at seven, so please be on time. Myra will be calling in every ten minutes until all of you are back safe and sound. By the way, I received an email late last night saying the general received a seven-figure advance to write a book on his experiences in the Iraq War. Bear in mind he's only been retired for six months and in his current position for three months, earning twenty times what he earned in the military. The man has expensive habits as we all know.

'I think that's about all for now. The car is waiting. Good luck, ladies.'

The women all hugged Charles as they headed out the door. Yoko stood to the side with Murphy and Grady next to her. She waved goodbye.

'I made some tea, dear,' Charles said when the sound of the limo could no longer be heard. 'I couldn't let you go with them, Yoko, but I do know how you feel. All I ask is that you be patient just a little longer.'

Yoko nodded as she took her place at the table. 'Will it be all right if I go out to the nursery today? I really should check on things.'

'No, you have to stay here. We can't risk anyone seeing you or knowing where you are. There's a manhunt going on. I hate to say this but the price on your head is enough to make someone turn in their own grandmother for the money. It's just too risky. And you cannot use your regular cell phone. If you absolutely must make phone calls, use the encrypted phone so the calls can't be traced.'

Yoko nodded again as she accepted the cup of tea Charles handed her. 'I'll clean up the kitchen. I know you have things to do. It was a wonderful breakfast. Is there anything I can do for you?'

'I've got it covered. Please don't fret, all your sisters will be back by ten this evening since I scheduled everyone's appointments for four o'clock. Return flights are within fifteen minutes of each other. If you need me for anything, just call me on the cell.'

Left to her own devices, Yoko, her stomach churning, finished her tea and poured a second cup. When she finished it, she cleaned the kitchen and turned on the dishwasher. She wanted to call Harry so bad. Was it a good idea or a bad idea? Probably a bad idea but she was going to do it anyway but not until she called the nursery to see how things were going. And she needed to check the messages on her private cell phone as well as the messages on the business phone in the shop.

The dogs lying at her feet nibbled on her slippers. Yoko smiled, knowing they wanted to go out to romp in the snow. It was safe, so she opened the door and the dogs ran through and immediately started chasing each other. She went back to the table and picked up the special cell phone to call the shop. Emily Li answered in her sweet voice. Yoko spoke English slowly so Emily would understand. She insisted all her employees speak English and when she had time, she tutored them.

Now, Yoko listened as Emily Li ran down a list of things, deliveries, orders, what was late, the bills that had come in. 'Any messages?' Yoko asked.

Emily Li giggled. 'Forty-seven messages from Mr Harry Wong. Three messages from a man who said he used to be your husband.' Emily Li giggled at that. 'There have been seven calls in total where no one speaks on the other end of the phone.'

Yoko thought her heart missed a beat. Her tongue felt thick in her mouth. 'I'm sure they were just wrong numbers. Did the man who said he used to be my husband leave a number so I can call him?' Emily Li read off a number and Yoko copied it down.

'What should I tell Mr Harry Wong when he makes his forty-eighth call?'

'The same thing you told him for the other forty-seven calls,' Yoko said smartly. She said goodbye and hung up. The dogs wanted to come back in so she opened the door and then carefully locked it once they were safely inside.

Yoko pondered her problem. Why would her ex-husband, who didn't even like her, call her? Not just once but several times. Everything had been settled legally. He'd left nothing behind so he couldn't be calling about personal possessions. Since he didn't like her, he wasn't calling to see how she was. She shook her head at the thought of the arranged marriage they both had to endure until she got the guts to call it quits. So, why was he calling? Maybe he needed money No, Japanese men were too proud to borrow money. Especially from an ex-wife. What? Why? She thought about Harry Wong and how much she cared for him even if she was playing, as Kathryn called it, hard to get. Harry loved her. He would never give up even if he had to make a hundred and forty-seven calls.

Yoko picked up the phone and called the number Emily Li had read off to her. 'This is Yoko. My assistant said you have been trying to reach me. Why is that?' She listened to a rapid-fire explanation in Japanese. She said, 'There must be some mistake. I know of no such people. Why would you be so generous with your information? Excuse me, *my* information. That is unforgivable. I am very happy we are no longer married. You think only of yourself. Now these people will come to my shop and pester me. You are a . . .' Yoko tried to think of a name that Kathryn or the others would use to describe her ex-husband but the only thing she could come up with was '*dud*. You are a *dud*. Do not call me again. You have brought shame on both of us. By the way . . . you . . . you, *dud*, I am going to get married to a very rich handsome man who values my honor.' When she hung up the phone, Yoko started to tremble. She ran to the living room and the secret staircase that led to the war room where Charles was. She was breathless when she galloped down the steps, the special phone still in her hand.

'Slow down, child. What is it? Yoko,' Charles said sternly, 'Take a deep breath and relax. Now, take another one. Tell me what happened.'

Yoko repeated the conversation she'd just had with her

ex-husband. 'Now they know where I am. I'm sure it was a simple matter for them to trace me. My people keep impeccable records. All they had to do was find out where my mother's ashes are kept. There are many people, friends of my aunts, who would be only too happy to tell others of my worthy marriage and my relocation, thinking they were doing a good thing. Who knows what sort of story the people doing the investigating told them? The man I was married to (Yoko refused to call him her husband) said three men came to talk to him two days ago. They could be here in Washington right now.'

'Yes, Yoko, they could be in Washington right now. You aren't in Washington, though. You're in Virginia and safe. No one knows you are here unless you told someone. Did you? Does Harry Wong know about this farm?'

'No, Charles, I told no one, not Emily Li nor Harry. No one knows.'

Charles smiled. 'I think, my dear, Mr Michael Lyons is very worried. By four-thirty this afternoon, he is going to be even more worried. Now, go upstairs and turn on the house alarm. It's just a precaution. Keep the dogs with you at all times. I'll be up as soon as I finish what I'm doing. Everything is under control.'

Yoko hoped he was right.

She curled up on the window seat in her room. She stared out at the snow, remembering the first time she'd seen the fluffy white miracle. As a child, that's what she'd called snow.

Childhood. It was all so long ago. She'd lived in a world of adults who had secrets and who whispered all the time. She'd tried so hard to be good so the whispers wouldn't be about her. The people she lived with, the ones she called aunts, were good to her. She didn't think they loved her but then maybe they did. They took care of her, fed her, sometimes even told her bedtime stories. They'd taught her how to cook and clean, how to pray, how to meditate. They taught her how to sew her own kimonos and sack-like pants she wore during the day. She'd learned enough to make her own way in the world but when she broached the subject, the aunts had closed in and said it was time for her to marry. Time for someone else to take care of her was what they meant.

The marriage was a disaster for both of them. Still, they tried and it was her husband who finally made the decision to go his own way. Secretly, she'd been glad.

Often, she'd wondered if she had told him about her mother and father, what his reaction would have been. Even now, she felt guilty at how she'd spied on the aunts, listened late at night when they talked of her and her mother. She'd run away but they found her and brought her back. They sat her down with a cup of hot tea and finally told her her mother's sordid story. The aunts had cried. She cried with them and like a brave little girl she told them she would find the man someday and make him pay for what he'd done. The aunts had smiled and patted her head.

But, here she was. Sitting here staring out at the snow. Here in this house she was loved and respected. There were no barriers here. Only love and kindness. The people who loved and respected her were willing to help her avenge her mother.

And, she had Harry Wong in her life.

Life was going to be so very good and very soon.

Yoko gathered the light quilt around her shoulders and closed her eyes. She hoped she would dream of her beautiful mother. She drifted into sleep, her face, her whole body serene.

Kathryn Lucas stepped out of the cab in front of the Pan Am Building in Manhattan. She leaned forward, paid the driver and gave him a generous tip. She looked like a high-powered mover and shaker in her Carolina Herrera suit, matching fedora, and Manolo Blahnik shoes. She carried an ostrich skin briefcase. She received more than one admiring look as she made her way into the building where she signed in and then took the elevator to the floor where Lucian Treadwell, the CEO of one of the major auto makers, awaited her arrival.

Kathryn looked at the Rolex on her wrist when she stepped out of the elevator into what she later described as the swankiest reception area she'd ever seen. She sashayed over to the receptionist who looked like a movie star and said, 'I'm Mary Clare Peabody and I have a four o'clock appointment with Mr Treadwell. It's now four o'clock.' Kathryn looked pointedly at her watch. 'I'm prepared to wait exactly three minutes and then I'll leave. Time is money as I'm sure you know.'

The movie star-receptionist mentally catalogued the cost of Kathryn's attire, taking in the Rolex watch, the diamond stud earrings and the diamond boulder on her left hand before she pressed a button with a long pointy nail and spoke softly. She looked up at Kathryn and said, 'Mr Treadwell's assistant is on the way to escort you to his office.'

Kathryn looked down at her watch. She held up her index finger indicating there was one minute left on her waiting time. As the minute hand started its final sweep, she looked at the receptionist and smiled. 'There are hundreds of CEOs in this city who would die to be named CEO Of The Year.' She was on her way to the elevator when the movie star-receptionist ran after her offering to escort her to the inner chambers. Kathryn let her doubt show for an instant and then followed her.

Halfway down a luxuriously carpeted hallway they met the man who was to escort Kathryn to Treadwell's office. Kathryn offered up an icy glare and said, 'You're late. Don't apologize because it won't get you anywhere with me. Time is money. Remember that.'

The aide, the assistant, whatever he was, literally danced a jig to turn around and lead the way farther down the hall. Kathryn hadn't broken her long-legged stride. At the end of the hall the man literally leaped ahead of her to open the door to Treadwell's office. He announced her in a squeaky voice.

Lucian Treadwell got up and walked around his desk, his hand outstretched. Kathryn ignored it. 'Tell your secretary not to interrupt us for the next twenty minutes. I don't like interruptions.'

Treadwell blinked. 'That won't be necessary. I cleared fifteen minutes for this interview.'

The minute the door closed, Kathryn tossed her fedora onto the leather sofa and sat down. The Herrera skirt hiked up showing a generous toned thigh. Then she opened her briefcase and handed a manila folder to Lucian Treadwell. 'This isn't an interview, Mr Treadwell, this is a coming-out party. Is that your wife and children in that picture on your desk?

What a lovely family. Three sons! You must be very proud. Your wife is lovely.'

Treadwell looked puzzled. 'Did I misunderstand, Miss Peabody? I thought you were here to talk to me about being named CEO of the Business World?'

Kathryn frowned and then shrugged. 'That's possible. The truth is we lied to you. Michael Lyons sent me. Now open the envelope and tell me what you think. You better sit down when you open it.' Kathryn looked at her watch again, hoping Charles really did have the power to turn the juice off in this office. She heard a high-pitched squeak that signaled a power surge. Two more squeaks told her he'd been successful. She yawned but never took her eyes off Lucian Treadwell.

Lucian Treadwell was a big man, well over six feet and probably weighing in at around a hundred and eighty pounds. He was wearing the requisite power suit with the requisite red tie. He was bronzed and looked fit. It was obvious he worked out. His age was 62 and he earned seven million dollars a year plus stock options. He had an impeccable reputation and was a deacon in his church.

The man's hands trembled slightly when he opened the envelope and pawed through the pictures and the reports. His face drained of all color. 'Where did you get this?' he asked in a strangled voice.

Kathryn wagged her finger. 'No questions, Mr Treadwell.' She watched as Treadwell ripped the material in front of him into shreds. 'Hey, I have tons of copies. If you want another one to rip up, here's one. Ooops, that one belongs to one of your club members. You know Josh Tappen, that retired military guy? You want to rip his up, too?'

'Who are you? What do you want? How much?' Treadwell asked through clenched teeth. His color looked pasty gray.

'Mister, you don't have enough money to buy me. What do I want? I want to see your face plastered all over the newspapers, above the fold. I want your sorry ass in jail for the rest of your life. That's what I want and that's what I'm going to get.'

'You can't just waltz in here and threaten me like this. I won't stand for this. This is all some kind of mistake. I'll have you arrested. I know the President of the United States. We dine together when we're in each other's cities.' The man's voice was so desperate sounding Kathryn almost laughed out loud

'Hey, I know the guy, too. I voted for him. Obviously that was a mistake seeing as how he socializes with the likes of you. You know what you are, Mr Treadwell? You are a slimy sack of poop. What's POTUS going to say when he finds out he dined with a pervert like you? Okay, enough chatter,' Kathryn said standing up and plopping the fedora on her head at a rakish angle. Gotta go now.'

'Just a goddamn minute. You can't come in here and . . . and . . .'

'Upset your sleazy world? Is that what you were going to say? Hey, I just did it. Your wife should be opening her envelope right about now,' Kathryn lied. 'I'd hire the best lawyer in the city if I were you.'

'You just ruined my goddamned life,' Treadwell roared. His face was a mottled red and purple.

'I ruined your life! I don't think so! You did that all by yourself. Well, my fifteen minutes were up seven minutes ago. I'm sure you have a lot of phone calls to make. Don't go too far, Mr Treadwell. You're being watched. I can see myself out.'

Outside in the hall, Kathryn thought she was going to faint. She leaned against the wall, her head down as she struggled to get her breathing back to normal. If she had one wish right now it would be to take a bath. The stink of the man was still with her as she made her way to the elevator that wasn't running. She turned to look at the receptionist in the dimness of the windowless reception area. 'Where's the stairway?' The woman pointed to the left.

Kathryn walked down eight flights of stairs in her spike-heeled Manolo Blahnik shoes. When she got to the eighth floor, she took them off and carried them in her hands as she walked down the other eight flights of stairs.

Outside, she hailed a cab and directed the driver to Kennedy Airport. Her job here was done. She called Charles and said, 'I'm on my way to the airport.'

Seventeen

A lexis Thorn, attired in Karl Lagerfeld from head to toe, entered the glass highrise on Peachtree in Atlanta. The time was 3:55. Just enough time to sign in and take the elevator to the 22nd floor where Adam Newhouse, CEO and CFO of Ultimate Toys, a billion dollar company and on the Fortune 500 list, hung his hat during daytime hours.

As she rode up in the elevator, Alexis let her mind drift to the dossier she'd read and memorized on the plane trip from Washington. She had seriously asked Charles if she and the others could be hypnotized after Yoko's mission so none of them would remember anything about the horrid people they were dealing with. Charles had responded just as seriously by saying it was 'doable.'

Alexis thought she was prepared but she knew she wasn't. She'd played one scenario after the other in her mind as to how to present herself and the contents of her briefcase to Adam Newhouse. Maybe she should follow Kathryn's advice and go straight for the jugular. Dump it all out, stare at Newhouse defiantly, and wait for the fallout.

The moment Alexis stepped out of the elevator the power on the 22nd floor went off. Good old Charles. How *did* he do that? Why she even bothered to ask that question, she didn't know. Charles could do anything he said he could do. *Anything*.

Alexis strode over to the receptionist, a grandmotherly type with rosy cheeks and wire-rimmed glasses. The perfect image for a toy company. She announced herself and the woman smiled warmly. 'Oh, dear, our power seems to have gone out. It's a good thing there are lots of windows on this side of the building. Mr Newhouse is expecting you, Miss Davis. Go to the hall on your right and go to the end, make another right and Mr Newhouse's office is the second door.'

Alexis returned the smile and started off. She walked slowly, enjoying the colorful photos of different toys the company sold. And to think the sleazebag she was about to see had something to do with toys children played with.

Adam Newhouse was fifty-nine years old, three years away from his expected retirement. In one of many interviews he'd given over the years, the man had said he started out in the company stock room packaging toys for shipment. He'd also worked in the mail room. 'Pulled myself up by my bootstraps' was his favorite expression. While working his way up the ladder he'd somehow managed to knock up the owner's grand-daughter to the dismay of the grandfather but everyone had put a good face on his little indiscretion. He'd married the granddaughter, a rather homely woman, and was the father of six children and a grandfather of three. Bootstraps my ass, Alexis thought as she rounded the final corner that would take her into Newhouse's suite of offices.

Alexis had seen pictures of Newhouse that *Atlanta Magazine* and the *Atlanta Journal Constitution* had run of the tycoon and she'd seen *other* pictures, pictures that made her sick to her stomach. She breezed into the office just as Newhouse reached the door. He was Mister Affability himself as he smiled and extended his hand. Alexis pretended not to see it. Instead, she mumbled her name and commented on the colorful toys sitting on custom made shelves.

The suite was lavish – custom leather furnishings, ankle deep carpeting, entertainment center, wet bar and luscious green plants. She knew there was a bathroom, fully equipped with Jacuzzi, shower and double vanities, because Charles had told her so.

Newhouse was portly and pasty white with brown splotches all over his face and a partially bald head. Even his plump hands were liver-spotted. A short man, probably with a Napoleon complex. His voice was deep and harsh when he asked if she'd like coffee, a drink or possibly tea. Alexis declined. 'Well then, shall we get right to it. I don't mean to rush you but I have a four-thirty in-house meeting that I cannot

132

be late for. I feel terrible saying that because being even nominated for CEO of the year is incredibly flattering. I had no idea I was even in the running.'

Alexis dug around in her briefcase. 'Oh, it won't take that long. You aren't. In the running that is. We just made that all up so I could get in here to see you. Here, this is for you, compliments of Michael Lyons.'

To his credit, Newhouse looked perplexed for all of a heartbeat. 'The movie star?'

'Uh huh. You have a lovely family, Mr Newhouse,' Alexis said as she inclined her head to one wall that held nothing but pictures of the man's family. Alexis watched him, her gaze sharp and intense as he made his way to his baseball-field-size desk.

'I read in the paper that all of your children are successful. Your sons are all in politics. I think I read that your oldest son is a congressman and another works for the Department of Justice, another son works in the White House. Your wife is on the board of the Red Cross. Your daughters married well into prominent Atlanta families.'

'What the hell is this?' The words exploded from Newhouse's mouth like bullets.

Alexis leaned back into the depths of the leather sofa and crossed her legs. 'That's a really good question, Mr Newhouse. What the hell is a man of your stature, a pillar of the community, doing getting his jollies off on a slavery ring? Those young women you're boffing in those pictures are only fifteen years old. You have granddaughters that age.'

'Who the hell are you? What right . . .' Spittle flew from the man's mouth. 'This is a lie! Someone superimposed my head on these pictures!'

Alexis laughed. How do you suppose they superimposed the rest of your body on those pictures? Oh, it's you, so don't deny it. My favorite is the one where you're practicing tonsil hockey. That's the one your whole family is going to see.'

For a round fat man, Newhouse was fast. He was up and racing toward her, his arms outstretched. Alexis was even faster and had the toy 22 from her briefcase in her hand, and pointed directly between the CEO's eyes.

133

Newhouse skidded to a stop and then backed up to his desk. He reached down to press a button on the elaborate telephone console on his desk.

'Power's off, Mr Sleaze. Try your cell phone.'

Newhouse reached for his cell phone and clicked it on.

Alexis laughed. 'There are some pigeons on your windowsill. Maybe you could send a message with one of them.'

Newhouse mopped at the mottled skin on his forehead and bald head. 'This is all some kind of ghastly mistake. I refuse to be blackmailed. What do you want? Blackmail is against the law.'

'You are so right, blackmail *is* against the law. The big question is, who are you going to tell? Were you thinking of offering me money to keep this all quiet? Mr Newhouse, there is not enough money in the whole world that could make me keep this quiet.'

Newhouse continued to mop at his head. The handkerchief looked sodden to Alexis. 'I can give you millions. Whatever you want. Just give me a number.'

Alexis smiled, the toy gun still in her hand. 'You want a number? Okay, try this, 404-530-6630?'

'What kind of number is that?'

'It's the Atlanta Police Administration office. You can call them any time of the day or night. Or, you can call Michael Lyons. We have your . . . *contributions* to Mr Lyons's organ- ization of which you are one of the founding fathers. What's it going to be, Mr Newhouse? I see you are at a loss for words. That's okay, I have to go now anyway. Do you think you might need some additional copies, Mr Newhouse? I have stacks and stacks. We'll be sending them out to anyone and everyone you said so much as hello to. Oh, by the way, if you try to skip town you won't get far. We red-flagged your passport. Do you know what happens to men like you who go to jail for the kinds of things you've been doing? Of course that's assuming you even get to jail. Society frowns on what you've been doing. You might well meet your maker ahead of schedule.'

'Get out of here and don't come back. If you do, I'll kill you,' Newhouse said hoarsely.

At the door, Alexis stopped and turned, the toy gun in her hand. She winked and said, 'Bang!'

Alexis could tell the power was still off so she high-tailed it to the nearest EXIT sign that was battery operated and clattered down twenty-two flights of stairs. She was so light-headed, so nervous, she had trouble punching in the numbers on the cell phone to reach Charles. She hated the shakiness in her voice when she said, 'I'm on my way to the airport.'

Just as Alexis was stepping into a cab on Peachtree, Isabelle Flanders found herself in a wrestling match with retired General Josh Tappen in Dallas, Texas, where he oversaw one of the country's largest oil companies. The general was huffing and puffing, obviously out of shape, as Isabelle struggled in his stranglehold. Suddenly, she let her body go slack. In a nanosecond, she kicked backward and made contact with his groin. She was free a second later. Oh, God, what was she supposed to do now? What had Yoko said? Chop his neck. Isabelle clasped her hands together and brought them down across the back of the retired general's neck. She danced backward, her breathing ragged as she debated her next move.

Charles had said there was a chance one of the men might get physical. 'You bitch! Who the hell do you think you are coming in here with this disgusting filth and trying to blackmail me! I'll call the police and have you locked up for the rest of your life!'

Isabelle laughed. She moved a tad closer and kicked out with her pointy-toed shoe. She caught the general in the throat. He gasped and rolled backward, his fat little fingers clutching at his throat.

The door to the general's suite cracked open and his secretary poked her head in. 'Is something wrong?'

Isabelle thought she was going to black out at the sight of the secretary. She managed somehow to trill with laughter. 'Good heavens no! The general is showing me how he used to disarm men in combat. I think we're going to use this scenario in our opening teaser. Your boss is quite a man!'

'Yes, he is. Well, keep up the good work.' When the door closed behind the secretary, Isabel fell against the door as she struggled to take deep breaths. When she had her breathing under control she said, 'You can kiss goodbye to that book deal on your army experiences you got seven figures for. I'm going to write a *picture* book of your *real* after hours experiences. I guarantee it will be a best seller. You can read it when you're in prison. Now get up or I'll break your ribs, cut off your dick and stuff it down your throat. I want to see what kind of man you are when a *real* woman has the edge. While I'm doing all that, I want you to think about all those little girls you paid for and then raped and sent out on the sex circuit. What's that nice family of yours going to think?'

The general struggled to his feet, his eyes murderous. He staggered to his desk and sat down.

'To think people like you are the defenders of our country.' Isabelle stared down the retired four-star general. Her gaze swiveled to the family lineup behind him. Four daughters and a wife. She just knew they were a nice family with no clue what their father and husband did. She hoped they would be strong when the dark stuff hit the fan.

Knowing she was safe on the other side of the desk, Isabelle leaned over and lowered her voice. 'You have no options, General. All of you are going to be exposed and sent to prison. I suspect you won't make it to the prison doors but I could be wrong. Someone will pop you, I can almost guarantee it. I also want you to know you offended me earlier when you offered to bribe me to keep quiet.

'Before I leave I want to tell you that you can run but you can't hide. Your passport has been red-flagged. We closed your bank accounts. You know, those special accounts you use to buy all those young Asian women. And of course your membership dues in that *skeevy* club you belong to. It's a cruel world out there for people like you. You might want to just sit here and wait for the authorities to come for you. What I wouldn't do if I were you is to call Michael Lyons. Well, goodbye, General.'

'Who are you?' the general rasped.

Isabelle thought about the question for a full minute. 'I'm the conscience of all those innocent young women you and those pigs in your little club turned into whores.'

In the cab, Isabelle called Charles's number and said, 'I'm on the way to the airport. Has everyone called in?'

'Everyone but Nikki,' Charles responded.

The man was cool, Nikki thought. And brazen. He was acting like she'd just shown him pictures of sailboats instead of the sick, perverted sex pictures scattered on his desk. 'So,' he'd said.

'So? That's all you have to say?'

He was beyond handsome. Royce Gardener, Chief Counsel to the Catholic Diocese of Boston, Chief Counsel to the state's baseball team and Chief Counsel to half the organizations and businesses in the city, sat behind his busy-looking desk, an amused smile on his face. Nikki couldn't decide if he was yanking her chain or not. Maybe the guy was an accomplished poker player. Maybe a lot of things.

'So you found out I have a private life outside this office. So what?'

'So what? So you're breaking the law. You're buying and selling human beings and you're forcing them to do obscene things, that's what. And let's not forget that you and your cronies smuggle these women into this country for your own pleasures. You're a sexual deviate, Mr Gardener, as are the others in your inner circle. Alphabet City is going to be on your butt within hours. You can't run. Your family is going to be destroyed. You'll be the main topic of conversation for years to come. You're going to go to prison. We have all your records.'

Gardener leaned back in his ergonomic chair and smiled. 'You keep using the word, we. Who exactly is we?'

Not only was he cool, he was smart, too, but Nikki knew how to play the game. 'Why don't we just say it was a slip of the tongue. I have copies of your bank records. All that money you flash around the world in those secret accounts. How about this? Josh Tappen, Lucian Treadwell, Adam Newhouse and Michael Lyons. Which one do you think will be able to keep his mouth shut? You know the drill, Gardener. First one to cut a deal gets points. By the way, I'm not here to take a bribe or to ask for anything. I'm just the messenger. We have thousands of those,' Nikki said, pointing to the

137

perversion that littered the desk. 'We tracked all your business transactions and moved your money for you. Don't thank me. It was a pleasure to do it. You're flat broke as of early this morning. We left you $64.22 in your account. We canceled all your credit cards, even your black American Express card. Your passport has been flagged. That's another way of saying you're dead in the water. How in the world are you going to pay for that fancy wedding you're throwing for your daughter in June?'

Gardener stood up, his fists clenched. 'Leave my daughter out of this and the rest of my family.'

Nikki looked around the luxurious office. The furnishings and paintings on the wall could have supported a family of five for a generation. The man himself was an endorsement to the fashion industry. 'You should have thought about your family before you got involved in that slave ring. I don't care if you're the second coming of Clarence Darrow, there's no way you or your colleagues can sweep this under the table. If you think that's possible, you're a fool.'

The amusement was gone. Evil leaked out of Gardener's eyes. 'What do you want? How much to shut you up? How much to burn this trash?' he said pointing to the pile of obscene material on his desk.

'Spill your guts. Names, dates, places. The percentage of everyone's involvement. Your own as well. Every member's profile. We'll match up what you tell us with the information we have and rest assured, we have plenty. By the way, there is no such thing as a safe computer. No matter how many safeguards you have in place there's always someone out there smarter than you are who can hack through it all. We have the King Grandfather of all hackers on our payroll.'

Gardener nibbled on his lower lip. He no longer looked amused or cool. Now he looked frazzled and worried. 'How do I know you'll keep your end of the bargain if I spill my guts?'

'You don't. That's a chance you have to take,' Nikki said coolly.

'I want to know who you are. Who do you represent?'

Nikki smirked. 'Privileged information, counselor.'

'Will you give me back my money and reinstate my credit cards?'

'Absolutely not.'

'How the hell am I supposed to live?'

'That's your problem, Mr Gardener. Oh, before we continue, if you alert any of your buddies to this little deal we're doing, all bets are off.' Nikki looked at her watch; 4:30. She wanted out of here. Her gut told her that Gardener was going to try to beat the odds and wouldn't say one word.

Gardener stood up and towered over Nikki. She rose immediately and headed for the door. Her hand was on the doorknob when Gardener reached her in three long-legged strides. 'Without a guarantee, I can't help you,' he said coldly. 'You don't know these people.'

Nikki turned around and jabbed her finger into Gardener's throat. 'Now, you see, that's where you're wrong. I *do* know those people. You don't know me and my people.'

'They'll find you and kill you. Once you're in, you're in. I tried to get out years ago but it wasn't possible.'

Nikki felt a chill race up her arms. With all the bravado she could muster, she said, 'Now, Mr Gardener, if you were a betting man, who would you put your money on? You just made the biggest mistake of your life.' She opened the door and walked through the outer office and then headed for the elevator whose door swished open. Thank God the power was on.

Nikki didn't relax until she was in the cab that would take her to Logan Airport. She called Charles and said, 'I'm running late and headed for the airport. He didn't go for the deal. I'll see you tonight.'

Eighteen

Michael Lyons scratched at the mysterious rash that covered his body. He'd used almost a gallon of some kind of anti-bacterial itch lotion but it wasn't helping. He looked in the mirror and was stunned at his puffy face. He squinted to try to see himself better and was sorry he did. His eyes were almost swollen shut, his lips were puffy and his nose had a scab on it from scratching. His lips appeared to be twice their normal size. Even his dick was swollen. Oh, he was going to look wonderful for the Academy Awards. Son of a bitch, he might have to cancel.

Nerves? Maybe he should go to a doctor instead of trying to doctor himself. Like that was really going to happen. There was no way he was going outside where people could *see* him. His daily domestic said the rash looked like a severe case of shingles, whatever the hell that was. She'd backed away from him as though he might be contagious which had angered him even more.

And now this fucking shit! He looked down at the cell phone in his hand, willing it to ring. He needed to get a new one. It worked and then it didn't work. It beeped when there were no calls and then he would get nothing but static for hours on end. He'd paid thousands for this piece of crap and it wasn't worth shit. He clicked it on hoping he would hear the dull buzz indicating the phone was in a working mode. He dialed Dan Boatman, cursing when the computer wizard didn't pick up. He canceled the call and dialed Paul Yarm from Five Star Investigations. When the detective identified himself, Lyons snarled, 'Well?'

Lyons scratched and scratched as he listened to the investigator say they'd located his daughter, but she was away. 'Out of town, the shop assistant said. We managed to check the calls stored on the answering machine.' He went on to say the business she operated was a profitable one. 'The workers speak limited English. Communication is difficult. Implied threats mean nothing as they know nothing. We have the entire nursery and flower shop under surveillance.'

Lyons scratched some more. 'How long as she been gone? Business owners don't go away without leaving a number to be called in case of an emergency. Sweat them.'

'Mr Lyons, we know what we're doing. Your daughter goes away quite often, sometimes for as long as a week. She calls in. As I understand it there are no emergencies in the flower business. She's been gone for over a week. Let's understand each other, Mr Lyons. We do not "sweat" the people we trace. We stop short of threats. More often than not, stern words work better. We contracted to locate your daughter and that's what we've done. The fact that she isn't here is not our fault. Legally and technically, we can walk off the job, bill you, and go on from there. We will continue with our surveillance until you tell us to stop but that's all we will do. Once the subject returns, we will notify you and send you a final report.'

Lyons started to sputter. 'Did she use a credit card? When people go away or travel, they use credit cards, gas cards, they make ATM withdrawals.'

'This lady has not done any of those things. No charges of any kind. The last time she used her credit card, which by the way is a Visa card, was back in June of last year when she purchased five pairs of house slippers. She paid the bill in full the following month. She doesn't have a gas card and she's never used an ATM machine. She deals in cash for her personal purchases. She pays the business bills out of a special account that carries a very low balance. There is one other thing. There were quite a few messages on your daughter's answering machine from a man named Harry Wong. Whoever he is, your daughter didn't see fit to tell him she was going away so he probably isn't important but we are checking him out. All we have so far is he is a martial arts expert. We think your daughter takes lessons from him because in one of the messages he says she missed class.'

'Well find out all you can about him. What about women friends?' Lyons was not about to give up.

'None that we know of. We've checked everything. These people, if they know anything, and there's no reason to suspect they do, do not talk to strangers. I have another call coming in, Mr Lyons. Shall we continue the surveillance or not?'

'Yes. Call me as soon as you know something. Put more people on it. Money is no object. I have to find my daughter.'

'Yes, sir.'

Lyons broke the connection.

Clad only in a pair of boxer shorts, Lyons started to swab his body with the smelly pink lotion again. Maybe he could find a doctor who would make a house call. Yeah, yeah, that's what he would do. He could use his celebrity and demand a house call. The only problem was he really didn't know any regular doctors. He knew dozens of plastic surgeons. Maybe they could help him.

Who the fuck was Harry Wong?

Lyons was about to click on his cell phone when it rang. He looked down at the numbers flashing on the screen. Lucian Treadwell. Lyons frowned and scratched. He muttered something that could pass for a greeting.

'What the hell is going on, Lyons?'

'Since you reside in New York and I reside in California, how the hell do I know what's going on? I'm not in the mood to play guessing games with you, Lucian. What do you want?'

'I'll tell you what I want, you son of a bitch! Some goddamn woman was just here named Mary Clare Peabody and she *knows*. She *knows*, you bastard! She gave me pictures! Are you listening to me, Lyons? Somebody cleaned out all my bank accounts. She's sending these pictures to my family. They invaded my computer. How in the hell did this happen? She said they red flagged my passport. Will you say something for Christ's sake!'

Lyons sat down not caring that the pink lotion was smearing all over the chair. He was usually a fastidious man but right now he didn't care about anything except what he was hearing. 'Who is Mary Clare Peabody?'

'I don't know. Everyone in the inner circle had visitors, too. This is going to hit the fan. I'm ruined. Royce Gardener called me and said *they*, whoever *they* are, only left him $64.22. He was always the weak link. I told you that. Did any of you listen to me? No, you did not. Newhouse is a basket case. We'll be on our way to California within the hour. We managed to scrounge up enough for air fare from petty cash but we will be arriving penniless. Send someone to meet us at the airport. Don't even think about trying to run because you are too well known. We'll find you no matter where you go. And you damn well better have a large chunk of money to divvy up among us. You're the fucking ring leader of this little show so you better start acting like it.'

Michael Lyons forgot about his rash and how badly it was itching. His chest was pounding and he couldn't breathe. He broke out in a cold sweat as he started to shake. The impossible had happened. He struggled to breathe, to get his nerves under control. He forgot about calling a doctor for a house call. Instead, he raced to his one operational computer to check on his finances. As he clicked and clicked he got sicker by the moment. His accounts here in the States all registered zero balances. One bank showed that one particular account was overdrawn by twenty dollars. Tens of millions gone with a few clicks on a rogue computer.

Fifteen minutes later, his breathing more or less under control, he started to itch again. He needed to blame someone. Boatman! Boatman was the only one savvy enough to pull off something like this. Where the fuck was the computer wizard? He reached for the cell phone and called again. A tinny sounding voice told him the customer he was trying to reach was out of his calling area.

Somehow Boatman must have teamed up with his daughter. It was the only thing that made sense.

Michael Lyons started to pace. He had millions in his safe. And billions in off-shore accounts. He also had foolproof passports with identities and backgrounds to assure him safe travel anywhere in the world. He knew the others weren't as fortunate and they would be left behind. Stupid is as stupid does, he thought to himself. He had another plus on his side. He was an actor and a master of disguise. Getting out of the country wasn't going to be that much of a problem. Perhaps it wouldn't be a problem at all. But, he needed to clear up this rash first.

He knew he could, if he wanted to, fund and spirit those in the inner circle out of the country. Would it be better to do that so they wouldn't talk or should he leave first and let them hold the bag? He simply couldn't decide.

How in hell did this happen?

Where was he going to go? Would he still be able to control and monitor his other business or would it all come crashing down? He squeezed his eyes shut as he tried to imagine the fallout in Hollywood and around the world. He knew he should contact his worldwide colleagues but he wasn't going to do that. The way he looked at it, it was every man for himself. He stomped his feet like a petulant child.

Argentina might be a good jumping off place. He'd always liked Argentina.

The phone took that moment to ring. Lyons wondered if it was safe to answer it. What the hell. It might be an important call. It might even be that bastard Boatman. He rolled his eyes when he heard the voice of Anna de Silva say she was staying at the Beverly Hills Hotel and wanted to make arrangements to meet. Like he needed this right now. He tried to be civil when he said he was suffering from a severe case of shingles and wouldn't be available till the following week. 'You can count on me for a million dollars, Countess.' They spoke for a few more minutes and then he ended the call and promptly forgot about it. He wouldn't be around when it was time to pony up the million dollars so what difference did it make?

As Lyons stalked off to check on the money in his safe, scratching and digging at himself, he knew he was living a bad dream. When he woke up he wouldn't have shingles and the members of the inner circle would be at home and not on their way to California and his bank accounts would still be as robust as they were a few days ago.

If he wasn't so scared and miserable he would have cried.

*   *   *

Ted Robinson grabbed his duffel bag off the carousel at LAX and then waited for Maggie's to appear. 'If this turns out to be a wild goose chase, I'm going to strangle you, Maggie.'

'Look, you made the decision to come with me. I was prepared to come alone but you insisted on coming along. You better not even think about blaming me if this doesn't work out. And, no, I don't want to talk about Alan Nolan. We talked him to death on the flight here. He's gone. He's not coming back. You agreed with me when we went back to his apartment to scout around. He took *everything* with him. He snookered me just the way I snookered him. He doesn't give a good rat's ass if the cyber café and bakery shut down or not. He just threw that in to make me think . . . whatever it was he wanted me to think. He did give up the name Lyons and that was on the money. He was bragging and trying to impress me. Now, shut up and let's find a cab and a hotel.'

Muttering under his breath, Ted followed Maggie who was dragging her suitcase on wheels. He didn't know if he felt like a fool or not. He was the idea person, Maggie was the follow along person. He took a few seconds to wonder how she knew that the Ladies of Pinewood were on the way to Los Angeles. When he'd asked her, she'd sniffed and said, 'Woman's intuition.' He'd shut right up after that. No way was he going to tinker or question woman's intuition. Not in this lifetime anyway.

As they lined up to wait for a cab, Maggie whispered, 'I don't want you to look right now but at three o'clock there are two ladies waiting. Guess who they are, Mister Robinson?'

'You told me not to look,' Ted hissed. 'Who?'

'Myra Rutledge and de Silva. Now, why do you think they're standing here at LAX? They're waiting for the others. I guarantee it. No, no, don't look. Just get in the cab. They aren't paying attention to us.'

Inside the cab, their sunglasses in place, Maggie said, 'Do not ever question my intuition ever again.'

'Okay, okay. Good work, Spritzer. You sure you didn't sleep with that guy Nolan?'

Maggie laughed.

*　　　*　　　*

145

As the cab rolled by, Myra Rutledge looked right at it. 'You know what really bothers me, Annie?'

'No, what?'

'Young people seem to think because you're *old* that you're deaf, dumb, and blind. Those two thought we didn't see them. Are they stupid or are we stupid? When someone tries so hard to be invisible, I always wonder why. Like sunglasses and baseball caps will alter their features. They must think we're doddering old fogies. I'm so glad we spotted them because it means our job just got harder. Forewarned is forearmed. I cannot wait for the girls to get here. They'll have some ideas about those two reporters and how to deal with them.'

Annie peered at Myra over the top of her sunglasses. 'Does our job getting harder mean it will get more *exciting*?'

'My dear, I think you can count on it,' Myra drawled. 'Oh, look, here comes Alexis! The others will be here soon.'

'Myra, you should have come to Spain earlier and dragged me here. My adrenaline is really kicking up. I'm loving every single minute. It's like you turn a corner and something beyond your dreams happens. Then you turn another corner and something even more unbelievable happens.'

Alexis hugged the two women, her eyes bright. 'Boy, do I have a story for you.'

'I've got one for you too, my dear. Those two reporters from the *Post* just rode away in a cab. They thought we didn't see them but we did.'

'Oh, shit!'

'Oh, poop, is right,' Myra said as she clutched at the pearls around her neck.

Nineteen

Nikki Quinn spun around so quick she lost her footing. An elderly man caught her in mid spin and set her firmly on her feet. Nikki blushed, thanked the man, and raised her eyes to stare at the arrival and departure monitors overhead. Was she crazy or had she just seen Royce Gardener as he perused the baggage area at LAX? Did he see her? She didn't think so. He appeared to be looking for someone, maybe the other members of Michael Lyons's inner circle.

Nikki fished around in her pocket for her sunglasses. Everyone's idea of the ultimate in disguise. She continued to make her way to the baggage area, stopping long enough at a kiosk to toss forty dollars on the counter for a wide-brimmed straw hat. She didn't bother to wait for change. She ripped off the tag, pulled her hair on top of her head, and plopped the bonnet on her head. Another sure-fire disguise. She walked a little faster now, confident that she would be the last person Royce Gardener expected to see in this particular airport.

There he was, tapping his foot impatiently as he waited. He didn't appear to be waiting for luggage. Most likely he was waiting for someone. She recognized Lucian Treadwell, Kathryn's man, immediately as he approached Gardener. You didn't need to be a rocket scientist to know they were probably meeting up to make their way to Lyons's house. Where were the others? Arriving on different flights just the way she and the other sisters were doing.

Kathryn! God, where was she? She racked her brain as she tried to recall who was getting in at what time but couldn't come up with the information. She was rattled and she knew it.

Nikki moved through the milling passengers as she headed

147

for the doors leading outside to ground transportation. If everything was on schedule, Myra and Annie should be waiting for her at the taxi stand. She grew light-headed when she saw them. She ran up to them, careful to keep her back to the doors. 'We have a problem. Gardener and Treadwell are inside by the baggage carousel. I have to get out of here before he sees me. Where are the others? Myra, where are the others!' God, she hated the panic she was seeing on her mother's face. 'What's wrong, Myra?'

Myra's grip on her pearls was fierce. 'We just saw Maggie Spritzer and Ted Robinson. They saw us, too, although we all pretended not to see one another. They were trying to be invisible just the way we were but Annie and I saw them. Alexis arrived just as they drove off. We have to call Charles. Nikki, you make the call but wait till you get in the cab with Alexis. Annie and I will try to head off Kathryn, Isabelle, and Yoko. Yoko won't be a problem since those people don't know her. This is beyond urgent so hurry, dear.'

'What can I do?' Annie said, her face alight with anticipation.

'This is not good, Annie. In fact, this is disastrous. We have to act like nothing is wrong. We have to look harried like everyone else. You've seen the pictures of the men just the way I have. Let's see if we can spot them. Nikki said they were by the baggage carousel. Ah, there they are. They don't exactly look like captains of industry, do they?'

'No, they don't. I think they look like they'd pass out if one of us came up behind them and said, boo! Slow down, Myra, there's a man joining them. I think it's that retired general. Do you want me to stay here and watch them. I can . . . ah . . . tail them if you think it's advisable. I'll just hop in a cab and do what they do in the movies.' At Myra's look of skepticism, she said, 'I'll just say, "follow that car!" Then I'll flash a wad of money. It always works.'

'Annie, we know where they're going. Where else could they go but Lyons's house?'

'Not necessarily. Maybe they're going to have a meeting someplace else. Maybe Lyons won't want them at his home. It could be a secret place where they won't be recognized.

Think about it, Myra. Someone has to keep tabs on them. Give me all the cash you have in case I have to bribe the driver. They always do that in the movies. Wads of cash.'

Myra suddenly spotted Kathryn and rushed forward. She pretended to bump into her, at the same time spinning her around. 'Those men are here, three of them. Treadwell, Gardener and Tappen. They're by the baggage carousel. Go back the way you came and try to head off Isabelle. And if you see Yoko, clue her in. Don't leave the airport until the men leave. Take a cab to the Beverly Hills Hotel and wait for us in the lobby.'

Kathryn didn't say a word until Myra ran out of steam. 'This is not good.'

'No, dear, it is not good. I didn't tell you the worst part. Maggie Spritzer and Ted Robinson are here, too. Annie and I saw them getting into a cab. They saw both of us.'

'Oh, shit!'

'I have to go now, Kathryn. Nikki is calling Charles. We're going to have to fall back and regroup.'

Kathryn nodded as she walked over to the arrival and departure monitor. She hoped she could head off Isabelle and Yoko. She started off, her stomach in knots.

Myra headed back to the baggage carousel, her thoughts in turmoil. Out of the corner of her eye she saw that the three men were gone and there was no sign of Annie so she headed for the door. She gasped when she saw the three men smoking and Annie standing alone, chatting with another woman who was also waiting for a cab. Myra motioned her over.

'I think they're waiting for the fourth man and transportation. They could have gotten a cab earlier but waved it off. I checked flight arrivals from Atlanta. I assume they're waiting for Adam Newhouse. There's a flight due in from Atlanta in twelve minutes. What do you want to do, Myra? If we don't follow them, we might never be able to find them again. Do we even need them?'

What Myra wanted to do was go back home to McLean, Virginia, but she knew that was impossible. Along with the others, she was committed to Yoko's mission. 'I guess we follow them. If they go to Lyons's house then we can either go back to the hotel or call the girls to alert them and we stay and do surveillance. Everything is going to hinge on what Charles tells us to do.'

'But, Myra, what if they do go there and then leave again? How will we find them?'

Myra took a deep breath. 'The authorities will deal with them. Our mission is Lyons. He's the one we have to keep in our sights.'

'What if Lyons leaves with the four of them? Since they have no money to speak of, it's logical to assume they came here to make a getaway with Lyons's help. What makes you think he isn't running scared right now just the way they are?'

'Because the man is too cocky. He never thought he would get caught. I don't know a lot about people like him but my instincts tell me he doesn't care about those four men. He's only interested in saving his own skin. He's buying time. He probably agreed to help them so they'd keep quiet until he can make his own plans.'

'You could be right, Myra. I'm just a novice compared to you. I think this might be a good time to commandeer a taxi so we can be in place when they leave. How much money do you have on you?'

'A little over a hundred dollars. How much do you have?'

'About the same. I rarely carry cash. Two hundred dollars isn't much of a wad. They always flash a wad in the movies,' Annie fretted. 'I'll go back into the terminal. I saw an ATM machine. Give me your card and pin number. That will give us another six hundred. You always get twenty-dollar bills so all those twenties will make a nice little bundle of money. Don't get your panties in a wad, Myra. I have four minutes till the plane lands. Another eight to ten minutes for Mr Newhouse to disembark and make his way here.'

Myra sighed as she handed over her money and ATM card. 'And to think just months ago you were sitting on a mountain in an old monastery watching the weather channel on satellite television. I should have left you there. Charles is not going to like this.'

Annie laughed. 'No, you don't wish any such thing. They're lighting another cigarette. It takes five minutes to smoke a cigarette. I read that somewhere. That means I have time.'

'Just go already. I'll keep my eye on them. Make it snappy, too. Don't stop to talk to anyone. Don't buy anything. I know you, Annie, you can be diverted.'

Annie glowered as she stalked off.

Myra wished she smoked so she could light up. She wondered if anyone was paying attention to her. She played with her pearls and watched the taxi line as she tried to imagine which one they should commandeer. She wondered what the brash, go-for-the-gusto, Kathryn would do. She smiled when she thought of Kathryn's response. She'd say money talks and bullshit walks. 'That works for me,' Myra mumbled as she envisioned the *wad* of cash Annie would have on her return.

Myra continued to watch the three men as they finished their cigarettes and started looking around. Tappen walked off, his gaze on the string of cars inching their way alongside the row of waiting taxis. Gardener walked over to where she was standing outside the door and peered inward. He looked down at his watch. The door whipped open and Annie walked through. Gardener muttered something as he stepped out of the way.

'Oh, my dear, how nice to see you again!' Annie gushed as she wrapped her arms around Myra. 'He's right behind me. Let's get a taxi.'

The two women moved then but could still hear Gardener say, 'About goddamn time you got here. The car is here. At least Lyons did that much. Let's get this show on the road.'

Annie ran ahead and opened one of the cab doors. The Pakistani driver hopped out and said, 'No, no! You go to head of line.'

Myra panicked. She was already in the cab. 'Annie, tell him money talks and bullshit walks. Flash him a hundred and get your tush in here. Hurry up, they're getting in the limo.'

Annie eyed the diminutive driver and flashed a hundred dollar bill. 'Get in the damn car and drive or I'll bop you in the nose. We work for the FBI so don't ask any questions. Now move!'

'Oh, God!' Myra wailed as the man in charge of the taxi stand held up his hand and shouted for them to get out of the

151

car. 'Two hundred,' she said to the driver. She leaned her head out of the car and said, 'CIA. Back off, mister. Hold all traffic for ten minutes. If you don't, I'll be back and arrest you.'

'You say FBI. Now you say CIA. I think maybe you lie,' the driver said.

'No, no, no. We work for CIA on Fridays and Saturdays, FBI the rest of the time. Follow that limousine and don't lose him. You get a bonus if he doesn't spot you. Furthermore, special agents are not permitted to lie.'

'Is like movie chase, no?'

'Damn straight,' Myra said as the taxi rocketed ahead. 'Don't lose that car.'

'You pay now!'

'Half now and half when we tell you to stop,' Annie said tossing five twenty-dollar bills onto the front seat. She made sure the driver saw the wad of cash in her hand. At the sight of the thick bundle the driver's foot clamped down on the gas pedal.

As Annie buckled her seat belt, she looked at Myra and said, 'I wish we had thought to wear trench coats. It would be so much more official.'

'Shut up, Annie!'

Ted Robinson opened the drapes on the motel window. Then he wished he hadn't. The sleazy room decorated in orange and brown looked even sleazier. What could you expect for $69.95 a night? He hoped the sheets and towels were clean. He looked over at Maggie who was busy on her cell phone calling all the major hotels in the city hoping to track down the ladies of Pinewood. Like those over-the-top women would really sign in to a hotel using their real names.

'Woohoo! They're at the Beverly Hills Hotel.' Maggie fixed her smug gaze on Ted and said, 'Oh ye of little faith. I knew they'd go first class. Rich people like them would never stay in a roach coach like this. Okay, let's go. Our rental car should be here now and I already have a map. C'mon, Ted, let's go. I don't want them getting away from us.'

'But you said . . .'

'Never mind what I said. Whatever it was I said when I

said it isn't important. I said whatever I said when I didn't know those women were coming here. Now that they're here and we saw them with our very own eyes, the game plan has changed. We have to follow them.'

'I thought we were going to go out to Lyons's house and try to bullshit our way in. We don't know why they're after him. Before we go half-cocked, we should know that. We could get our asses in a sling if . . .'

'Ted, does it matter to us what he did? No, it doesn't. Yes, it would be nice to know but it isn't going to change anything. We're after the women. We want to catch them red-handed. This is our *coup de grâce*. We're here. They're here. This is it, Ted! I can feel it in my bones.'

Ted planted his body against the door. 'It doesn't feel right, Maggie. Something's wrong. We need to get in touch with Lyons.'

Maggie put her hands on her hips and glared at Ted. 'Get real, Ted. Movie stars do not list their telephone numbers in the phone book. There's no way to get his cell phone. If you insist on alerting him, you do that and I'll tail the women. What's it gonna be?'

'Okay, okay, but it doesn't feel right to me. My gut tells me they know we're here. You have no idea how smart those women are. Even Jack Emery said they're smart. My gut tells me those fucking gold shields are here, too. My gut is also telling me Jack Emery and that kooky ninja friend are also here. It's going to turn out to be a regular goddamn reunion. You just wait and see. How are we going to deal with all that?'

'You're serious, aren't you?' Maggie's voice held awe at this declaration.

'Hell, yes, I'm serious. I wouldn't be one bit surprised to see that Martin guy and your new best friend Nolan pop up out of nowhere. We're reporters, not super spies.' His voice turned stubborn. 'We need to see Lyons first. We need to know why those women are after him. When we explain who we are and that we're on his side, he might prove invaluable to us and the story we write.'

'Ted, did it ever occur to you that Lyons might have done something horrendous and that's why those women are after him? No way am I going to align myself with him. Those women wouldn't be putting it all on the line for something like unpaid parking tickets. Whatever it is, it's serious. We're better off sticking with the women. Think Pulitzer! A double whammy so to speak. I'm right and you know it. Now, can we get on with it?'

'Okay, okay, but this is a mistake. We checked Lyons out and he's squeaky clean. He's never so much as spit on the sidewalk. He's what his PR people say he is, a nice down home guy who made it big in Hollywood and shares his good fortune with others who are less fortunate.'

Maggie sniffed. 'This is Hollywood, land of make believe. He did something somewhere along the way and those women are going to bring him down for it. It's our job to bring *them* down. Now are you going to shut up and come with me or are you going to sulk and go your own way?'

'You can be such a bitch sometimes. You aren't always right, you know.'

'I got us this far, didn't I? Without Alan Nolan we'd be back in Washington freezing our tails off.'

Maggie was right and Ted knew it. 'All right, let's go.'

Twenty

The knuckles on Charles Martin's hands were white, almost translucent. As he listened to Nikki he clenched his teeth so tight he thought they would crack. His mind racing, he tried to figure out how the two *Post* reporters got downwind of this mission. Just because they were in California at the same time as the sisters didn't necessarily mean they knew what was going on. He refused to believe they were smarter than he was. They could be there for something as simple as capturing the dirt on the stars in preparation for the Academy Awards. The *Post* would run tidbits every day to drive up interest in the waning viewer war. He managed to unlock his teeth and asked, 'Where's Myra?'

'She and Annie are still at the airport waiting for the others. I haven't heard from anyone since we arrived at the hotel. I tried calling but neither one of them are answering their cell phones. Oh, wait a minute, Charles, here they come. Give me five minutes and I'll call you back.'

Nikki walked to the door of the bar and waved wildly. Kathryn, Yoko and Isabelle made their way to a small seating area. All three of them looked grim. Nikki felt her heart start to flutter.

'Where's Myra?'

'Chasing the bad guys with a Pakistani taxi driver,' Isabelle said. 'I need a drink. Before you say it, there was nothing we could do about it.'

'I'll second that,' Kathryn said. 'We have to call Charles.'

Nikki motioned to the waitress and the women ordered drinks. 'I just got off the phone with Charles. I have to call him back. Myra and Annie are . . . are tailing those guys? What were they thinking?'

155

'I don't think they did a whole lot of thinking, Nikki. They reacted instead,' Kathryn said. 'They were wired, I can tell you that. The creeps took off in a limo. Limos don't drive very fast so their driver should be able to keep up. That's all I know, Nikki. I'm not worried about Myra and Annie. Those two can take care of themselves. I'm worried about the fact that those two reporters are here.'

The drinks arrived. Nikki paid with cash. 'I really have to call Charles. He's going to go thermonuclear when he hears about Myra and Annie,' she said gulping from her vodka and tonic to fortify herself.

Charles picked up on the first ring.

'It's me. What do you want us to do, Charles?'

'Where's Myra?' Charles barked, ignoring the question.

Nikki gritted her teeth. 'Kathryn said Myra and Annie commandeered a cab and followed the perverts who sped away in a limo.'

'They what?' Charles exploded.

Nikki squeezed her eyes shut as she gulped at the tart drink in her hand. 'You heard me, Charles. I wasn't there and I seriously doubt the others could have stopped either one of them. Tell us what you want us to do.'

'The only thing you can do is abort the mission. It's been compromised.'

'Charles, for God's sake, that's spook talk. Talk to me in English. Tell me why. We can handle this. We're here. Don't act in haste.'

'No, I don't think you can handle it. This has gone wrong from the onset. Those two reporters are there for a reason and the reason is all of you. Somehow, someway, one of us miscalculated and they picked up on it.'

'Do you want us to try and find them? We can start calling the hotels and motels. It will take a while, though. This might be a good time to trot out those damn gold shields you have on that mysterious payroll of yours.'

Charles ignored the reference to the gold shields. 'That would be an exercise in futility since there are thousands of hotels and motels, and if they're as smart as I know they are, they wouldn't register under their own names. I want you to

abort the mission. That's an order. Get word to Myra immediately.'

'With all due respect, Charles, isn't that our decision to
make? Right now, five of us are here. Majority rules but I will
put your order to them and call you back. I'll do my best to
reach Myra but I can't promise anything.' Nikki ended the
call before Charles could protest further. She wondered why
he hadn't responded to her mention of the gold shields.

Nikki licked at her lips. 'Charles says we should abort the
mission.' The announcement was met with stony-faced
silence. 'We have to take a vote,' she went on. 'Majority rules.
Raise your hand if you agree with Charles's order.' When no
one raised a hand, Nikki said, 'Well, I guess that takes care
of that.' She looked around, stunned at all the movie stars
walking around. Any other time she might have gawked the
way the tourists were doing. Not today, though. She had other
more important things on her mind.

'We can't sit here forever,' Isabelle said. 'I don't think it's
a good idea to go to our hotel either. We better find some low-
end dive to hang our hats till we figure this all out. Those
reporters will call around to see where we're staying. This is
just my opinion but I think it's okay for Myra and Annie to
be staying here at this ritzy place. That's expected. As far as
those reporters know only Alexis is here. We can leave a
message for Myra and Annie and call them later when we're
settled. We need a car, too.'

'There's a car reserved in the name of Mary Clare Peabody
and Charles gave me the I.D. to go with it. It should be here
waiting for us,' Kathryn said. 'We can talk in the car. All these
people milling around here are starting to make me nervous.'

Yoko was wringing her tiny hands. 'I am so sorry this is
happening. I didn't know . . . I didn't think . . . perhaps Charles
is right and we should forget all this and go back home.'

Alexis threw her arm around Yoko's shoulder. 'Hey, it's just
a little hiccup. We'll figure it out. We're going to get him. We
didn't come halfway across the country to turn around and
run back home with our tails between our legs.'

'Let's go,' Kathryn said as she slung her duffel bag over
her shoulder.

Fifteen minutes later the gutsy ladies of Pinewood were cruising the streets of Los Angeles like they owned them.

'You have gun?' the taxi driver demanded.

'What's it to you? Just drive and pay attention to the road,' Annie said.

'Is against the law,' the driver blustered. Annie threw a twenty dollar bill on the seat.

Myra fingered her pearls with both hands.

'You need to drive a little faster, driver. That limo is getting away from us. Look, pull over and I'll drive,' Annie ordered.

The Pakistani was outraged at the suggestion. 'No woman drive this taxi.'

'Then do what I tell you and speed up or I'll . . . I'll rip your heart out through your nose and then I'll shoot you.' That was good, Annie thought. Good thing she remembered Charles saying that. She dropped another twenty on the front seat.

Myra's pearls broke. She unbuckled her seat belt and tried to pick them up. She mumbled over and over, 'Charles is going to kill us, Charles is going to kill us.'

The driver cowered in his seat. Annie thought she heard him say, 'crazy Americans.'

'Myra, Myra, get up. The limo is slowing down. Look, the driver of the limo has his blinker on. Okay, Mr Patel, drive right on by and pull over as soon as you can.'

'You get out of my taxi then?'

'No, you're getting out! I'm going to buy this taxi from you. Pull over. Make it quick. You people move so slow. Myra, forget the damn pearls already.'

The driver pulled to the shoulder of the road but he stubbornly refused to get out of the taxi. 'Taxi belong to company. Can not sell it.'

'Sure you can. I'll shoot you if you don't get out.' Annie was already out of the car and walking around to the driver's side. 'Myra, get in the front seat.'

'Here,' Annie said, scribbling out a check and handing it to the driver. 'We're . . . ah . . . we're leasing this fine vehicle. You need to call a taxi for yourself, Mr Patel.'

The driver got out of the car. Annie towered over him by a good two feet. For some reason the man didn't seem intimidated. He did take the check, though.

'Hijack. You hijack my taxi. Police come.'

'You stop saying things like that right now or I really will shoot you. I'm not hijacking your taxi. I'm *leasing* it. Look at the check. It says *lease* on the message unit. Now, skedaddle and if you call the police I will personally . . .' Annie fished around in her brain for a Kathryn response and finally came up with what she thought was suitable. 'If you do call the police, I will find you and kick your ass all the way back to Pakistan. You got that?'

The Pakistani ran down the road. Annie shrugged as she tried to figure out why getting his ass kicked scared him more than having his heart ripped out through his nose. 'You ready, Myra? You got all your pearls?'

Myra settled herself in the front seat and buckled up. Annie waited for a break in traffic and made a U-turn. Cars honked and curses could be heard through the open car windows. Annie ignored them as she headed back to the driveway that led to Michael Lyons's estate.

'You're enjoying this aren't you?' Myra snapped.

'What's not to enjoy? But to answer your question, yes, I am enjoying this little caper. We should have a game plan,' she said swerving into the driveway.

'Maybe you should have thought about that *before* you *leased* this vehicle. We should call Charles. Annie, this is not a good idea. In fact, it's a terrible idea.'

'I know but we don't have anything else going for us right now except guts and bravado. For someone who is in charge of this organization, you aren't very observant.'

'I've had those pearls forever. They were my grandmother's. I feel naked without them. I have to call Charles. What's that mean, I'm not observant?'

'You can have the pearls restrung. I know an excellent jeweler. Why do you insist on worrying Charles? Don't you have any faith in our ability?' She sounded like she was discussing the weather. 'By being observant I meant you should have picked up on the car behind us. I think someone's been following us. I said *think*, Myra. This spy stuff is new to me so I might be wrong. Like I said before, don't you have any faith in our ability?'

'Not one damn bit,' Myra snapped. 'No one is following us because no one knows we were stupid enough to practically steal a taxi. We . . . got away . . . clean.'

'I love it when you get cranky, Myra. Oh, there's a guard house with a guard. How shall we play this? Bear in mind there is going to be a lot of testosterone in that house. This might be a good time for an epiphany of some sort.'

'I should have pushed you off that cliff in Spain. God, why didn't I do that?' Myra muttered under her breath.

Annie brought the car to a complete stop at the guard house. 'Countess de Silva to see Mr Lyons. This is an emergency, hence our arrival in this taxi. My limousine had a bit of a problem so the kind driver of this taxi . . . allowed us the use of it. Please explain all that to my dear friend Mr Lyons and please stress the word *urgent*.'

Myra Rutledge, also known as the CIC, or the Cat in Charge, said, 'I'm calling Charles.'

Back at LAX, Jack Emery and Harry Wong stepped out into the California sunshine. They headed for the Hertz rental he'd reserved, got in, opened up the map and perused it. Harry chattered non-stop.

'I thought I'd be able to smell orange blossoms. Isn't California known for its orange blossoms? What the hell are we doing here anyway, Jack? I know you said the girls needed us but I think you need to tell me why. Ah, Jack, look out the window.'

'Harry, will you shut up long enough for me to read this map. We have all afternoon to talk.'

'Jack . . .'

Jack tossed the map on the dash. 'What?' he stormed.

'There's a man at the window who looks like he wants your attention.'

Jack swiveled around to see a tall muscular man motion for him to roll down his window. His heart pumping, Jack turned on the engine and pressed the button that would lower the window. 'Yeah.'

'Mr Emery, welcome to California! It's nice to finally meet you, Mr Wong. I've heard all about you,' the man said pleasantly.

'Aren't you supposed to be talking into your sleeve or your collar or something?'

This one was young, probably new to the job, unlike the seasoned guys back in Washington. Jack knew in his gut the man had one of the special gold shields somewhere on his person. Hopefully it was stuck up his ass. Obviously no one had told him he was supposed to snap and snarl. He was wearing his government issued aviator sunglasses. Someone should tell those guys the glasses were a dead giveaway. Plus he smelled like a cop.

The smile stayed on the agent's face. 'Or something. I have a message for you.'

'Yeah, I bet you do. I bet I even know what the message is. Is it, get back on the plane and go home? I can't do that. I have things to do and places to go. Me and my friend here like being up front right from the gitgo.'

The good looking guy threw back his head and laughed. The sunglasses didn't even budge. It was a nice sound, Jack thought. 'Wrong.' He handed Jack a slip of paper that was folded. Jack unfolded it and read: 'Spritzer and Robinson in L.A. Do what the messenger tells you to do.' It was signed, CM. CM had to mean Charles Martin. Like he was really going to fall for this. On the other hand, maybe it was for real. Now that he was out of the closet and on the Pinewood ladies' team, Martin might really be trying to warn him. 'How do I know this is for real?'

'The sender of the note said you would say that.' The special agent smiled showing a glorious row of sparkling white teeth. 'He said if you did ask, I was to tell you he is looking forward to walking Nikki down the aisle and handing her over to you.'

'He said that, did he?'

'Yes, sir, he did.'

'Okay, what's our next move? We've eliminated the need to knock each other's heads off, right?'

'Yes, sir. There are those in the Capitol who have long

memories. I'm not one of those people. I don't even like Washington. No offense, sir.'

'None taken. I'm not real crazy about the place myself. You should think about relocating yourself, this place is going to go into the ocean sooner or later and then all those sharks and barracudas in Washington will eat you guys up. What now?'

'Your call, sir. By the way, the agents in D.C. are the ones who alerted me to the arrival of the parties in question. I planted a homing device on their vehicle. I know where they're staying, the make of the car, how much their room cost and I even know where they are right this minute. A colleague is following them. I can take you to them. I can haul their asses to wherever you want them delivered or I can fade away into this glorious sunshine and pretend we've never met. It's your call, Mr Emery.'

'Listen, I need to think about this a few minutes and I have a few calls to make. I'll have an answer for you shortly. By the way, what's your name?'

'Call me Six. It's an old navy term for covering your ass. That's what I'll be doing.'

'I knew that,' Jack mumbled. Like hell he did.

The agent stepped away, offered up a sloppy salute of sorts, and then lit a cigarette.

'What the hell was that all about, Jack? Jesus Christ, what are you involved in? Who is that guy? Look, all I want is Yoko. You can do all this super spy shit on your own time. I just want my girl.'

Jack turned to Harry and his face was grim. 'Well listen up, you dumb shit. Your girl is involved, just the way my girl is involved, in all this super spy shit. Now shut the hell up while I think. Let me say right now, this is not a good thing. I was not expecting this. Right now I don't know what to do so shut the fuck up until I decide. Don't even breathe, Harry.'

Jack squeezed his eyes shut and tried to think. When nothing came to him, he hit the speed dial on his cell phone and waited for Nikki to pick up.

Twenty-One

'What now, Super Sleuth Spritzer?' Ted Robinson demanded. 'We've been up and down this road ten times. Are we going in or are we going to drain the gas tank?'

Maggie's grip on the steering wheel was fierce. 'I'm thinking, Ted. You need to keep quiet while I make a decision. Take a nap or something.'

'Look, Maggie, we dropped everything to come cross country. We're on shaky ground with the executive editor we report to. I say we send the story now and the editors can fill in the gaps as we call them in. Assuming we can fill in those gaps. If we file the story now, we'll be the first ones out of the gate. The paper will hold the story until we give the okay.'

'What if we don't get anything to fill in the gaps? Then our story is *out there* and by out there I mean at the paper. You know how many people are going to read it before it goes to print. We have to get in Lyons's house and warn him, that's all there is to it. Okay, let's go back and go right up to the guard house and . . . and announce ourselves. I've never heard of a movie star that turns away good press.'

'There's a first time for everything. I'm for anything right now that will get us off this road. All right, let's give it a try. If we don't get in to see the man of the hour, what then?'

'Then we wait for Rutledge and de Silva to come out. Then we try again and allude to the security guard who will then allude to Lyons that we're here to warn him and maybe then he'll agree to talk to us. It's a gamble, what can I tell you. If you have a better idea, I'd like to hear it.'

'We're flying blind. We don't know what he's done. All we know is those women from Pinewood *know* what he did, and are after him. In my book that just ain't good enough. Damn,

163

you hit that pothole again. That makes nine times in a row. You know it's there, why don't you steer around it? You're going to break an axle and we'll be stuck out here.'

'Stop whining, Ted. Okay, I'm going to turn around and we're going to attempt to get in to see Mr Lyons. I said attempt, Ted.'

'I can't even begin to imagine what that guy could have done to bring down the wrath of those vicious women. Which brings me to my next thought, where the hell are they? It occurs to me, and it should have occurred to you by now, that maybe those damn women are setting us up.'

Maggie waited for a break in traffic before she made a U-turn in the middle of the road. 'Oh, they're out there, trust me on that. There's no way they set us up. No one knows we're here. Those two old ladies are simply the first string. The others will move in for the kill when the old ladies give the signal. That has to be how it's going to work because nothing else makes sense. Your problem is you think like a man. Rutledge and de Silva soften up the guy and then when the time is right, the Pinewood cavalry arrives. They're way off their own turf now. My woman's intuition tells me they're a little nervous just the way you and I are nervous.'

'Maybe so but I'd feel a whole hell of a lot better if I knew where those women are right this minute.

Maggie chewed on her lower lip as she pulled into the shale driveway that led up to the secluded guard house. She took a deep breath and muttered, 'I would, too.'

'How much longer are we going to cruise these streets? I feel like I know Los Angeles like the back of my hand,' Kathryn snapped.

Nikki took her eyes off the road for a split second. 'Until we come up with a plan. We don't even have a base of operations. Charles told us to abort the mission. We're flying solo here, Kathryn. We should call Myra again. Do it now, Kathryn. Maybe she'll answer this time.'

Kathryn was still in a snapping, snarling mood. 'Maybe you should turn your cell phone back on, Nikki. If you see

Charles's number pop up, don't answer it. All right, all right, I'm calling Myra.'

Nikki was driving blindly, up one street and down another. Finally, she turned into what looked like a residential neighborhood and pulled to the curb. 'We need to talk right now and make some kind of hard fast decision.'

'No answer,' Kathryn said snapping her cell phone shut. Nikki's phone beeped. She looked down at the number and clicked it on. 'Jack!' She listened, her hand trembling on the phone. The others leaned over the seat as they tried to understand what was going on.

'I know they're here. Myra saw them at the airport. Charles told us to abort the mission but . . . we voted to continue. We think Myra and Annie are at Lyons's house but aren't sure. They're not answering their phones. Charles is livid. Actually, he's beyond livid. We're in a car sitting by a curb in a residential neighborhood, and no one is following us, Jack. We've been driving aimlessly trying to decide what to do. You're *here*! Here in California! With Harry Wong! You didn't tell him, did you, Jack? Please, tell me you didn't tell him. No, Jack, you didn't have to tell him. Why didn't you take a damn ad out in the *Los Angeles Times* for God's sake. No, no, I don't want to hear that. Wait a minute, yes, I do want to hear that. There's a gold shield here and he's your new best friend. Are you sure about that? Okay, okay, what's the *bad* news. The reporters either found the tracking device the gold shield put on their car or it fell off. Yeah, that is bad news. That means you don't know where they are. Is there any *good* news? You're going to call Ted Robinson? Where are we exactly? Hold on a minute.'

Nikki turned around. Do any of you know exactly where we are?'

'Brentwood,' Kathryn said.

'We're in Brentwood, Jack. I'm worried about Myra and Annie. We're going out to Lyons's house. I forgot to tell you those men are out there. That's five against two, Jack. I don't know if Annie and Myra can bluff their way through something like this. I'll call you when we decide what we're going to do.' Before Jack could reply, Nikki closed her cell phone. It rang almost immediately. She ignored it.

'Yoko, Harry is here and Jack told him everything. I guess he's okay with it. Are you okay with it?

Yoko smiled for the first time in days. 'Absolutely.'

'You heard my end of the conversation. There's a gold shield out here and he appears to be on our side. He planted a tracking device on Robinson's car but either it fell off or the reporters found it. Our guys lost them. Spritzer and Robinson could be anywhere. What that means is they are definitely onto us. We may find ourselves in the position of having to take care of them one way or the other. Do we vote on this or go where angels fear to tread?'

It was a unanimous vote to forge ahead.

Nikki took a deep breath as she turned her signal light on and moved into the slow residential traffic. 'Read the map, Kathryn, and tell me where to turn.'

From the back seat, Alexis said, 'We need to chat this up a little. Let's try to figure out where we made a mistake. Was it our mistake or Charles's mistake? I want to know.' The others agreed.

'Maybe our mistake was going to see those four guys and tipping our hand. Maybe we should have gone straight to Lyons. Maybe the mistake was Charles hacking into Lyons's computers and records. It's been a sloppy mission from the gitgo,' Isabelle said.

'There are two ways to look at that. Those four guys along with Lyons make up the inner circle of his little organization. There's no doubt at all that Lyons is the Rainmaker. The four of them headed here like homing pigeons which proves my point. We have all five of them under one roof so I'd have to say it wasn't a mistake,' Nikki said. 'You take out the inner core and hopefully the domino effect will spring into action. We can't lose sight of our true mission which is Michael Lyons. The rest of it, as ugly and perverted as it is, is up to the authorities. We're leading the way. All they have to do is step in and clean up the organization when we're finished with Lyons. The plan is to leave all the information Charles gathered at the residence. This is just my opinion,' Nikki said.

'And if we get caught?' Alexis asked.

'Then we get caught,' Kathryn snarled. 'We've all known

from the beginning that getting caught was a possibility. This time around is no different. Just stay alert and let's do what we do best, get Yoko's revenge, move on, and don't look back.'

'With Jack and Harry here along with their new buddy, the playing field is a little more level,' Nikki said as she pulled up to a stop sign.

'I'd agree if those two reporters weren't here. I hate being the voice of doom and gloom but those two can screw up everything,' Isabelle said.

'Only if we allow it,' Kathryn said. 'I, for one, have no intention of letting that happen. Whoa, whoa, slow down, Nikki. Make a left at the next intersection and that's going to take us right past Mr Lyons's house.'

'So we're just going to bust in and hope for the best. We're going for the gusto, is that it?' Isabelle said.

'That's it,' Alexis said.

'Then, let's do it! Call Jack and tell him we're going in.'

Maggie Spritzer tried her best to charm the guard standing outside his little hut but she wasn't having any luck. Charming Alan Nolan was a walk in the park compared to this stone-faced giant with the gun in his holster. 'I'm sorry, Miss, but Mr Lyons called down earlier and said I wasn't to admit anyone to the big house today. He's not feeling well. Mr Lyons made a point of saying absolutely no reporters were to be admitted. Move up a little and you can turn around. Next time before you make the trip up here, call ahead for an appointment.'

Maggie wasn't about to give up. 'But we're with the Countess and her companion. They're expecting us. She's going to pitch a fit.'

'Then maybe you should call her on your cell phone,' the guard said calling her bluff. Maggie had no other choice but to pretend to make the call. 'I guess she turned off her phone. Are you sure you can't call the house phone up there?'

The guard's hand moved to the butt of his gun. 'I'm sure. Now turn around and leave the premises.'

'I sure hope you don't get into trouble over this,' Maggie said.

'Let me worry about that. You can leave your cell phone number and if anyone up at the house calls about your arrival, I'll have them call you.'

Maggie thought about the request for all of one minute. Finally, she decided she had nothing to lose. She gave the guard her cell phone number and name. She watched him copy the information onto a yellow pad. 'Thanks for nothing,' she said speeding off down the shale driveway.

'I could have told you that would happen. Now what, fearless leader?' Ted groused.

'We learned one thing, Ted. Rutledge and de Silva are still in there, and it's been a while. If they had left, the guard would have said so.'

'That's true but it isn't helping us. For all we know those two women could be there on legitimate movie business.'

'Get real, Ted! We'll just find a good spot along the road and wait it out. Sooner or later, the others will come out here. The second string. Or, if you prefer, the enforcers. Then if you think you're up to it, we storm the guard and take matters into our own hands.'

'Are you talking about the guard with the gun?'

'That's the one!' Maggie said, her voice full of bravado she was far from feeling.

'There's only one thing missing in this mess.'

'What's that?' Maggie asked as she scanned both sides of the road that ran past Lyons's driveway so she could pull over and park.

'Jack Emery and those goddamn gold shields.'

Maggie shivered.

Inside Lyons's mansion, Myra and Annie were running out of conversation. They were literally babbling as Lyons pretended to be attentive.

'My dear, I feel so bad for you. I do wish you would allow me to call a doctor I know. He can give you a shot to curb the itching. I seem to recall they treat shingles with some powerful antibiotics. It won't be a problem to make the call. I'm also sorry we can't take the pictures today. Another time,' Annie said in her best motherly voice.

'I'll be fine, Countess. I just want to go back to bed.' Hint, hint, hint.

'But, Michael, how can you do that with your guests? I can take them back to our hotel. It won't be a problem. You won't get any rest as long as you have company. Men don't know how to care for someone who is sick. I insist, my dear. We insist, don't we, dear?' Annie said, addressing Myra.

'In fact, they can use our two-bedroom suite at the Beverly Hills Hotel since we have to leave tonight. Oh, dear, I said that already. I do apologize for coming out here unannounced but I didn't know what else to do. People make too many demands on my time. I'm just going to leave my check with you and then you can make the photo arrangements with the foundation when you're feeling better.'

If these women didn't get out of here soon he was going to kill them. He itched so bad he wanted to claw his skin off. He nodded as he tried to usher the women to the door. 'Yes, yes, that will work. I really don't feel well, Countess, but I will be happy to do what you want as soon as I feel better. I also appreciate the invitation to accommodate my guests but they're leaving in an hour or so. They're having lunch right now and then they're leaving.'

Myra knew they'd blown it. She wanted to cry. She reached up for the pearls that were no longer around her neck. She raised an eyebrow in Annie's direction. 'I think we should allow Mr Lyons to return to bed. Write him the check, Countess.'

Annie frowned as she dug around in her purse for her check-book. She looked down at the balance under the last entry. She had exactly $33.11 in what she called the kitchen grocery account. She scribbled off a check for five million dollars and handed it over with a flourish. She couldn't resist a parting shot as Lyons marched them toward the door. 'You can die from shingles, Michael. I do wish you would allow me to send a doctor out here for you.' She wondered if what she'd just said was true.

'Die?'

'Oh, yes, it's one of those creeping mystery ailments doctors can't get a handle on. They say they have cures but they don't.

169

My gardener had the same thing. One minute he was scratching and complaining about the pain with the blisters and then he just dropped down into a bed of pansies. I have to tell you, I cried. What will the world do without you, Michael? We all love your films. Surely you don't want to be known as the famous actor who died from shingles. It's such an ugly word. It's like the difference between Federal Express and mail from the post office. Well, it's your body,' she blathered on.

'Good luck at the Academy Awards,' Myra said.

They were almost to the door when Lyons moved over to the window. Myra looked at Annie. The look said, stall as long as you can. I think the girls are here.

Twenty-Two

Nikki drove the car up the long driveway leading to Michael Lyons's house. The guard stepped out of his hut the moment Nikki stopped the car. She got out of the car at the same time Yoko stepped out of the back door.

'This is not a turnaround road, Miss. This is private property. You'll have to leave right now. Pull to the right and turn around.'

'Some other time,' Nikki said walking around the guard. Yoko stepped forward, her right hand like a claw. She jabbed her fingers into the man's neck and he crumpled.

'Who has the duct tape?'

Alexis climbed out of the car ripping off strips as she made her way over to Nikki and Yoko who were dragging the guard into his little house.

'Homey,' Nikki said looking around. 'It's heated and cooled. TV, VCR, radio, mini fridge, all the comforts of home. Lots of girlie magazines. Maybe when we leave we'll set fire to the magazines. Look at this,' she said ripping a sheet of paper from the yellow pad. 'Maggie Spritzer's cell phone number! She's been here. That's okay, we'll deal with her later.'

Alexis and Yoko rolled the guard over to the corner while Nikki confiscated his gun, and his cell phone. Then she ripped out the phone lines and turned off the electrical breaker that controlled the electronic gates. 'I can open the gates manually.' The last thing Nikki did was close the door to the guard house and lock it using the key on the guard's key ring. She took a moment to look around to see if there was a sign that said, Closed, or, Off Duty. There weren't any.

Nikki ran ahead and opened the gate. She raced back to the

car and drove through, then sprinted back to close the gate. Anyone driving up would assume the power was still on and they were locked out. She sailed up to the main house, her breath coming in hard little puffs.

'Show time, ladies!' Nikki said as she brought the rental car to a full stop behind the yellow taxi sitting in the driveway. 'They're still here,' she hissed. 'Get the bags!'

'Got 'em,' Kathryn said getting out of the car. The others followed suit.

Nikki took a moment to walk over to Yoko. 'Are you ready, Yoko? Are you sure you can handle this?'

Yoko looked serene. 'I have waited my whole life for this. I am more than ready. You all promised that I could *do it*.'

Nikki, their undisputed leader, said, 'Quick, fast and as dirty as you can get. I have the guard's gun. If we have to, we use it. Let's go! Fifteen minutes and we're out of here.'

'Michael! Yoo hoo, you have company! Do you want Myra and I to . . . to shoo them away? Oh, my dear, you're looking so ghastly. My goodness, there are five of them and they look so . . . so *determined*. They must be fans. Quick, Michael, do you have any pictures of yourself? That's probably all they want. If you get them, I'll sign them for you. My goodness, listen to that doorbell. I declare, I think they're leaning on it,' Annie babbled.

'What the hell! How did they get past the guard? I told him no visitors. Yes, yes, get rid of them. I have pictures but I don't . . . I don't know where they are. Just open the door a crack and speak through the crack. I can't handle visitors today.'

Myra opened the door a crack and then stepped backward. She looked at Michael and said, 'Your fans are so . . . *pushy*. How do you stand it?' The door swung wide to allow the cavalry from Pinewood to blaze through the open door. Isabelle locked the door.

'*Hello, daddy!*' Yoko said bowing low.

Michael Lyons thought nothing in the world could phase him but seeing his daughter, a true replica of her mother, stunned him, leaving him speechless. And if the reports he'd gathered were true, she was here to kill him. He wanted to say something but he couldn't make his tongue work. Then he looked into her eyes and knew this tiny creature would show him no mercy. His shoulders sagged.

'Where are the others?' Nikki asked brandishing the guard's gun.

'Either in the dining room or the kitchen. They're staying out of sight and haven't made a sound. Be careful,' Myra said. The girls raced off, leaving Yoko, Myra and Annie alone with Michael Lyons.

Yoko advanced a step and then another. 'I understand you've been looking for me, *daddy*. Well, here I am.'

Still speechless, Lyons stood rooted to the floor as he tried to figure out what was going on. He finally found his voice. 'What do you want?' He couldn't believe the strangled sounding voice was his own. 'What?' he screamed.

'I'm here to avenge my mother. My mother was Suki Naoki. You remember my mother, don't you?'

'Yes, yes, I remember your mother. She was very beautiful,' he said, his voice cracking with desperation. He looked around wildly as he finally figured out what was going on. He almost blacked out when he saw the members of his inner circle walking toward him at gunpoint.

'And you killed her,' Yoko said.

'No. No, that's not true. She died but I didn't kill her.'

'You turned her out on to that . . . that sex circuit. Oh, yes, you killed her.'

The four men looked whipped as they took in the scene playing out in front of them. It was Josh Tappen, the retired general, who roared a denial and accused Lyons of setting them all up for his own purposes. The women ignored the outburst.

'Yoko, watch the time,' Kathryn said as she unzipped her duffel bag and pulled out a jug full of clear liquid. Alexis did the same thing. Yoko nodded.

'Strip,' Nikki said waving the gun around. No one moved. 'They're not listening, Yoko,' Nikki said in a sing-song voice. 'This might be a good time to tell them we're all PMSing.'

'I can fix that,' Yoko said in the same kind of sing-song voice. She leaped in the air, her legs and arms going in all directions. The four men fell to the floor within seconds. Lyons started to squeal like a stuck pig when she advanced on him.

'The lady told you to strip. That goes for you, too, *daddy*. Do it!' The men hastened to obey the order.

'What . . . what are you going to do?' Lyons asked.

Yoko pulled on a pair of latex gloves. 'Where's the brush?'

'Right here,' Isabelle trilled as she handed it over.

All the men eyed the two jugs with the clear white fluid. One of them was brave enough to ask what it was.

The ladies of Pinewood smiled.

'Krazy Glue. *Industrial* strength,' Yoko said. She snapped the gloves into place and picked up the brush. 'Who wants to go first?' No one moved.

'Don't mess with us, we have no patience. Didn't you hear her when she said we're all PMSing. Nikki, shoot their dicks off?' Kathryn ordered as she shoved Adam Newhouse forward. They all cowered like beaten dogs.

Yoko dropped to her knees and painted a wide swath on the hardwood floor. Isabelle and Alexis pushed and shoved Newhouse until they had him glued to the floor. It took three minutes to glue all the men to the floor.

'They're stuck in place. Hurry, Yoko.' Isabelle said. The brush dipped in the Krazy Glue moved at the speed of light. Ears were glued to their heads, lips were sealed, their hands were glued to one another, legs glued together and to each other. 'You forgot the most important place!'

'No, I was saving it for last.' The ladies of Pinewood smiled as the brush moved again. 'Are you sure there is no solvent that will unglue all my hard work?' Yoko queried.

'Nope. No solvent. They're stuck here forever! Oh, my, you have almost a whole jug left. What are you going to do with it?' Kathryn asked.

'Waste not, want not,' Yoko said as she splashed the remaining glue over the five men. The women clapped and clapped. Annie, whose eyes were big as saucers, started to laugh and couldn't stop.

'Who has the records?' Alexis asked.

Isabelle opened her duffle bag and dumped the contents on

the floor but far enough away so the glue wouldn't trickle onto them.

'Our work here is done!' Kathryn said dramatically. 'Eighteen minutes. Not bad. Come on, we have to get out of here.'

Myra opened the door and then slammed it shut when a sharp, piercing sound whipped through the air. Off in the distance they could see red and blue flashing lights.

'The police are here!' Myra said quietly. 'You all know what to do.'

Twenty-Three

Maggie was half dozing behind the wheel of the rental car when she felt Ted poke her elbow. 'It's them! They just whizzed by. A big SUV. Nikki Quinn was driving. The car was going too fast to tell if the others were in there. It looked full, though.'

Maggie licked at her lips. 'This is it then! Pulitzer, here we come. How do you want to play this, Ted? We need a plan here. Do we file the story first or call the cops first? Make sure the camera is charged. Just one picture is worth a thousand words. Tell me what you want to do first!' She sounded so annoyed and yet excited that Ted felt befuddled.

'Unless they're expected, which I don't think they are, how are those women going to get past those electronic gates? You met the guard. The one with the gun. He's not going to open those gates to anyone. There are five of them. They're like fucking commandos. You've seen them in action, they're heartless.'

'Trust me, they'll find a way,' Ted said.

Maggie digested the information. Ted was right. 'We're wasting time. We have to take them by surprise. Let's check out the guard. If they disabled him, we call the cops. It will take them at least seven or eight minutes to get out here. We've already wasted five minutes. Those women aren't going to stand around patting each other on the back. When they finish whatever it is they're doing they're going to split. That's when we take our pictures. The California cops can nail their asses to the wall. We get the rest of our story, call it in, email the pictures and hop on the next plane to D.C. and wait for our Pulitzer. Damn, I thought this day would never come.'

Always a thinker, Ted said, 'Don't you think this was all a little too easy?'

'Easy? Easy? Are you crazy? No, I do not think this has been easy. It's been damn hard. Sometimes you catch a break like now. That's how you have to look at it. Get your cell phone ready so you can call the police. The laptop is on. All I have to do is hit Send, and it's all over. You ready?'

Ted watched the flowing traffic. He didn't trust himself to speak so he nodded. Maggie was on the road a minute later. The driver of the car she'd cut off blasted his horn and gave her the finger. Maggie gave it right back.

Maggie slowed just long enough to turn onto Lyons's driveway. She put the pedal to the metal and screeched to a stop outside the guard hut. 'He's not here! Maybe he escorted them up to the house.' She was out of the car a second later. 'The hut is locked. Ted, did you hear me, the hut is locked. Maybe we should break it open.'

'What's that *we* stuff? I'm not breaking my shoulder for you or anyone else.'

'Then kick it in, Ted. We have to hurry. I think we should call the police right now. I'm going to do it, Ted, while you kick in the door.'

Ted was about to lift his foot when he heard a hard thumping sound inside. It was all the impetus he needed to lash out at the door. He was stunned when the flimsy door gave way. Both reporters gawked at the duct-taped guard. 'His gun is gone,' Ted hissed.

'I see that. Take that tape off him while I call the police but before I call them, take his picture. Better take a couple.'

Ted snapped the pictures from different angles. He winced when he ripped the duct tape from the man's wrists, ankles and mouth. The guard got to his feet and charged out of the door. 'I'm going to get fired for this. Taken down by a bunch of women! Mr Lyons is going to be so pissed,' he said as he staggered over to the gates to open them.

'Oh, oh,' Maggie said. 'Look who's here!'

Ted whirled around to see two cars. Jack Emery glared at him through the car window. All he had to do was see the aviator glasses on the man in the other car to know who he was. 'Son of a fucking bitch! I told you this was too easy. Hit that Send button. *Now*, Maggie!'

177

Maggie fumbled in her backpack and yanked her laptop out. Her hands were shaking so badly she missed the Send button twice before she finally made contact.

Jack and Harry Wong leaped out of the car. Jack could see the guard running up the driveway, saw the laptop in Maggie's hand and the worry in Ted's eyes all at a glance. He looked over at his new best friend and pointed to the two reporters. 'Take care of them. Rip their guts out if you have to. Read them their rights just to be on the safe side.'

'My pleasure,' the man drawled as he pulled two pair of flexi-cuffs from his pocket.

'We didn't do anything. Why are you arresting us? We freed that man. Those women had him trussed up like a Christmas turkey. Look for yourself, there's the duct tape they used. His DNA is on it. What's the charge?' Maggie shouted.

'I haven't decided yet but something will come to me. Now shut up and let me do my job.'

'I don't have to shut up. This is a free country or it was the last time I looked. Well, guess what, buddy, we filed our story and there's nothing you can do about it. And, we called the police, too. What do you have to say to that?' Maggie blustered before the special agent picked up one of the strips of duct tape and plastered it against her mouth.

'What I think, lady, is this. You just made the most serious mistake of your life.'

'Fuck!' Ted said.

'You want the tape, too?'

'No, sir, I don't.'

They all heard the sirens before they saw the flashing blue and red lights.

There were three police cars. Two raced through the open gates, the third one stopped behind the special agent's car.

Special Agent Bert Navarro had his credentials in his hand when both L.A. cops sauntered over to where he was standing. He held them out. 'These two are my prisoners,' was all he said. The two L.A. cops whispered among themselves before they handed Navarro's creds back to him. They nodded respectfully and got into their car and headed to the main house.

'Okay, you two, into the car.' Navarro pulled out a second set of flexi-cuffs and handcuffed the two reporters to the doors before he climbed behind the wheel to head up to the main house. He could hear the brouhaha going on inside even before he got out of the car. He didn't bother to knock or ring the bell. He opened the door and stepped inside. He stepped around the L.A. officers who were arguing with Jack Emery. It wasn't time for him to intervene. He walked over to the area in question and looked down at the men glued to the floor. Then he looked around at the seven women who glared at him defiantly. 'Is that what I think it is?' he asked of no one in particular.

'Krazy Glue,' Kathryn said. '*Industrial* strength.'

'That would mean the floor has to be sawed away. Then some very strong men will have to carry the slab holding the men to a tow truck of some sort so they can be transported . . . to *somewhere*. I don't see any other alternative.' He sounded like he was discussing a flat tire.

'That's pretty much how I see it,' Kathryn said. Special Agent Navarro allowed himself a small smile that Kathryn returned. Then she winked at him.

Special Agent Navarro stared at the attractive woman from behind his sunglasses. Now, here was someone he'd like to get to know better. She'd winked at him. Considering the circumstances, he thought the wink was pretty damn bold. He fought the urge to laugh.

A verbal war seemed to be going on by the front door. The L.A. cops were claiming jurisdiction while Jack Emery was shouting to be heard over the melee. 'This is my collar. I've been tracking these women for years. I have all the paper-work to transport all seven women back to Virginia. You can argue until the cows come home but nothing is going to change. The women go with me. You get to keep the floor and the guys stuck to it. Give me any shit and you'll be walking a beat some place in the desert.'

Suddenly a new voice was heard. 'Tell me I'm not seeing what I'm seeing!'

One of the L.A. cops cursed loudly. 'Who the hell let that reporter in here? Get him out of here! Christ Almighty, this is going to be splashed all over the front pages by morning. Kaminsky, didn't you hear me, kick his ass out of here!'

Jack Emery looked at Harry Wong who was busy making moon eyes at Yoko who couldn't seem to take her eyes off the man on the floor. Her father.

'The shit's going to hit the fan on this one. Someone has to call this guy's studio. You do it, Carpenter. If the mayor shows up, don't let him in here until we figure out what the hell is going on. Who did this?' the cop in charge asked, wincing as he looked down at the floor.

The room grew quiet. It was obvious the men on the floor couldn't respond so the cop who appeared to be in charge and who had asked the question looked at the women who just stared at him, their expressions blank. He turned to Jack who wiggled his eyebrows. 'We have a plane to catch. My paperwork is in order. Having said that, Harry, cuff the ladies.'

Harry fixed the flexi-cuffs on all seven women. Jack herded the women toward the door. He held his breath, hoping no one was going to look too close at his paperwork. The women moved quickly.

Agent Navarro, sensing trouble, moved just as quickly, his special gold shield in his hand. He raised it high enough so everyone in the room could see the special emblem. 'Don't even think about it, gentlemen!'

To Jack he said, 'Take your prisoners and leave, Emery. I'll stay here to oversee the . . . cleanup.'

Jack opened the door and the women filed out. Flashbulbs popped and cameras clicked. The pictures appeared on the six o'clock news. By midnight the photos had whipped around the world, claiming the Virginia Vigilantes were under arrest. Web sites appeared instantly. Viewers were asked to vote guilty or not guilty.

Jack urged his group forward but stopped at Navarro's car long enough to yank open the door and glared at Ted Robinson. 'Take a good look, asshole. I hope you'll be happy when that shield dumps you at your new home which, by the way, you are not going to like. The *L.A. Times* scooped you, you crud. They have the pictures.'

'Jack . . . Jack wait!'

'Don't ever talk to me again, Ted. You, too, Maggie. I don't ever want to see you again.' He slammed the car door shut and moved forward.

'Get in the car, ladies. We're heading home. I engaged the services of a private jet. I sure hope one of you can pay for it. I don't want you saying anything until we're in the car and on our way. Tell me you understand.' Seven heads bobbed up and down.

The moment the car was in gear, the windows closed, and they were on their way, Myra said, 'What did Charles say?'

'He said not to worry about him. He said you all know what to do,' Jack said.

'What did we do wrong?' Alexis asked, anger ringing in her voice.

'We didn't pay enough attention to those reporters,' Nikki said.

'You'll never have to worry about them again. Agent Navarro, who, by the way, is a very nice guy, has their future in his hands. I'm sorry about the cuffs, ladies, but they have to stay on till we're airborne. I'll have to cuff you again before we leave the plane. It's going to be a circus so be prepared. You'll have to spend the night in jail but you'll be arraigned at eight tomorrow morning.'

The rest of the ride to LAX was made in silence.

The moment the rented Gulfstream leveled off at 30,000 feet, the women all started to talk at once. What was never supposed to happen had happened. They were now felons. They would spend the night in jail with criminals and be arraigned in the morning. No one had a clue what the next step was.

Nikki was sitting next to Jack. 'I don't know how to thank you, Jack. You always come through in the nick of time. God knows what would have happened to us if you hadn't showed up when you did.'

'Krazy Glue, huh?'

Nikki smiled wearily. '*Industrial* strength, Jack. And, there is no known solvent to loosen or remove it. I'm going to lose my license to practice law.'

'I know,' Jack said quietly.

'You might want to distance yourself from us after the arraignment tomorrow. It won't do your career any good to be seen with any of us, me in particular. It is going to be a circus, isn't it? I hope Myra is up to it.'

'Nik, you have no idea. It's going to be a free fall. Don't worry about my career. I don't think you have to worry about Myra either. She's a tough old gal. Alexis is the one I'm worried about. She already did a stretch in the slammer. I'm working on it, Nik. Relax. Try to get some sleep. It's going to be a very long night. I'll be right here.'

Jack looked around the luxurious cabin. Harry and Yoko were cuddling together. Alexis, Isabelle and Kathryn pretended to be asleep. He knew they weren't. He also knew their brains were whirling and twirling. Myra and Annie were talking quietly. Neither seemed overly alarmed. In fact they looked peaceful and contented. He thought about that for a moment or two. He didn't move, though, until he was certain Nikki was truly asleep. He made his way down the aisle to where the two older women were sitting. Each had a glass of bourbon on the rocks in her hand. He joined them.

'We certainly owe you a debt of thanks, Jack,' Myra said.

'I was going on sheer guts. That piece of paper is pretty much worthless. I think it was special agent Navarro who paved the way for it to work. It's not going to be easy, Myra. When we step off this plane it is going to be a free fall. Nothing in your life as you've known it can prepare you for what's coming up.'

'I think we can handle it, young man,' Annie said.

'I sure as hell hope so, because it will get ugly.'

'Then we'll get ugly right back. You're supposed to be our enemy, Jack. I hope you can play the part when we go public.'

'I can do it, Myra. I'll be going up against Liz Fox. The man or woman hasn't been born who can outthink, outwit, outlawyer Lizzie Fox. Nikki told me she contacted her as soon as the dark stuff hit the fan. She'll be waiting for you all when we land. Whatever you do, do not, I repeat, do not open your mouth to anyone but Lizzie. Don't even talk among your-selves because someone might be listening. From here on in you're all the media's new darlings.'

182

'We understand,' Annie said.

Jack stood up. He couldn't remember when he had felt this tired. He made his way back to his seat. Nikki was still sleeping soundly. He wondered if he would ever be able to sleep again. Sooner or later, someone was going to get downwind of his involvement with the ladies of Pinewood. He closed his eyes and was instantly asleep.

As the rented Gulfstream sliced down the runway at Dulles Airport, a team of twelve detectives, warrant in hand, broke open the door of the Pinewood farmhouse. They worked industriously for the next four hours. When they left the farmhouse with nothing in their hands, they fixed a padlock to the door and locked it. Grumbling and complaining among themselves, they made their way back to the station to file their report. The report read simply. *Nothing out of the ordinary found. There were no occupants in the house.*

The passengers aboard the Gulfstream gasped when they looked out the windows. Hundreds of people with microphones and cameras stood against the metal barriers waiting for the passengers to disembark. Several dozen police officers walked the perimeter, their hands on their gun butts.

Jack stood up. He helped Nikki to her feet. 'Listen to me. Your lawyer is out there waiting for you with the hordes of reporters. You're big news now. Do not try to hide your face. Let them see the flexi-cuffs. Hold your heads up and if possible, look defiant. Nikki, lead the way. I'll bring up the rear. No talking. The officers will lead you to the police van. Get in calmly, say nothing.'

'We know what to do, Jack. Let's just get this over with.'

'What about me?' Harry said.

'You leave with me, Harry. Everything I said applies to you, too. Don't open that yap of yours, understand?'

'I got it, Jack. Tell me this is going to be okay.'

Jack took a moment to look into Harry's eyes. 'Only a fool would tell you something like that.'

'Aw, shit!'

Twenty-Four

Charles Martin stepped from the recently installed cable car, locked the gears and looked around. Even from where he was standing he could see the sparkling blue Mediterranean below the mountain, the beautiful refurbished monastery that was now his new home. To his left he could see the recently installed pool, the tennis court, the helicopter pad that was still being worked on. His heart heavy, his step weary, he made his way to the old monastery that had been Anna de Silva's home for so many years. He felt guilty and he knew he shouldn't feel that way but he did. Here he was, safe and sound on this beautiful mountain while the women he loved with all his heart were sitting in jail.

It wasn't that he was a coward, far from it. But every member of the Sisterhood, and himself included, knew this very day might come at some point in their lives. It had been Myra and Annie's idea to make this mountain fortress a getaway. He'd vetoed the idea in the beginning but eventually they'd worn him down.

Charles thought about the endless supply of money it had taken to make this mountain safe and secure. It was supposed to be for all of them should the authorities ever close in on the group. The best-laid plans of mice and men, he thought sadly. He was the only one to walk on the mountain while the others fought for their lives across the ocean. A lump settled in his throat. How was he going to carry on alone? Who would he cook for? Who would he plan for? He missed them so. Ached with love for Myra.

If there was anything to be proud of it was that everyone had followed his orders to the letter, even Myra who he thought might balk at the eleventh hour. And here he was, all alone to carry on.

Charles looked down at his watch, calculated the time difference between Spain and the United States before he raced into the monastery. Time to turn on the television to see what was going on in the States. He picked up his feet and literally ran the remaining distance to the heavy wooden door that would take him to the main part of the monastery that was considered personal quarters. Fifteen thousand square feet of personal room.

It wasn't quite home. Perhaps in time . . .

He knew Isabelle's blueprints had been followed and no questions asked by the local contractors who were glad of the work. Later, he would check out everything because he knew certain things still needed to be done.

Sanctuary.

He didn't bother to slow down or look around. He just wanted news of his girls.

As ugly as it was, Charles loved seeing the satellite dish outside the kitchen window. Sitting high on the mountain like this it should give him excellent television reception. When he turned on the television set in the kitchen to CNN the picture exploded onto the screen. The reception was beyond belief, the clarity magnificent. A pity he had no one to share this moment with.

A second later he was glad he was alone.

His jaw slack, his eyes wide, he watched as his ladies walked down the stairs of the Gulfstream that had brought them from California to Dulles Airport. They looked tired and disheveled but their heads were high, their hands handcuffed in front of them. They walked in single file, police officers alongside. Reporters shouted questions which they ignored. He saw Jack Emery and Harry Wong bringing up the rear of the parade. So far so good, he thought. He continued to watch as the women were herded into a police van. He flinched when the van door slammed shut. He continued to watch as the excited televison reporter took that moment to recap what he'd probably been saying for hours.

Charles propped his head in his hands on the counter-top

and watched, all signs of weariness gone. The reporter with a thinning blow-dried hairdo looked down at his notes before he spoke. *'The two reporters, Maggie Spritzer and Ted Robinson of the* Post, *filed their story right before the infamous seven vigilantes were arrested. Within hours the women have become household names. They have managed to push Michael Lyons, Hollywood's Golden Boy and nominee for best actor at this year's Academy Awards, and four associates to the back pages. We know there is a scandal brewing but at this moment we're waiting for the head of Lyons's studio to hold a press conference. Rumors have filtered out that the infamous seven vigilantes, as they're being called, used a liquid similar to industrial strength Krazy Glue to glue the five men to Lyons's floor. We're told there is no solvent that can extricate the men and the entire floor had to be dismantled and transported to an undisclosed destination . . .*

'The two Post *reporters who filed the story are among the missing and a spokesperson for the* Post *said they are doing everything in their power to find their two employees.*

'For those of you just tuning in, the infamous seven vigilantes include socialites Myra Rutledge, heiress to a Fortune 500 candy company, Countess Anna de Silva whose bank balances rival those of Bill Gates, lawyer Nicole Quinn, architect Isabelle Flanders, Alexis Thorn, a personal shopper, Kathryn Lucas a long distance truck driver, and Yoko Akia owner of a nursery and flower shop. The Post's *star reporters linked them to several unsolved crimes, one having to do with the home invasion of the National Security Advisor here in the nation's capital where he was beaten so severely he had to be hospitalized and resign from his office.*

'I was shown the front page of the morning Post *whose headline reads, FEMALE VIGILANTES TAKE THE LAW INTO THEIR OWN HANDS!*

'We've also been told that Elizabeth Fox will be representing all seven women. For anyone in the area who doesn't know who Elizabeth Fox is let me be the one to tell you. More than a few of her colleagues have called her a female Clarence Darrow. Her track record is impeccable. That means she's never lost a case. Several prosecutors have told me they lose

sleep when they're forced to try a case against her. In this case, the prosecution will be handled by Jack Emery whose credentials are just as impressive as those of Miss Fox. He's been called a barracuda while Miss Fox has been called a shark.'

Charles turned down the volume and sighed. He was bone weary, jet-lagged, worried sick and yet he was hungry. He didn't know how that could be, it just was. He looked around at the kitchen Myra had helped Isabelle design. It was beautiful with all the ancient brick, the stone floor, the diamond pane windows, the fresh flowers on the windowsills, the colorful crockery sitting on the shelves that had been carved into the brick walls. The table was huge, with twelve chairs. Charles wondered who would sit in them. A yellow bowl in the center of the table was filled with fresh fruit. Charles opened the refrigerator to see a fully baked ham, a roast chicken, a bowl of salad, assorted cheeses, soft drinks and some delightful Spanish beer. He wondered if he had the energy to eat.

He'd called ahead when he was airborne, to the padre at the bottom of the mountain, to have his nieces ready the house for his arrival. He knew when he got to his room there would be fresh sheets on the bed and flowers on the night-stand.

In the end, Charles decided he was too tired to eat. His shoulders sagging, he walked out of the kitchen and down a corridor that would take him to the room meant to be shared with Myra. The bed looked incredibly inviting. He'd been right about the flowers, too. The windows were open, a gentle breeze blowing the sheer curtains inward. He kicked off his shoes and fell back on the bed. It was supposed to be fail safe but something had gone awry.

He had failed to protect the sisters.

Jack Emery entered the courthouse through the basement. When he'd said it was going to get ugly he hadn't known just how ugly until he saw the circus outside the courthouse. His heart beat furiously in his chest as he rode the elevator up to the courtroom where Myra and the rest of the Sisterhood would be waiting. Which judge was he going to draw? His stomach heaved at the thought, then heaved again when he saw Lizzie Fox ahead of him. She waved as she headed for the rest room. She's probably going in there to apply her war paint, Jack thought.

Jack slammed through the courtroom doors and took his place at the prosecution table. His second chair was a gutsy young guy who looked like Adonis and flaunted it. He was sharper than razor wire and Jack liked working with him.

The courtroom was filled to overflowing. He'd had to fight his way down the hall to get here. He'd successfully managed to ward off questions and get into the room in one piece. He was frowning when he looked down at Spiro Artemos who was looking at him curiously. 'Is it my imagination or are those people on the side of those women?'

'You got that right, Jack. The tide turned during the night, thanks to the media. Women all over the world woke up to start their day hearing about those vigilantes. Fox is going to shred us.'

'No one is going to shred us, so stop talking like that. We have them dead to rights. They were caught redhanded.'

'Oh, yeah, turn around and take a look at what's coming in the door.' Jack turned and gawked. Lizzie Fox was so gorgeous, so sexy, Jack felt his mouth start to water. She didn't walk, she strutted on legs so long they looked like they went all the way to her throat. She was dressed in a skimpy suit whose short skirt could have been stuffed in her ear, a blouse open way too far. That blouse beckoned every man in the courtroom. She positively reeked of power, money and beauty. A trifecta. Jack felt sick.

'Whatever you do, don't look her in the eyes or you're dead,' Spiro said. She's going to strut herself and we're dead. We're dead, Jack.'

'If you open your mouth again, you're going to find my foot in it.'

'All rise!' the bailiff shouted. Everyone in the courtroom stood. 'The honorable judge Cornelia Easter presiding.'

Jack gripped the edge of the prosecution table. Son of a bitch! He risked a glance at Lizzie Fox who was frowning. *Oh, lady, you should only know we're both on the same side.*

Judge Easter rapped her gavel so the buzzing would stop. A door opened and all seven women were led into the courtroom to stand next to Lizzie Fox. The women in the back of the courtroom cheered with calls like, 'You go girls! We're on your side!'

Jack didn't want to look at Nikki but he had to. She looked so cold, so distant in her orange jump suit and manacles. He wanted to run to her, to tell her he'd do anything in the world to make this go away. Instead, he turned away, his eyes burning.

Judge Easter banged her gavel. 'One more outburst like that and I'll clear the courtroom!'

Judge Easter wiggled her hand.

'Jack Emery for the prosecution, your honor.'

'Elizabeth Fox for the defense, your honor.'

'This is a simple arraignment, counselors. Let's keep it simple. How do you plead?'

'Not guilty,' the seven women responded, one by one, in clear, high voices

'The State asks for remand, your honor?' Jack stated.

'Your honor, that's ridiculous. My clients are respected members of the community. At best the charge is circumstantial. My clients were unlucky in that they were at the wrong place at the wrong time. There's no reason for remand,' Fox said, her bosom rising and falling in indignation.

Jack retaliated. 'They're rich and they can flee the country. I don't care if they are friends of the governor. That's what you're going to spew next, right, Lizzie?'

Lizzie blanched, her eyes narrowing because that's exactly what she was going to do.

Judge Easter frowned. 'Let's not make this personal, Mr Emery. Approach, counselors.'

Both lawyers walked to the bench. 'Convince me you need these women jailed, Mr Emery. I also want you to think about what you just said. I do not want the governor calling me and telling me how to run my court. Is that clear?'

It was time to pretend he was a good lawyer. 'Your honor, those women are rich. They can flee the country at a moment's notice. Two of them have their own Gulfstreams. Do you know

189

how much those babies cost? Millions, that's how much. If you've read the charges, your honor, you'll understand why I have to object. The public is going to view this as the rich get what they want if they can pay for it. Celebrity always wins somehow.'

Lizzie Fox sniffed. 'Your honor, just because a person is rich doesn't mean they're going to flee. My clients are law abiding citizens. These charges are trumped up. This is a grievous miscarriage of justice. It's a simple case of my clients being at the wrong place at the wrong time. Innocent until proven guilty. My clients all pleaded not guilty. If you set bail or incarcerate them, they are tainted forever. Come on, Jack, loosen up.'

'Spare me the theatrics, Lizzie,' Judge Easter said. Jack, she's right, it's circumstantial. I did read the charges and find them a bit mind boggling. How about if I confiscate their passports? Will that make you happy, Miss Fox?'

'Hold on here, your honor. That doesn't make *me* happy. *Remand*, your honor, they can afford it.'

Lizzie Fox ignored Jack's outburst. 'No, but I'll take it. No bail. They walk out. Bail has a stigma attached to it.'

'And well it should,' Jack said. 'Those women broke the law. I'm not happy with them walking around free as the air.'

'Allegedly broke the law, Mr Emery. First year law, 101,' the judge said coldly.

'Remand and electronic bracelets, your honor. Passports mean nothing. I can give you the names of two people who can get you a passport to anywhere in the world for a thousand bucks a pop. Make me happy, too, your honor.'

'If you can do that, why aren't those men in jail?' Judge Easter asked.

'Because no one filed charges against them,' Jack retorted.

'Step back, counselors.'

Jack walked back to the prosecution table and sat down. Lizzie Fox did the same thing.

'There will be no bail but the defendants are asked to surrender their passports at which point electronic ankle bracelets will be issued. I'm also instituting a gag order on everyone involved in this case.'

Jack stood up and bellowed, 'I object, your honor. You're showing these women gross favoritism.' He whirled around and shouted to the reporters in the back of the courtroom. 'Make sure you get that down word for word.'

Judge Easter banged her gavel. 'One more word and I'll cite you for contempt.'

'I don't care, this is not justice.'

'One thousand dollars!'

'Why don't you make that two, your honor?' Jack bellowed.

'Five thousand! How do you like that, Mr Emery?'

'I damn well don't like it. Lock me up. I'm supposed to be an officer of this court just the way you are, your honor! I demand remand!'

'Ten thousand!' Judge Easter roared. And two days in jail! Turn yourself in at eight o'clock tomorrow morning. Post your fine when you check in. Cash, Mr Emery, no check.'

Jack's second chair reached for his sleeve. 'Give it up already.'

Jack risked a glance at Liz Fox and was stunned to see that she was stunned. Well, good, he'd played his part to the hilt. He saw a small smile tug at the corner of Myra's mouth.

'Next case!'

'Nice going, Jack,' Spiro Artemos said as he started to pack up his briefcase.

Jack knew the electronic bracelets would be faulty. He looked over at the women, careful to keep his expression neutral. He was stunned when Myra gave a slight nod of her head. *She knew. Goddamn it, she knew.* It was all he could do not to laugh. Then he made the mistake of looking at Judge Easter who winked at him. Fighting the laughter bubbling up in his throat, Jack started to choke. Spiro pounded him on the back.

Jurisprudence my ass, Jack thought as he struggled through the crowd of people who all suddenly seemed to want a piece of him. Spiro followed close on his heels.

'I thought it went well except for the gag order which is going to drive Lizzie nuts seeing as how she pleads her case to the public every chance she gets. This case is a prosecutor's dream. Bet you ten bucks the fashionista of jurisprudence is headed for Neiman Marcus to lay in a new supply of court-room apparel. It wouldn't hurt you to update your wardrobe either, Jack,' Spiro said. An edgy note crept into his voice. 'Did you think she looked a little *too* smug there at the end? I can shop for you while you cool your heels in jail.'

'Does it matter?' Jack asked as he tried to figure out how he was going to see Nikki. He wasn't. It was that simple. He felt lower than a snake's belly as he forged ahead to the parking lot, reporters and photographers dogging his every step as they shouted questions they knew he wasn't going to answer.

Lizzie Fox had a charming voice that could be melodious if she so chose. Now, she was elated as she stared at her clients who were being fitted with monitoring devices on their ankles. 'No bail. I didn't think the judge would go for it. Easter is one judge I hate going before. She's the only judge I can't get a handle on. She's one contrary, cranky curmudgeon. I didn't think she'd go the monitoring route, however. I like it that she rescinded her order to surrender your passports. Since you can't leave the farm, I guess she thought the device was sufficient. She filed the order to rescind that particular order immediately. So in Fox versus Emery, we won that one.

'The order clearly states you can't go farther than seven miles in any direction. If what you told me is accurate, that should encompass your entire acreage at the farm in Pinewood. We'll be going back to court in about ten days. I'll take care of everything. I've arranged transportation out to the farm for you. It's going to be a circus. The media of the world will be camped outside your gates so be prepared. If any of them get adventuresome and go over the gates, call the police immediately.

'I want you all to go home, clean up, wash the stink of your holding cells off you, have a nice dinner and then go to bed. I'm on top of everything. I don't want you to worry about anything. Oh, one last thing: Do not take any phone calls from the press.'

'My dear, I don't know how to thank you for all you've done for us,' Myra said.

'I hope you feel the same way when you get my bill. Goodbye, ladies. I'll be in touch.'

The women looked at one another and then around the smelly, dirty room where they were being outfitted with the ankle monitors. Yoko was the last to be fitted.

A female officer opened the door and said, 'Follow me. Stay close and ignore the hordes out there. Your driver has the engine running. The doors will open, hop in and you're on your way home.'

And that's how it worked. The only thing the officer left out was the mention of the parade that would be following the van to Pinewood.

'This is unbelievable,' Myra said an hour later when the van raced through the gates to Pinewood. 'There must be two hundred cars and trucks out there.'

Safe in the kitchen, the door locked, the alarm system on, Myra looked around and said, 'It's so quiet. Even when Charles was in the war room, I know he was here. He's always been such a presence and now he's gone. All of you, stop looking at me like you are. I am not going to fall apart. Now, this is what we're going to do. We're going to follow Miss Fox's orders. We'll all meet down here and prepare dinner. That's when we'll turn on the television and not one minute sooner. Scoot!'

The moment the young women were upstairs and out of eyesight and earshot, Myra looked at Annie and grinned. They gave each other a high-five. 'It went just the way Charles said it would.'

'I was never in jail before. It was such an experience, Myra. The people we met behind bars were so interesting. I do hope they get a sympathetic judge when their cases come up for hearing. And to think I missed out on all your other adventures.'

'Annie, go get cleaned up. I want to sit here a minute by myself. You don't mind, do you?'

'No, of course not. Charles is fine, Myra. This is no time to be selfish. These little ankle bracelets are certainly different from my regular jewelry,' Annie mused as she headed for the stairs.

Myra leaned back and closed her eyes. They snapped open a nanosecond later when she heard a voice that thrilled her to her very being.

'Mom, I am so proud of you. Lizzie and Aunt Nellie really kicked some ass in that courtroom. It happened just the way Charles said it would. You did it, Mom. The press is going wild.'

'Darling girl, how nice of you to appear right now. I'm a little worried. I know it worked just as Charles said. I understand this house was searched. They didn't find the war room or we would have heard about it. Charles . . . what would I do without him?'

'Mom, Charles is fine. He's feeling just the way you are. He misses you, too. I'm not telling you something you don't already know. The next few days are going to be very trying so be prepared. I'll be here, Mom. You need to get some rest now. I'll check in with you later. Right this moment, Nikki needs me.'

'Go to her, Barbara. Console her. She needs a friend right now.'

'See you later, Mom.'

'I'm going to count on it, darling girl.'

Energized and happy, Myra made her way to the second floor where she shed what she referred to as her smelly jail clothes and showered. Life was going to go on one way or the other.

Day four of captivity found the ladies of Pinewood perplexed, awed and excited when they read the news online and watched the twenty-four-hour news programs.

'Did you read the *Post* this morning?' Alexis asked. When the others nodded, Alexis burst out laughing. 'That cartoon of us wearing bustiers, spike heels with guns blazing made me laugh my head off. And that one headline that said, "At last, someone is taking charge!" I loved it. The *New York Times* said we were household names. They did a poll of some kind and every single woman they polled said they knew who we were.'

'I counted over a hundred web sites that feature us where

people are voting. Meaning they approve of us or disapprove. Approval is in the high 90s,' Isabelle said.

'The best is the article in the *Post* about the White House. To discuss the National Security Advisor, I'm sure. I'm just as sure that our names came up a time or two,' Nikki said.

Annie beamed as she poured coffee for everyone. 'Did any of you see the article in the *Los Angeles Times* that said various women's groups in the L.A. area started a defense fund for us? At the same time, there was no news on our . . . our visit to Mr Lyons's house. Why do you suppose they're downplaying all that?'

'Because if they broadcast what we did it gives us credibility. We broke up a slave and porno ring, something the authorities haven't been able to do. Every mother in America would be thanking us if they knew,' Myra said. 'What's even more strange is the *Post* hasn't mentioned their two missing star reporters the past few days. I do hope Charles is following the news.'

'Count on it,' Nikki said.

Murphy and Grady both reared up suddenly, extra protective since their return from the kennel where they had been boarded during the trip to California. Neither dog liked the throngs of people outside the gates. 'Mail's here,' Yoko said going to the door. 'The mailman is blowing the horn. I think he wants to come through the gates or he wants us to go out there. Maybe he has packages.'

'I'll go,' Kathryn said.

'I'll go with you,' Nikki said.

Five minutes later the women stood around the mail truck, stunned at what they were seeing. 'Twenty-four sacks of mail, ma'am,' the driver said to Myra. 'I've got a dolly and I'll truck it in for you. This is all the truck could hold. There's twice this much back at the post office. I'll bring it out tomorrow.'

When all twenty-four sacks covered the kitchen floor, the driver tipped his cap to Myra and said, 'Just leave the sacks by the gates and I'll pick them up tomorrow. Happy reading, ladies. By the way, my wife is on your side. I am, too.'

'Thank you, Malcolm. Your endorsement means a lot to us,' Myra said.

Kathryn, with Isabelle's help, emptied all twenty-four sacks. All they could do was gawk as the others picked up letters at random. 'They're from all over the world,' Alexis said, awe ringing in her voice.

'I'm going to make more coffee,' Annie said. 'And I'm going to lace it with . . . with whatever I can find. Does that sound like a plan, girls?'

The others ignored the question as they ripped at the envelopes.

An hour later, Myra called a halt to the letter reading. She looked around at the sisters and said, 'People want to *hire* us! For high dollars. I had one that said money was no object and we could name our price.'

'Here's an official looking one from Interpol saying they'd like to interview us to exchange ideas. Exchange ideas!' Nikki said rolling her eyes.

'I read one from the German government that said they would give us carte blanche if we walk away free. They said they would pay us in U.S. dollars,' Yoko said.

'Coffee's gone,' Annie said as she tipped a bottle of bourbon over the women's cups.

'Who are you kidding, Annie? The coffee ran out two cups ago. We're snookered in case you haven't noticed,' Isabelle said, holding out her cup for a refill. Annie poured lavishly.

'What are we going to do with all these letters? We can't answer them, that's for sure. Some of the letters have money in them,' Nikki said.

'What time is it?' Myra asked.

'It's ten minutes past one, and yes, we missed dinner hours ago. Who cares?' Alexis sing-songed.

'Whose turn is it to check the computer in the war room?' Kathryn asked.

'I think it is my turn. I will do it now,' Yoko said.

The others sprawled on the floor, their legs at awkward angles. 'I hate this ankle bracelet,' Myra said. The others agreed as they talked about what was going to happen to them in the coming days.

They heard Yoko before they saw her. 'Here, I printed it

196

out. Yes, yes, I locked up everything. What does it say? I do not know how to decode it. Nikki, what does it say?'

Nikki ran her fingers over the words wishing she hadn't consumed so much bourbon. She labored over the coded email. When she thought she had it right, she read it aloud. It says, 3 a.m. Wheels up at 5:05. Do you want me to read it again?'

'No, dear, once was enough,' Myra said happily. 'Stick your legs out, girls, and let me take off your ankle bracelets. Nellie showed me how to do this. We spent one whole afternoon practicing until I got it right. No one is going to know we're not wearing these horrid things. Go to the barn and bring in seven of the barn cats. Yoko, put out enough food and water to hold all of them until Nellie can get here to take them back to the barn. The kibble is under the sink. Annie, fix five or six litter boxes. The litter is in the pantry. Go, girls, go, but be quiet.'

Tears rolled down Yoko's cheeks as she started to fill bowls full of cat food. Myra watched her and wanted to cry right along with her. 'Call him, Yoko. You have to give Harry the opportunity to say yes or no. Go back to the war room to make the call but make it to Jack who will then call Harry. Harry's phone might be tapped. We can't be too careful at this stage. Go, dear, I'll finish this up.'

By the time Myra finished filling the cat bowls, the others were back with the cats. Myra carefully fitted the ankle bracelets onto the cats' necks and then set them down. She smiled from ear to ear. 'That's going to drive the people who are monitoring us crazy. Cats are all over the place.'

Annie looked around, an expectant look on her face. 'Should we pack? No one said anything about luggage.'

'Your purse and your toothbrush, Annie. That's it. Our funds were transferred months ago. Get your things, girls. It's time to leave. Kathryn, go around and turn out all the lights. Thank God there's no moonlight tonight. We go out the laundry room door. We have a long hike ahead of us so make sure you're wearing hiking boots.' The sisters looked down at their feet. Sneakers.

'Then let's go,' Myra said. 'Charles is waiting for us.'

'Just like that! You're walking away from the house you lived in all your life and it doesn't bother you?' Nikki said.

'I can't let it bother me, dear. Charles told me not to look back. I don't want you to look back either.'

'Wait! Wait! I have to get something.' The others waited as Nikki sprinted up the stairs to return with Willie, Barbara's teddy bear. She stuck it inside her wind breaker. 'Okay, I'm ready now.'

The women left Pinewood like silent ghosts, the two dogs on leashes beside them. They all knew how to obey orders; no one looked back. They made their way across the fields to the old Barrington Farm that was now Judge Easter's new home, where they would find a Chevy Suburban. Kathryn would drive them to the airport.

The drive was made in total silence.

At the airport, the women climbed out and clustered together. Charles said the pilot would find them and escort them to the plane. They waited.

The voice when it came startled all of them. 'Hurry,' was all he said. The women ran across the darkened tarmac. Halfway up the portable stairway they all turned when a voice came out of the darkness.

'Jack! Oh, Jack!'

'Harry! You came!'

'Hurry, hurry, girls. You can canoodle on board. Nice to see you, Jack. You, too, Harry.'

Murphy and Grady yipped their pleasure as they leaped up the stairs.

Five minutes later, the sleek silver Gulfstream lifted off into the dark night.

Their destination: a monastery on top of a mountain in Barcelona, Spain. There, the Sisterhood could carry on their work as they followed *The Rules of the Game* – and hired out to the highest bidder.

Epilogue

High atop a mountain in Spain.

Charles Martin looked around his new kitchen. He was preparing a celebratory dinner for his beloved ladies. As yet he hadn't told them it was a celebratory dinner. He was saving that to go along with the dessert.

They were chattering; the settling-in period was now over. The month-long adjustment period was prologue and now they were restless. He could see that restlessness in their faces. Understandably so. He himself was chomping at the bit to get back into the swing of things. They wanted to know what, if anything, was coming next. Well, he was just the one to tell them. He looked over at Myra and smiled. She wiggled her eyebrows and winked at him. He felt himself flush. Myra had such power over him. He continued to watch her smile as her hands went to the pearls he'd had restrung one week after her arrival.

Brash and blunt as always, Kathryn Lucas poked a finger in Charles's direction. 'You know something, don't you? Come on, Charles, don't make us wait. At least give us a hint, a clue to sink our teeth into. For starters, who are all those people out there in the compound that came up on the cable car? What are all those buildings that are being constructed going to be used for?'

'All in good time, my dear,' Charles said. Kathryn pretended to pout but it didn't last. It was hard for all of them to be anything but happy on this beautiful mountaintop with the golden sunshine bathing them in its glow, the wild flowers that looked like rainbows, the sea down below, this fortress where they were safer than they'd ever been.

'Charles, it's two hours till dinner. Let's go to the war room and *talk*,' Nikki said. 'It's cruel to keep us in suspense like this.'

Charles laughed. He knew this was going to happen. He gave in gracefully, and said, 'Where are the boys?'

'Perfecting their tennis game.' Nikki laughed. 'Neither one of them has taken a vacation, a true vacation in over ten years. They're living it up these days.'

'You better call them if you want them at our meeting.'

Kathryn opened the kitchen door and said to Murphy, 'Go get Jack and Harry.' Both dogs raced off. Jack was always good for a treat and Harry was an expert belly rubber.

'Gentlemen, follow us,' Charles said as he led the way out of the kitchen, down a corridor to a massive mahogany door with a steel insert. The door opened at a touch of a finger. The heavy doors moved soundlessly and then closed just as soundlessly when the last man walked through. Jack was the last man.

The air here in this part of the catacombs was damp but not unpleasant. The stone steps were dry, the air quality normal. The area was well lighted.

This was the first time the sisters had been down here. Even though they'd begged and pleaded, Charles had been adamant. All he would say was, 'When it's ready, you will be the first people to see the room.' Excitement was at an all-time high.

Harry Wong looked at Jack who shrugged. This was a first for both of them, too. His glance seemed to say 'when in Rome' . . .

Another massive set of doors opened. Kathryn was at the front of the line behind Charles. First she gasped. 'Holy shit! We're home, girls! Look! This is just what we left in Pinewood!' The others brushed past her, their eyes wide and incredulous. Myra and Annie smiled from ear to ear. Harry and Jack looked like they were in shock.

'Welcome to Barcelona, ladies and gentlemen. Please, take your seats.'

'So this is what you've been doing for the past year and a half,' Alexis said, looking around at the room.

'It's different in the sense that the equipment has been updated. There's nothing we can't do here. Before we get down to business, I'd like to update all of you on what's happening back in the States. For starters, you're all fugitives. The authorities aren't quite sure what to call Jack and Harry. That appears to be an ongoing situation. The rest of you, myself included, are fugitives with a price on our heads.'

'How much? How much?' Kathryn demanded.

'Ten million each. I think that's just for publicity purposes, and to sell more papers and magazines. It's unclear who would pay that much money to catch you all. Regardless, there is a price.'

'Well, damn!' Kathryn said.

'Judge Easter, who we can never thank enough, is fine. She's not been tied to us in any way. Miss Fox is fine also.

'Mr Michael Lyons and his associates are in prison. There are no precise details. The press and the government are keeping all that information close to their vests. At some point there will be a trial. Then again, there might not be a trial if the men get snuffed out while incarcerated which is what I think the authorities are hoping for. Needless to say, Hollywood is making no comment. This is where I have to ask Yoko if she feels she's been avenged. Yoko?'

'Yes. My mother can now rest in peace. I, too, am content with the resolution. I wish to thank all of you for helping me.'

Charles stepped down from the bank of computers to approach the table. He stood behind Myra, one hand on her shoulder, the other hand holding a batch of papers. He looked around, delaying the moment as long as he could until Nikki literally screeched at him. 'What, Charles?'

'I have here in my hand a stack of invitations.'

The women all groaned. Jack and Harry looked at one another and shrugged.

'Ladies, ladies, these are not invitations to some tea party we are going to RSVP to. These are invitations requesting your services. They're from all over the world. I might add there is even one here from my own government. For money, ladies!'

'Hired guns?' Jack said

'Hired minds,' Charles said.

'Are we going to do it?' Isabelle asked.

201

'That's up to all of you. But . . . if you vote to do this, you must train. You've got to be fit, at the top of your game. You've all made a start by learning the language of this country. You will be learning other languages as well. In short, ladies and gentlemen, you are going back to school for one full year. Commando school. Those buildings being constructed outdoors are going to be your training quarters.'

'Oh, my God!' Alexis said. 'Do I have to learn to climb a rope and roll around in the mud, and jump through tires? I saw that in a movie.'

Charles smiled. 'The answer is, yes! If you vote to continue, I will respond to all these invitations and put our new clients on a wait list. How say you all?'

No one stopped to think or weigh Charles's words. Nine hands shot in the air.

'Ladies and gentlemen, let me be the first to welcome you to *The Rules of the Game*, and our next mission. One year from today. Welcome aboard!'

'And now, sisters . . . and brothers,' Myra said, one hand on Charles's shoulder, the other on her pearls, 'let's have that special dinner you promised us.'